Steve Braker

African Ivory

A William Brody

Action Thriller

Table of Contents

Chapter One 1
Chapter Two 15
Chapter Three 37
Chapter Four 49
Chapter Five 65
Chapter Six 77
Chapter Seven 85
Chapter Eight 105
Chapter Nine 125
Chapter Ten 137
Chapter Eleven 151
Chapter Twelve 169
Chapter Thirteen 177
Chapter Fourteen 201
Chapter Fifteen 209
Chapter Sixteen 221
Chapter Seventeen 227
Chapter Eighteen 235
Chapter Nineteen 249

Dear Reader,

This is the fourth book in the William Brody series. I sincerely hope you enjoy African Ivory, as much as I have enjoyed the journey of writing it.

The poaching industry in East Africa has become an epidemic. The losses are at such a rate we may well lose these wonderful creatures within our lifetimes. I don't know about you, but I would hate not to be able to show my grandkids an elephant.

I mention the Sheldrick Trust in this book. It's a fantastic charity that really helps the orphaned elephants. My family have been staunch supporters for many years. Whenever we go to Tsavo, we pop in to see the baby elephants they are looking after. If you want to get more information, then please visit their website: http://www.sheldrickwildlifetrust.org.

The Pokomo tribe mentioned in African Ivory are real and live on the Tana River. I visited them when I was looking for crocodile eggs in the delta. They are a gentle tribe, living peacefully in the environment.

Tana River, although a bit remote, is opening up to tourism. There are several lodges there now. The wildlife is spectacular, especially the birds. It is known as the center for birdlife in East Africa.

I hope you enjoy the read. Please get in contact or visit the website *https://www.stevebrakerbooks.com* I also have a newsletter with special offers.

Yours

Steve Braker.

steve@stevebrakerbooks.com Drop me a line.

William Brody African Ivory

Map Kenyan Coastline

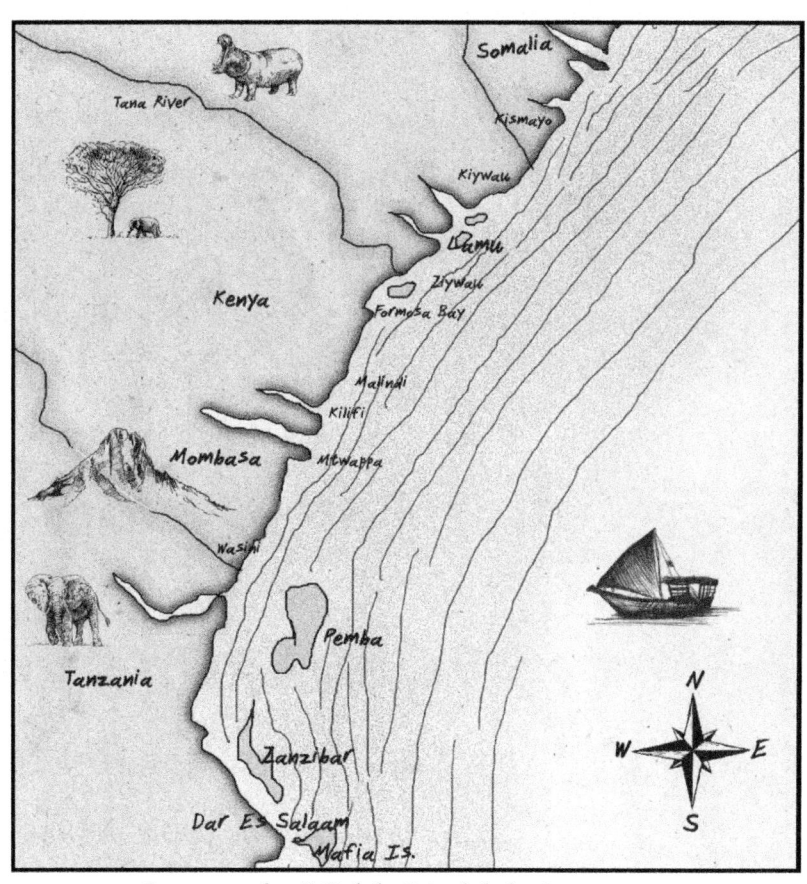

Cover art by J Caleb @ jcalebdesign.com

Chapter One

The torturing hot African sun was directly overhead, beating down on the bleached, arid, dust-filled savannah. Everything it touched seemed to shimmer, radiating remorseless heat. There was no escape. This was not a place to be; only mad dogs and Englishmen were out at this time of day. The small group sheltering under the acacia bushes were neither mad nor Englishmen. But they were here. Greed the major factor for their presence in this unforgiving landscape.

Tsavo National Game Reserve was either hot and dry or wet and flooded. Full of wildlife: from the giant Rothschild giraffes (with their extended necks and distinctive orange and brown fur), to the gangs of unruly warthogs running through the bush, with their twenty offspring chasing each other's short, wiry, curly tails. The current season was the hot one. Everything stood still. The heat was intense, burning the red dusty soil, making it so hot your head felt like it would burst. Water was scarce, down to a few soured, mud clogged pools. But change was in the air. Huge black clouds gathered in the far distance over the Taita Hills. When it finally broke, the deluge would come, washing the heat away, changing the dust to thick red mud. Flowers would rush to enjoy their short time to bloom. The watering holes would fill, and the great migration to the south would start. But now there was no respite. The deserted plains carried on forever in every direction, small stubby bushes and acacia trees the only haven from the intense sun. The savannah was as quiet as a graveyard at this time of day. Everything that walked, flew, or slithered knew to stay still and hide away until the sweltering ball of heat in the sky moved through its arc. Only later would there be some relief.

Under the cobalt blue, cloudless sky a nearly seven-foot-tall, gaunt, ebony tribesman was standing stock still. Perched on one leg, motionless. Frozen in time. Thick plaited curled ringlets of hair covered in cow grease hung down his back. A red and black tartan robe was draped over his shoulder and secured at the waist with a long leather thong. On his hip hung a fourteen-inch, brown, battered, hide scabbard, holding a razor-sharp blade. His feet were wrapped in sandals made from old car tires, with more leather wrapped around his ankles. From head to toe, this formidable warrior was covered in beads of many different colors: wrapped around his neck in bands, plaited into his dreadlocks, around his wrists and ankles, all making for a very impressive sight. Finally, in his right hand, was a wicked-looking spear with a six-foot-long, worn mahogany shaft and a blackened steel point. He was standing with his eyes closed, head cocked to the left and mouth slightly open. The puffs of wind gusting across the arid savannah had suddenly changed direction, veering almost 180 degrees. This could be trouble. The Masaai warrior was not concerned for himself. He had carefully smeared buffalo dung all over his body before they had left. It was the Muzungus, the stupid white men, that would cause the trouble. If he could smell their sweat, the prey, about 40 yards in front of them, would pick up the scent in seconds.

The small group of six hunters stood very still, hardly breathing, willing themselves not to sweat. But the burning heat directly above had removed any chance of that. Their clothes had been sodden almost as soon as they had left camp eight hours ago. Seven men trudged through the pre-dawn wilderness, waiting for the day to begin. Large wet patches appeared under their arms and stretched to belt straps, backs became soaked and itchy under the light-weight packs each member carried. The stench of humans wafting in the wind was like a mushroom cloud from a nuclear explosion to anyone or thing that lived downwind.

The tall warrior slowly motioned for them to retreat. He whispered, "Eh Muzungu, Rudi Nyuma." 'Go back.'

A short, squat guy in white safari pants and jacket full of useless pockets was head of the team. Standing at the front of the group, he looked up surprised. "No chance. We've been tracking these beasts for five days. This is the perfect opportunity. We can bag them and be out of this godforsaken place."

The warrior said, "Boss. No, that's wrong. The bull will smell us, any closer and he'll charge. We cannot win a head-on fight with this one. He is old and will be cunning. I can sense his presence very close by. We need to be cautious."

The white hunter said, with a gloating smile. "He is no match for me. This rifle is a Ruger Tropical 675 loaded with a 600 Nitro Express Elephant Stopper. Nothing can get past us."

The warrior looked at the gun. "Boss, you think that small thing can really stop this beast if he is mad? And soon he's going to be madder than hell."

The white Muzungu said conceitedly, "You people don't understand. We know more about guns and killing than you ever will. We move forward, now!"

The warrior had seen this since he had signed up with this group two weeks ago, the arrogance of these people they never learned. The guns, the bullets, and the safari pants seemed to make them think they were invincible. "OK, Boss. Your life, not mine."

The warrior moved forward towards the edge of the thicket. Through the mass of twisted branches, it was possible to see the small herd of elephants chewing on the acacia bushes. Three large females, about twenty years old, covered in the red dust of Tsavo, calmly waiting for the sun to move across the sky so they could venture out again. The largest one was flapping her huge gray ears trying to get rid of the heat, standing with closed eyes, dozing serenely, whiling away the afternoon. She stood almost fourteen feet tall from her round flat feet to the top of her head with two long beautiful white tusks either side of her dusty, wrinkled trunk. The second and next in age leant against a broken acacia tree. Before getting tired, she had ripped the larger branches off trying to find some soft, moist, green bark to quench her thirst. The youngest of the females was watching the calves intently, always concerned for their safety. Lions had tried to take one of the babies entrusted to her a couple of weeks ago. The memory was vivid in her mind, like the long jagged rip marks along her flank, bearing witness to her bravery. She had stamped one of the beasts into the earth to save her calf.

The kindergarten was enjoying the shade of the small trees in the mid-afternoon sun, their paper-thin ears flapping gently to release the heat. The youngest calf had settled around the base of the trees, laying on his side, trying to feel the coolness of the dusty floor. The second was greedily suckling at its mother's teat.

The wind wasn't blowing. It was gently puffing across the arid landscape. Occasion miniature whirlwinds spun off across the dust, only to disappear in an instant.

This the warrior knew was dangerous, too unpredictable. If one of these monsters got the scent, they would charge without warning. The mothers would protect the babies to their last breath. Plus, the male was around somewhere. The warrior knew this, as he had smelled him about twenty minutes earlier, somewhere in front of them and to the right.

The Masaai and the head Muzungu slowly crept forward pace by pace. The Ruger Tropical elephant rifle had one shot, then a reload. This could take up to 30 seconds under calm conditions. Under pressure, who knew?

The tall ebony warrior was from the plains of Masaai Mara in Western Kenya. As had all of his brothers, he had been named after sixteen seasons had passed. Before this, the immature boys had been called Layonis, the lowest of the low, just a dog's body. Every boy yearned for the ceremony. His father had presented him to the Ol-Oiboni, the witch doctor, then the ritual had begun. It was long and tiring. The boys were taken into the bush by a council of elders and put through a grueling routine of marches and hunting. After two weeks, the youngsters had changed they were now almost men. Only one last thing remained. On the great day of the full moon, they were taken to the river and smeared with mud. A cow was bled. The blood was rubbed into their long snaking dreadlocked hair and smeared on their faces. As the moon rose over the river valley, the terrifying witch doctor appeared in the clearing. He danced around them chanting and screaming, his lion's head mask with huge polished canine teeth glinting from the surrounding fires. One by one, the soon to be men were led to the ceremony. An elder stood beside each new man with a large earthenware bowl. The boy lay on the floor and spread his legs. His father appeared in the night and shouted, "Lemasolai." As he did this, the elder poured cold water over his head, and the witch doctor cut a good inch of his foreskin off with one swift slice. The loop of bloodied skin was then threaded on a leather thong and tied around his neck, where it still hung today. He was now a Moran, a Maasai Warrior called Lemasolai.

At sixteen he already stood nearly six feet tall and was highly skilled with a spear and his knife. Lemasolai's father Meitinkini trusted him with the highly valued cows the family-owned. But as was the way of his tribe, he had been sent away. A Moran is still a 'Kijana' until he kills a lion, only then can he return to the family and take a wife.

This had been over a year ago. Since then, he had wandered around the Mara and then through the plains all the way to the west, finding himself on the borders of Tsavo, some four hundred kilometers from home. The game park was a massive area the size of a small country, policed by the Wildlife Service, which was severely underfunded and corrupt. Lemasolai had hung around the tourist centers looking for some work, becoming a guide of sorts, talking to the visitors in his broken English, making tips here and there. One evening, he had met a fellow Masaai tribesman from the Mara. The two kindred spirits had spoken about their travels. The new friend offered him a job as a tracker. Lemasolai jumped at the chance. He enjoyed tracking, his father had trained him as a boy. When he has sufficient skills his father had sent him out to follow the warthogs, buffalo, and wildebeest across the plains, then slyly creep up on the prey and kill it with his spear.

But now he was here. This was not what he had bargained for two weeks ago when this trip had started.

As far as he was concerned, they were tracking and hunting large prey. All he had to do was follow the prints in the earth and the signs leading this group of 'Muzungus' to the beasts. Lemasolai had no idea about poaching. He had never been to the cities. He could not read or write. He was from the Mara on his pilgrimage to kill a lion. Then he would go home, build a Manyatta, and take a young wife. His life was simple.

The Muzungu was keen to move forward, but Lemasolai knew it was not a good idea. The small herd would get spooked and make off into the savannah. Although they were big, when an elephant wanted to, it could move faster than a man could run and for longer too.

As they crept through the sparse undergrowth, the Muzungu said between pants, "How much further?"
Lemasolai looked at the smelly heap of flesh with disgust. "Bwana. We have to move slowly. There's a small clearing ahead. We must go around, staying in the bush for cover."

The white, squat man said with frustration, "Look, I can't see anything. The clearing is so small we can just cut across the center. It's quicker."

The warrior looked on in dismay. "No, Boss. I don't know where the bull is. We can't go for the females. They're out of bounds. We never kill them. The bull we can find. He smells old. You can take him. There will be other young males around to take over the herd."

The Muzungu just sneered, "You get me close to them, then I'll find and take the bull."

The bright sunlight beat the earth on the edge of the clearing. The space was no more than twenty feet across, a patch of brilliant light with shadows on either side. It looked like a torch beam shining from above on a dark night. The warrior knew that moving across this open space was foolish. They would have to run quickly, and it would expose them.

Against his better judgment, he stepped out into the clearing. There was silence. All the creatures were sheltering from the midday sun. Even the birds seemed to have had enough and crept off into the shadows for some respite. Lemasolai moved swiftly, taking long silent strides across the burnt earth to the far side. He cleared the edge and immediately settled down on one knee. The herd was about twenty yards ahead, easily seen through the thicket. The stinking Muzungu marched across the clearing. It sounded like twenty fat drunkards leaving a bar. The man must have stepped on every stick there was. Lemasolai was amazed the elephants had not heard the sound.

The two intrepid hunters settled in the gloom of the final acacia thorn bushes.

The white man panted. "Listen, you show me the bull. He must be close. We'll take him before he knows we're even here."

Lemasolai looked down on the little man with the big gun. "OK. I think I can smell him to the east. We must move around the edge. Do not make any noise. If he hears us, he'll charge. We're so close to the females he'll not hesitate."

They edged slowly to the east, moving one foot at a time. The air was still. Even the small puffs had given up hope and stopped.

Finally, the air in the tracker's sensitive nostrils could detect a faint putrid scent. This was an old man. His teeth were rotting in the gums, and there was a problem with his gut. Lemasolai had smelled old animals like this before. They had lived a long life. He guessed this bull was maybe sixty seasons old. Time to move on and let a young buck come in and take over the females.

The impressive old African bull elephant was about thirty yards in front of them under a small acacia tree, standing at over eighteen feet to his huge shoulders. Once he had been an impressive specimen of his species; now he was sick and old. But his huge white tusks still hung as a reminder of earlier times. The bull stood still with eyes closed, dozing in the afternoon heat. Patiently waiting, as he had for so many years, for the sun to pass its zenith. Then he could push the females out of the shade, and his harem could head for the watering hole, the best part of the day.

Lemasolai stood back in the shadows as the small fat Muzungu took his place for an easy shot to finish the bull. He strained to bring the Tropical Ruger rifle to his shoulder, then took careful aim. Close up, this beast was huge, but one shot with the Nitro 600 bullet could stop anything. The white man steadied himself. This was his fifth elephant. The trade was good. The weight of the tusks on this male would fetch a small fortune in the markets of Shanghai. Although the bull was old, he had bright white tusks, each one about six feet long, nothing broken or scarred. The hunter smiled to himself. The ivory on this beast must weigh over two hundred pounds. This was well worth the sweat and toil.

He breathed in deeply, the site on the barrel raised slightly above the elephant's head. Then as he exhaled, the long round barrel slowly dropped through its return curve. As it reached the center of the bull's head, he gently squeezed the trigger. The gun fired with an enormous kick, throwing the man backwards. The bullet left the end of the barrel faster than the speed of sound. The 600 Nitro Express was designed for this job: killing elephants. The 900-grain cartridge sent the half an inch lead bullet out of the barrel at 2400 feet per second. It took less than a tenth of a second to hit the animal just to the right of its left ear, causing massive damage to the old bull, but it was not an instant kill shot.

The bull knew he was going to die soon. The bullet had caused irreparable damage. But he was not dead yet. The old elephant lowered his head, letting out a guttural, primal roar as he charged at the small white human in front of him. The ground shook as the four tons of flesh covered the thirty yards in no time. Certainly not enough time to reload with another 600 Nitro Express. The white man threw his gun aside, pulling his revolver. It was a waste of time. The bullets hit the bull, but it didn't even slow him down. The Muzungu turned to run, but as he did the gigantic old male speared him through the back with his right tusk. The bull's eyes were going, but he could still just make out movements and colors. The end was near.

The six-foot-long tusk went straight through the center mass of the fat 'Muzungu,' then on as the elephant continued its death charge through the thicket. The white body was picked up and forced into the barbed acacia trees, ripping the safari jacket with all the pockets off the body, exposing and tearing the pale white flesh to pieces. The three-inch thorns tore huge gashes across the fat Muzungus' face as he screamed in pain. The trees forced the body to slide further onto the long tusk. The hunter screamed one last time as his body was shredded. The huge bull stopped violently, swinging his head from side to side. The white man's carcass was thrown through the air, landing in a bloody heap in the middle of the clearing he had crossed a few minutes before. The bull had his final moments. He reared and stamped on the body, crushing it into the red Tsavo dirt.

Lemasolai had stood in the darkness of the bush and watched with terror as the bullet had failed to achieve its goal. He was so glad he had covered himself in buffalo dung and was almost invisible to the huge angry beast. He could do nothing as the Muzungu was speared, and ripped through the thorns, and finally thrown on the ground and trampled.

He now watched as the huge bull felt the damage of the bullet to his skull. He slowed and faltered, losing his step, no longer able to stamp his foot on all that was left of the human who had killed him. It was his end too. His movements slowed, then the majestic beast staggered to the left and the right, like a drunken man wandering home to his Manyatta. The bull had the final insult though. His legs crumpled, and he fell sideways onto the flattened remains of the white hunter.

This all happened in a few seconds. Suddenly, all hell broke loose. There were more huge bangs from the other side of the thicket. Then a smaller rat a tat tat of many small shots all firing at once. Lemasolai ran through the bushes only to witness the other five guys pouring round after round into the rest of the herd. The females desperately moved forward, trumpeting in distress, trying to protect the two small calves, but to no avail. The bullets kept coming. The poachers were hosing them with machine-gun fire, like a keeper in the zoo on a hot sunny day. One of the others loaded another Ruger Tropical and fired into the mass of animals. It took less than thirty seconds to slaughter all the elephants.

Then absolute silence.

The second in charge, a small, wiry Muzungu with slanted eyes like he looked into the sun all the time, came forward. He had done none of the shooting. Now Wai Chan Quai was all business. He shouted, "Quickly, that noise will be heard for twenty miles in all directions. We have to move fast!"

He walked over to Lemasolai. "Where is your guy, Johnson? Your man, where is he?"

Lemasolai just looked at him with a blank expression. He could not understand. Killing the old male, that was fine. But why kill the females? No one killed the females. They were the line. You never killed your lifeline. It was like killing yourself. He stared at the man with the slanted eyes.

He was shouting. "Where is Johnson? Show me, Johnson!"
Lemasolai just pointed behind him.

Two men were dispatched to the scene and returned in seconds with a report.

When Wai Chan Quai heard what had happened, he just shrugged. "Cut the tusks quickly, and find the gun. Then we move. Fast now!"
The two guys ran back into the thicket carrying a long-handled axe to cave the old bull's skull in.

The team were brutally efficient. After an hour they had four sets of grisly, bloody tusks on the ground in front of the Chinese man, combined with sixteen larger feet and eight tiny bloody ones from the calves. The Tsavo dust was covered in gore, and huge swarms of flies were greedily feasting on the fresh meat.

Lemasolai had taken the opportunity to move back into the bush. By the time the Chinese man had noticed his disappearance, he was already over three miles away, jogging under the burning sun. This was not the place for him. It was full of evil omens. You did not do what these mad white men had done.

The dollars in his robe felt heavy. When he had been given them, he could only think of going home and showing his father the things they could buy. Even better than the lion he had failed to find. But now, if he ever told his father what had happened, he would be disowned from the Manyatta, forever sent into the bush to die alone. The Maasai were warriors, not killers of female animals. That could only bring the wrath of Enkai on his head. She had sent all the cattle in the world down the bark rope from the sky to be cared for by his people. This was not caring, it was destruction. Enkai would curse him and his family for generations.

After another two miles, the moran slowed. The bundle of dollars was hot in his robe. Lemasolai took the cash out and stared at it. All he could see was the baby elephants dead and bleeding, with the mothers lying beside them dying. The warrior prayed quickly to his god, then dug a hole in the red Tsavo earth and stuffed the cash in as an offering. He stood with tears in his eyes, looking up into the clear blue sky begging Enkai for forgiveness and to look after the animals. Then with a heavy heart, he jogged off, hoping he could forget this terrible sin.

Chapter Two

The water splashed, then the head disappeared into the depths. Gumbao stood watching where his friend and boss had just disappeared. There was now an hour to wait, with nothing to do but sit and stare at the ocean. Gumbao sat in the shade of the overhead canopy. Two 100hp Yamaha outboard engines behind him, silent now, but he knew with a click of the starter they could be moving at forty knots in a matter of seconds. The deep blue ocean stretched out all the way to the horizon. The ocean in all direction was empty; not another boat in sight. They were moored just off the coast of Kenya, some 160 miles north of Mombasa, and 25 miles south of Lamu. Three miles to the west was a small coral outcrop called Ziwayu. The place was occupied by seasonal shark fishermen. The island was just a tiny, barren rock sticking out of the ocean with reed huts for shelter. The boat was anchored above what his boss called a bomma, a massive mountain under the ocean.

Gumbao was proud of his boat. It was a 32-foot long fibreglass-hulled speed boat, with a beam of only six and a half feet. She sliced through the water like a knife through butter and could handle some of the worst weather the Indian Ocean could throw at her. He had taken ownership of the craft more by way of salvage than purchase. The original owners had been Somali pirates that Gumbao and his boss Brody had run into a year or so ago. The pirates had come to a sticky final end. Gumbao had been the lucky marine salvager on hand to relieve them of their property. He grinned his wide toothless smile as he thought of the day, then took a crumpled pack of cigarettes from his torn, grubby cut-off denim shorts and lit one with a paper match. Life had been good. Mr Brody, his boss, always seemed to have some money and was generous with it.

Gumbao enjoyed the simple life. He was not exactly sure how old he was. Life had started in the back streets of Old Town Mombasa. His mother, a well-known local prostitute, had left him outside a mosque, wrapped in an old dirty blanket.

Life on the narrow, rubbish-strewn streets had started as soon as he could run. He begged and stole what he could to get by. A born athlete, he was faster on his feet than most with quick, nimble fingers, essential for this line of work. Then one lucky day, he had been stealing fish in the local market when a huge hand grabbed his shirt collar. The hand proceeded to wrap itself around his scrawny neck. The skinny, half-starved kid was picked up by the fisherman he had been attempting to relieve of some fish and thrown bodily onto a boat. Another guy grabbed him and chucked him below, slamming the hatch shut, leaving the street urchin in total darkness. Within minutes, an engine started and they were heading out to sea. Gumbao was then a member of the crew, fed and worked night and day for three weeks plying the coast. When the fisherman returned to Mombasa, he had been offered his freedom, but refused. This new life had a lot more excitement for a young lad than running the streets of Old Town.

Now he was here. His hair was white and he had several teeth missing. But he was alive, had a full belly, and was the proud owner of a boat. As far as Gumbao was concerned, life was good.

Sixty-five feet below, William Brody was floating above the huge rock. After back rolling off the boat. he had finned quickly to the anchor line. The current racing north instantly seized him and tried to carry him away. On the surface, it was running at over seven knots. He grabbed the line, then emptied his Buoyancy Control Device (B.C.D.) of air. The lead weights around his waist started to slowly pull him below the surface. At six feet, he duck-dived, emptied his lungs, and pushed for the bottom. At around fifty feet, the large rock he was heading for diverted the current. The enormous block of limestone was clearly visible from forty yards away. The water along this coast was as clear as glass. It took about another two minutes to safely arrive at the top of the bomma.

A few days earlier, Brody had been out sailing in *Shukran*, the old wooden dhow he and his crew lived on. The depth sounder started bleeping like a mad robot as she passed over this coral outcrop. Hassan, another member of the crew, had noted it as a definite place to take a look at.

As Brody neared the coral, he blew some air into the B.C.D. to get neutral buoyancy. Now the exploration could begin. He felt like Speke or Lugard, the first Victorian Explorers to open up this country, seeing things for the first time, places no white man had ever set eyes on before. This area was not dived at all. A tingle went down his spine like a rush of cold water as a small burst of adrenaline hit his bloodstream. He was probably the only person on the planet that even knew this place existed.

The fish swirling above the corals did not bother with the newcomer. They had never seen a diver before, but his bright red wetsuit fit in with all of their garish colors. It was strange to be at this depth all alone. The only sound was the air leaving his mouthpiece as it created mushroom-shaped bubbles that headed for the surface. Although he was some seventy feet down, the four-millimetre full wetsuit did its job. The water was about 65 degrees, a comfortable temperature. Off to the left, the plateau spread out to about sixty feet, covered in a multitude of corals both hard and soft, even some lovely, rare, dark-green and golden-brown fans, stretching up towards the surface, slowly wafting in the gentle current moving over the top of his personal mountain.

This was a pleasure trip, just to enjoy the sights of a pristine coral reef. No fishing. The six-foot-long deadly spear gun was on the boat. Just looking at mother nature at her best. All around him was color. The brown thorn corals, full of damselfish, snaked across the top of the stone mountain. Large flat sandy areas sat in-between. Swimming above the outcrops were thousands of small fish. Each one seemed to be vying for attention with bright colors, stripes, and orange spots. All the fish big and small milled together, staying just close enough to the holes and crevices to be able to race back inside if a predator approached. Long-necked bright blue and gold ribbon eels, about as thick as his finger and up to four feet long, stretched out of holes in the rock, their mouths agape and black beady eyes staring. In the sandy patches oddly shaped and blandly colored crocodile fish lay partially covered. Three or four at a time in a line, as if waiting for the lights to change before they moved on, their long snouts, with large black spots, protruding and bulging eyes on top of bony heads swiveling as Brody floated above. This place felt like an alien landscape full of strange and wonderful creatures, with Brody hovering like a spaceman just above the planet's surface.

He reached the edge of the plateau and peered into the abyss of blackness below. It seemed to go on forever. He knew it was at least another three hundred feet to the bottom. A fat shimmer of water raced up from the depths. He shivered as it washed through the wetsuit. The thermocline like a cold breeze blew up from below. Larger fish idled in the up-welling, enjoying the day. The water surged from the ocean bottom, full of life-giving nutrients feeding the reef and its occupants. About twenty feet away slowly drifting in circles, six blacktip reef sharks lazed in the current. Their tails finned against the current, almost invisible against the gray ocean backdrop, with dead eyes and very sharp teeth, waiting for the evening when they would head to the reef to hunt.

Brody wandered back across the enormous bomma enjoying the sights. The computer on his arm beeped four times, telling him his total bottom time was up and to head for the surface. He lazily swam over to the anchor, checking it was not stuck too firmly in the rocks, then slowly started heading for the surface. From this depth, it would take another fifteen minutes to get back to the boat. But he was in no hurry. A flat-headed remora, looking for another large fish to attach its flat head too, followed him up the rope swimming around his waist, good company for the six-minute safety stop.

After handing his dive jacket and cylinder to Gumbao, Brody climbed the ladder onto the boat. Gumbao said, "All OK, Boss?"

Brody, as usual, said, "No worries, Gumbao. Let's head for *Shukran*. I'm starving."

Gumbao fired up the engines while Brody went forward to pull the anchor.

As they headed back towards the small island in the distance, where *Shukran* their old wooden dhow was moored, Gumbao said, "Boss, we should take the boat out tonight and find some swordfish."

Brody replied, "Where do we find them?"

Gumbao pointed east. "Boss. We head out that way, about 25 miles, until we hit the North Kenya Banks."

Brody said, "Shit, Gumbao, that's a bloody long way, and we go at night!"

Gumbao smiled. "Hey, Boss, you getting soft. If we leave around 4 this afternoon, we'll get there before the sun goes down. Fish all night. When the sun comes up, we race back here for breakfast. Hakuna Matata," 'No problem'.

Brody nodded. "Sounds like a good plan. I haven't caught swordfish before."

Thirty minutes later they were nosing into the lee side of Ziwayu Island. Out of the wind was a huge golden sandy beach. Just off the island in deeper water, *Shukran* sat at anchor, gently rising and falling with the slight swell.

She was a 40-foot long, wooden, ocean-going fat-bellied dhow. Made from dark mahogany and mvule from the ancient forests of Tanzania. On deck, ropes were coiled neatly ready for use, spigots and pulleys made from the same hardwood were kept greased, and the brass and copper fittings shone in the early afternoon sun. Large colorful cushions festooned the fifteen-foot-wide bench seat at the stern. Below, dark stained lockers contained all the crew needed for day to day living in the open. In the centre of the stern, jutting out some six feet into the dhow, an intricately carved tiller sat silently, connected to the heavy wooden rudder deep in the water which in turn was hooked onto the last rib of the boat. Above was a wooden roof reaching forward some fourteen feet, offering shade from the sun and shelter from the rain.

The scoured, planked deck stretched out in front of them some fifteen feet wide and forty feet long. At midships, the lateen sailing boom was supported by the thick tree trunk mast, then laid on the roof of the rear cabin. Hassan had spread the triangular, patched sail to dry and offer some shade from the bright morning sun. The engine room, below the rear cabin, was spotless, not a drop of oil or grease out of place. The old Yanmar 120hp engine stood proudly in the centre, bolted through the floor to the fat mangrove ribs. This small piece of paradise was home for Brody and his crew: Gumbao and Hassan.

Brody jumped aboard *Shukran* and immediately shouted. "Hassan, Habari Gani?" a traditional greeting in Swahili.

Hassan replied from behind his cooking pot set in the shade. "Habari Boss, Karibu lunch na kahawa." He then handed Brody a steaming cup of strong, sugary Arabic coffee, called 'Kahawa Thungi,' he had been brewing on the stove.

Brody said, "Asante," Thank you in Kiswahili.

Hassan went on. "Boss. How was the dive? Did you see those lovely fish you keep telling us about? Allah put them there to eat not to be looked at. I hope you speared one for our supper?"

Brody replied, "Hassan, not this time. This was just pleasure. No spears today. Anyway, you know I never spearfish with my tanks. That's not fair!"

"Boss, those fish don't know fair!"

"That's true. But I do like an even fight, where I don't have all the aces."

Hassan wandered off back to his cooking pot, mumbling about Allah's gifts and how fish were just food.

Brody grabbed a bucket of freshwater and tipped it over his head to get rid of some of the salt, then shouted down to Gumbao who was on the speed boat tying it off to the stern of *Shukran*. "Gumbao, bring the tanks up. We can refill them now before we leave for the night fishing."

Hassan asked, "Where you going fishing at night Boss?"

"Gumbao says if we go out east for about twenty-five miles there are some rip currents where the swordfish live. I've never caught one before and want to give it a go. Meant to be a hell of a fight. Some of them get to over 1000 lbs."

Hassan, unlike Gumbao, was the cautious one of the crew. He always saw the dangers. "Boss. You sure you want to go all the way out there in the night time? There's only a small piece of the moon tonight. It will be black, you won't see anything."

Brody replied, "Ah, Hassan, we'll be fine. You can stay here and watch *Shukran*. We'll be back just after dawn."

"I'll pull *Shukran* out to deeper water and watch you on the radar, make sure you're ok."

Brody laughed, "OK, my friend, we'll not get lost."

Gumbao set the mini Bauer Dive Mate compressor on the deck and checked the 1hp engine for oil and fuel. Once he was satisfied all was in working order, he jerked the long starter rope. The small engine spluttered, not sounding too happy. Gumbao adjusted the fuel and air mixture, making it spring into life. Once it was purring happily, the dive tanks were attached. The small compressor could fill the aluminum cylinders to 3000 psi in just over 14 minutes.

Hassan brought him a bowl of chili fish soup and ugali, a lump of maize meal mixed with boiling water, a staple from the coast of Kenya.

"Brother, you're mad heading out at night. Why do you take our Muzungu to dangerous places?"

Gumbao laughed. "Hassan, you're young and cautious. We need to keep this man happy. He loves adventure. We can't cage him, or he'll just leave and never come back."

"Eh, Brother, you push too hard. One of these days I'll not be there to save your ass."

Gumbao slurped his soup. "Don't worry. You're like a wife I have back in Pemba, always nagging about how safe life has to be. That's why I never go there anymore. I'll bring him back."

The afternoon passed swimming in the shallows off the beach and drinking cold Tusker, the local lager, it was about the only beer you could buy. At their last stop in Mombasa, before heading north to explore the Lamu Archipelago, Brody had fitted an electric fridge run off the alternator on the 120hp diesel engine. This had brought a whole new dimension to the dhow. Hassan, the self-elected first mate and cook, could now store foods for longer, and Brody had ice-cold beer.

Just before 17:00, Gumbao climbed up from his work on the speed boat. "Boss. I've filled the fuel tanks, we have two rods and bait, plus some cold beers in the cooler box. I'm ready to go."

Brody answered, "OK. Five minutes." He then said, "Hassan, can you move *Shukran* to the outer edge of the sandbank and anchor her? You can watch us on the radar screen."

"Will it reach that far Boss?"

"I think so. It said in the manual it could see for about 25 nautical miles. I want a backup. You never know what can happen out there."

"OK, Boss, no problem. When it all goes wrong, I'll come and collect you," Hassan said with a broad grin.

Brody jumped aboard the smaller boat as Gumbao gunned the engines, eager to get moving. Immediately, the boat raced off into the distance, up on the plane moving through the slow evening swells at 35 knots.

Hassan stood on the deck and watched them go. He knew Gumbao well. They had been friends on Pemba Island back before Mr Brody had arrived. Gumbao was an old fisherman who lived for the sea, any excuse and he was gone.

After starting the small diesel engine of *Shukran*, then pulling the old steel anchor from the sandy bottom, he maneuvered the dhow out into deeper water, where the island would not get in the way of the radar. Hassan was an accomplished mariner. The rules in his home village of Pemba had been: if the schoolmistress did not pass you at the age of ten, your father got you back to learn fishing. Hassan had been terrible at school, so fishing and boats had been his trade from a very early age. His smart sister Zainab was heading for the mainland in Dar-Es-Salaam for university. But he was restless and could never sit in those hot classrooms looking at dry, dusty books when the ocean was calling his name.

Shukran motored about 200 yards off the small rocky outcrop. Once clear, he knocked the engine into neutral and ran to the bow, releasing the anchor into the calm blue waters. It dragged along the sandy bottom for a few yards before the spade-shaped end dug into the soft bottom. The craft slowly swung herself on the anchor, finding the gentle current pushing to the north. Once all was settled, Hassan turned the Lowrance HDS10 navigation equipment on. The set-up sequence took a few minutes to run its course, finding satellites to pinpoint their location. When the machine was ready, he quickly found the only moving target on the green blinking screen and clicked on it to maintain monitoring. The boat was still moving at over 25 knots. Gumbao was mad! They would reach their destination before the sun went down. Why always the rush?

Just as the sun headed down in a golden, fiery ball behind the mainland, Hassan noticed two blips appear on the radar to the west. They seemed to suddenly arrive on his screen out of the large block of solid mass which was Africa. He watched with interest as the little green blobs floated onto the display. They were about four miles to his south, keeping a safe and wary distance from the small island he was moored near. After watching for a few moments, he realized they had come out of the Tana river delta system. This he knew was a massive, lawless, swampy area full of crocodiles, hippos, and big snakes, not a place for boats to be. The head of the Tana river ran through a small village called Kipini. Gumbao had taken him there a few days earlier for some supplies. Kipini was a dusty, frontier town. The old shopkeeper was fast asleep on his rickety porch when Hassan had arrived. The old Swahili man was very happy to open the small shop for them, probably his only customers of the day. Hassan had bought flour, chilies, and some whisky for Gumbao, along with his smokes. As they were leaving on the speed boat, some hippos had meandered along the beach in the early morning sun, heading back into the river system before the sun-cracked their skin.

The small green dots wandered across the screen, apparently heading for deeper water. As usual in the ocean around here, it was better to be missed than noticed. A light could easily be seen from eight miles away. You never knew who was going to arrive, so Hassan put all the lights out, then sat watching the screen as the boats passed him by in the darkness.

Brody and Gumbao were hammering across the flat ocean, weaving along the sides of the low swells trying to find a path which would not make the hull smack the waves. Gumbao was a fine seaman, so could adjust the boat's speed and direction to give them as smooth a ride as possible. However, his wild side often got the better of him. There was no sitting down on the boat; one hand was always holding something. Brody was ready for the inevitable slap of the hull against the front of a wave, then the lurch forward as the powerful boat suddenly slowed down, like hitting a deep pothole in the road jarring up through your spine.

The fast speed boat reached the rips just before darkness. They were a little further out than Gumbao had expected, more like 30 miles offshore. As they approached, it was immediately apparent as the water changed. Large long waves seemed to move across the top of the ocean perpendicular to the rest. It created what looked like a wide freeway running north to south, with defined edges and rough tumbling waves in the center. It was an eerie sight with calm water either side.

Gumbao said, "Boss, you take the controls, I'll run the lines out the back. We stay about this far off the side of the rips. The swordfish swim on the edge of these currents just below the surface."

Brody took control and steered the boat to about fifteen feet from the edge of the waves, and cut the engine down until they were moving at six knots through the water.

Gumbao set the lines, attaching the brightly colored lures, with four razor-sharp barbed hooks hidden inside, to the six-foot-long teaser lines. Once he was satisfied everything was ready, he threw the lures in the wash from the engine, letting line off the back of the boat. When the shiny lures were bouncing along on the surface some eighty feet behind them, the brake and ratchet on the reel were set.

The only thing left to do now was watch and wait. The boat slowly trawled along the edge of the rip current, hoping to find a fish that was hungry, and a bit stupid. Brody cracked a bottle of Tusker and Gumbao lit a cigarette. This could be a long boring night doing nothing, or it could suddenly get very busy if a large fish took the lure.

The powerful craft easily cut through the water with only the dim lights from the instruments showing. Quiet, oily dark water on the starboard side and rough whitecaps on the port. The engines were humming, pushing them against the current at trawling speed. With no radar and only a hand-held G.P.S., they were committed to the night. The sun had dipped behind the horizon about two hours ago, then almost immediately the boat had been plunged into total darkness. The moon would not come up for a couple of hours, and even then, it would be a small sliver of light giving little or no benefit. Although it was still a sultry night, a shiver went down Brody's back as the darkness descended. The boat was an insignificant speck, lost in the enormousness of the uncaring sea.

As the night wore on, they both fell into thought. This was the way of the fisherman: waiting and waiting, bobbing on the surface, hoping for something to find a tiny brightly colored float in a vast ocean, and then think it a good idea to swallow it! It was like gambling in a casino;

the odds were stacked against you. At around midnight, the reel on the port side started whining as the line went out. There was immediate panic for a few moments, then Gumbao shouted, "Shit, Boss, its weed. Forget it, bloody stuff."

They settled back down into their reverie. Brody was thinking of all the times he had sat on boats during his Special Boat Service days, usually cold and wet, with night vision binoculars searching a lost coastline for lights or hunched over the radar waiting to see the drug smugglers with their high-powered cigarette boats race onto the screen. It was the same as fishing, from zero to high alert in a second, everyone on an adrenaline high, rushing to their stations. The two S.B.S. semi-rigid ribs powered with two 250hp Mercury engines would race across the ocean to intercept the overpowered smuggler's craft. When the S.B.S. were close to the fast-moving vessel, the gunner in the bow would put some 30 caliber rounds across their bow. A short gun battle usually ensued until the smugglers realized they were not just a rival gang trying to steal the contraband. Finally, they would board the boat and tear it to pieces looking for the magic white powder so many people would kill for.

Gumbao sat at the stern, ever watchful of the reels. He could not see the lures. They were lost in the darkness. But the reels and the rod tips were telling him what was going on out there. If a swordfish hit, they would scream at him. Then he would flick on the large flashlight above the canopy, and they would fight the fish to the boat.

Hassan had watched Brody and Gumbao until they had reached the outer limits of the radar. That had been around 18:30, the final glimpse of them speeding through the water. As the green blob had faded, he marked the spot out of habit and waited. The rips must be further than Gumbao thought. Mind you, his friend did not think in terms of miles or kilometers. It was usually time. A fisherman here said he would be back around nightfall or in a couple of days. They had no idea of the actual distance covered, so on Gumbao's side it had been a guess.

He sat dozing with the screen on beside him. The night sky above was clear, the Milky Way like a bright cloud of sparks and light shining just overhead. He had loved the stars at night since he was a child. They offered a wonderful escape for his imagination. On Pemba Island where he was born, there were not many choices for a young lad: either study hard in school and try to get to the mainland for university or fishing. Hassan and books had not worked out well at all. Every day was just as hard as the last, with frequent beatings for not knowing the Koran as all the other pupils did. On his tenth birthday, the teacher came to the two-room family house in the village and explained to his father that education was just not working. The following day, Hassan was a fisherman, on the boats long before sunrise out in the forty-five mile Pemba channel between the island and the mainland, hunting for fish, not returning until after dark. This had been his life for over ten years. Then he had been given his own boat and guided occasional tourist trips for extra income. But he always found time in the slow rhythm of village life to head out to sea on a lovely evening and just sit in the pitch dark. A couple of baited hooks over the side, staring up at his beloved stars. A wave washed against the hull of *Shukran* bringing him back from his dreams. All that could be done now was to sleep. When the speed boat came back into the radar's sights in the morning, he would watch its approach. When it arrived, he would give Gumbao a piece of his mind.

Brody looked at his watch as his last beer went down, it was going to 02:00. They had been chugging along for hours, nothing happening. Now he had no beer and another three and a half hours before the sun would start to poke its head up in the east, giving enough light for them to head home. All around them it was pitch black. Nothing but the hum of the engines and the splash of the waves on the hull as they continued to trawl up and down the rip current. Every hour or so they would turn the boat 180 degrees and head back the way they had come, into the wind. They had fresh spray on their faces. Now they were heading north with the wind, so they washed along lifting and dropping with the waves. Gumbao had pulled the lures in a couple of times and then reset them. All they could do was wait and hope.

Suddenly, the starboard reel started screaming really loud. The rod almost bent double. This was one hell of a fish. Brody and Gumbao jumped to life.

Gumbao shouted, "Stop the boat, Boss. This is huge."

Brody pulled the throttles to center, putting the boat in idle. Then shouted, "What's happening Gumbao?"

He didn't answer. He was busy pulling the other line in. As suddenly as it started, the reel stopped screaming and sat silently as the rod straightened up.

Brody said, "What the fuck is this, Gumbao?"

Gumbao looked up. "Boss. I've no idea. I've never seen anything like it."

A few seconds later, a bright light lit the water about one hundred yards behind them.

Gumbao said, "Boss, we've hooked another boat. Those bastards went over our line, and it went into their prop."

Brody said, "Shit, man, we'll have to go over and sort this bloody mess out."

Gumbao reeled in the line as Brody reversed the speed boat over towards the other craft. As they got closer and came into the light, the crew on the other boat started shouting. "Stop! Stop! You cannot come closer!"

Brody yelled back. "Look, we need to untangle the line. I want my lure back."

The crew carried on shouting. "Stop, do not come any closer!"

Brody asked, "Why? Do you need help? We can assist in untangling your prop so you can get on your way."

He turned to Gumbao and said, "Switch the light on."

Suddenly, they could see the boat in front of them clearly. It was about 35 feet long, a shallow draft cargo boat, more for use on rivers than the ocean. As its bottom was so flat, it was wallowing in the water. The waves were picking and dropping it. The bow was dipping so low the splashback from the waves was washing over, letting water into the boat. There was a big green tarpaulin amidships, and the fiberglass hull sat heavy in the water, loaded to the maximum.

Brody shouted again, "Look. I can see you need help. We can come alongside and untangle your prop before you take on too much water."

A guy appeared in the light. He was a small thin, wiry Chinese. He shouted back, "No, just cut your line and leave. Don't come any closer."

This pissed Brody off a bit. "Hey, I want my lure back. It cost money, and now it's dangling off your boat, I'm coming over to get it. I can dive in and cut it free, then we can both go our separate ways. No harm no foul."

One of the crew had been working on the prop, and another had untied one corner of the tarp to get a knife. Suddenly a small gust blew the tarpaulin back a good four feet. Brody looked in horror. The boat was full of tusks. He could see rhino and buffalo plus six massive elephant tusks.

The Chinese guy immediately saw the problem. This could not go on he reached behind him, pulling something from his belt. Brody senses were now on high alert: a strange encounter in the ocean, and witnessing these smuggler's crime. He instantly knew they were in mortal danger.

Brody shouted, "Gumbao, cut the line!"

He rammed the engines into gear the boat surged forward as Gumbao slashed at the remaining fishing line.

Then the bullets came. Brody strangely thought, *"That's a Heckler and Koch."* They raced away from the smuggler's boat. Just as Brody was reaching for the light switch, the halogen bulb above his head smashed as a bullet went through it, showering them with glass. Then

33

more peppered the rear of their craft. Brody slammed the throttles to the full and started weaving the boat across the ocean to escape the hail of bullets attacking them like a swarm of locusts.

They cleared the circle of light and raced off into the darkness as fast as the boat would go. After about another five minutes, the port engine stuttered, then stopped. Brody took it out of gear, lifting it up out of the water to create less drag and ploughed on at half the speed heading north. Then the second engine sputtered and stopped. They had no light and no engines, sat like ducks waiting to be shot in a bathtub.

Brody said in the silence, "Can you hear anything?"

"No, Boss."

"You sure? nothing at all?"

"Hey, Boss, there is a noise from the south that way."

Brody craned his ears, opening his mouth slightly to improve his hearing.

There was a faint humming coming from the south. They sat waiting to see if it would get louder. If they were found helplessly bobbing in the water, it would be a one-way fight, fast and furious. Brody looked around for a weapon. The only thing he had was his heavy stainless-steel dive knife. He figured if they came, he would dive into the water, then try to board the other boat. He knew it was useless. Whoever they were had automatic weapons. But he would not go down without a fight. He could probably get one or two of them. But after another ten minutes, it was silent. The smugglers had left.

Brody let out a sigh of relief. "Shit. That was close. They were ivory smugglers. Must be out here meeting a larger ship. There was at least a ton of ivory on that boat."

"Hey, Boss, we were lucky. Those guys don't take prisoners they treat everyone like a Tembo."

"What's a Tembo?"

"Ah, Boss, that's elephant in Swahili."

Brody sat for a minute in thought. "So, what do we do now?"

"Boss, we wait for the light, then fix the engine and go home."

Gumbao relaxed in the seat, then dozed off within a couple of minutes. Nothing seemed to stress him. Brody looked at his watch. There would be no sleep for him. The sun would be up in about an hour, then they could get the engine running and head back to the mainland.

Chapter Three

The water to the east slowly turned a crimson blood red. Then the clouds above the horizon glowed silvery-white as the sky started to turn from black to its clear blue for the day. As the sun climbed, the light spread across the empty ocean, reaching the quiet speed boat drifting in the northerly current.

Gumbao said, "Boss, lift the second engine let's have a look."

He clambered out over the stern and sat on the engine cover, looking at both engines in the early morning glare.

Brody said, "Bugger. Gumbao, look. There's oil coming out of somewhere. Has to be the gearbox. A stray bullet must have hit it."

Gumbao moved lower to the waterline. "Boss, it's here. This engine's messed up until we can get a new casing. She won't start. Must be seized by now."

The second engine had a hole in the cover the size of Gumbao's thumb. When they took the cover off, the bullet had punctured the cylinder head, killing the engine for good. It was impossible to work on an outboard in the water. To remove the gearbox from one engine and put it on the other would be a hell of a job. They had the tools, but could not remove the parts.

Brody sat in the morning sun, contemplating their problem. They were drifting north at six knots along the Kenyan coast. His Garmin hand-held G.P.S. gave him a position just off Lamu. This meant that after six or seven hours they would be on the border with Somalia. Another nine hours and they would be off Kismayo, a hot zone for people like him. Brody had been to Somalia many times undertaking extractions. Back in the day, during his Special Boat Services tours, he had worked all over the country. One mission had taken him directly to Kismayo, where he had grabbed a local cleric that was causing too much unrest. If he was found adrift in a boat by the local pirates, his life would not last long.

The second challenge was the ominous dark clouds forming out to sea. The winds on the east coast of Africa come either from the south-east or the northeast, depending on the time of year. Currently, they were coming in from the northeast off the hot Indian plains. This meant the weather always blew in off the ocean onto the shore. A storm was coming. How long and how bad it would be was anyone's guess. But he could clearly see the sheets of rain causing a long grey shaft from the clouds to the ocean, two miles or so further out to sea. The tops of the ever-growing waves marching towards them were starting to get knocked off. This was not a good situation.

Brody had been a soldier for many years, most of his grown-up life. He had joined the Royal Marines at 16, the earliest age possible. During his career, he had seen many dire situations and learnt always to be prepared. Gumbao was a good mechanic. He dealt with all of the engines for the boats so always carried a full tool kit. If they were on land, the position would be very simple. Put the boat on the beach, dig a hole in the sand to remove the broken gearbox, then replace with the gearbox from the other engine, and away you go.

In the ocean, it was different. They could not get to the gearbox of the outboard engine, as it hung out over the stern of the boat. There was nowhere to stand. Anyone attempting to remove the gearbox would have to swim or tread water while trying to undo bolts, and dropping anything would be a complete disaster.

Gumbao and Brody put everything they could find on the open deck in front of the steering console. There were wrenches and screwdrivers for the job, that was not the issue.

Gumbao let out a low whistle. "Boss, let me jump in the water. I can try to hold on and undo the bolts."

"Just try, Gumbao. See if you can find anywhere to grab a hold."

Gumbao jumped over the side with a rope tied around his waist. Within seconds, he was washed off the back of the boat and started drifting away in the current. Brody hauled him back on board.

Brody shouted, "Shit, that current is strong. We need a new plan."

The cold rain slowly dragged itself across the dark gray ocean, the long shaft of water finally hitting them with huge drops smashing against the deck, soaking everything instantly. The wind got stronger, gusting at over 10 knots. There was nothing they could do; the boat was now being tossed around in the waves. Standing up was difficult, let alone working outside in the water. The two miserable men settled down, huddled under the dripping canopy, to think and wait out the squall.

Hassan had been up before dawn, eagerly watching the screen waiting for the faint green blip to appear. He would then start making coffee and breakfast. But the hours had ticked by. At first, he was not concerned. But now, four hours after sun up, his gut was gurgling, a sure sign something was wrong. His good friends could be lost at sea. The boat had two engines for a reason. If one went down, the second could be used to get home. The radar could see about twenty-five miles, so even if they were limping home on one engine, he would have seen them by now.

At noon, Hassan decided to up anchor and head out to find his friends. He started the engine, heading off into the east. The sea was calm here, but some bad weather was approaching. It did not look too serious. *Shukran* could handle herself in most conditions. He was not very concerned. Once the fat-bellied dhow was underway, he tied off the rudder holding the boat into the wind, then hauled the sail and the boom to the top of the mast. *Shukran* was a dhow, so used a lateen sailing system. These boats were meant for the tropics and sailing in the trade winds, not really designed for agility. With a lateen sail, you had to haul the thick wooden boom, as well as the sail, to the top of the mast. This took some time. Finally, it was done. After securing one side of the boom to the running rail, he pulled the sheet to release the sail, then turned her stern to the wind.

Shukran took off, running as close to the wind as he could hold her. He constantly monitored the screen, looking for any sign of the lost boat. Hassan knew the fat-bellied wooden dhow was a displacement boat so could only go at 8 knots maximum. Covering twenty-five to thirty miles would take about three and a half hours minimum. With the storm coming in, that could double.

Brody and Gumbao sat miserably, huddled down on the open deck, waiting for the weather to pass them by. The wind thankfully was blowing them towards the coast. But the current was taking them north at a steady six knots. If lady luck was on their side, the boat would be blown onto the islands of Kiwayu about thirty miles north of Lamu. If she was not smiling down on them, it would mean a landfall at Kismayo, the first port of Somalia, and becoming the guests of the Al-Shabab.

Brody had the germ of an idea. He was a Special Boats Operative so did not do mountains much. However, he had been on a training course where the instructor had shown them how to make rescue slings from lengths of rope. One thing they had plenty of was rope. He took a twelve-foot length of anchor line and tied a bowline loop at each end, then fastened the center to a cleat on the inside of the speed boat, finally putting a loop either side of the engine. He then made a shorter loop, attaching it high on the center canopy struts above his head. With smaller lines, he tied all of the tools they would need to parts of the boat. If anything was dropped, it could easily be pulled back on board.

Finally, he put a slip knot on a length of line and dropped it over the first propeller.

Then with a triumphant grin, he said, "Gumbao, we can do this. I've made a sling to stand in and another to go under my arms. You can tighten or loosen them so I can stand. The rain is slackening off now. I think the squall will pass very soon."

"Boss. I'll go. I'm the mechanic here. Let me try."

"Fine, but this will take ages. We go in shifts. We are both soaked from the rain. There is no sun right now, so it's bloody freezing!"

Gumbao struggled over the side and into the water. Once he was arranged, although the current washed him from side to side, it was at least workable.

Brody tightened the line to get him in the correct position, Then handed the wrench to undo the six bolts holding the seized gearbox in place. This took longer than he had thought. The current was pushing the boat along, and water was rushing under the hull, which constantly pushed against Gumbao. He could not drop anything. As each bolt came loose he had to stop and pass the wrench back to Brody, then, with shivering, numb fingers, slowly pull it free. The rain was still pouring, and the boat was being tossed around, but he persevered. When the last bolt came out, Brody reached for it and safely placed it on the deck. Then the difficult part, removing the gearbox. It had a long shaft the length of the engine. With the rain pelting them and the rush of the water under the hull, the cold was becoming unbearable. Gumbao slowly inched the gearbox out. At long last and with his head completely underwater, he was able to pull the end of the shaft free and pass it gratefully up to Brody on the deck. That was the first one. This might work.

Brody shouted above the noise of the tropical downpour. "Come aboard, Gumbao. It's too cold. I will do the next one."

Gumbao agreed and climbed onto the deck, frozen and shivering.

Brody jumped into the cold water next to the second engine. He put his feet into the slings, looped the second rope under his arms, and started working as fast as he could. The rain and wind were going to make this cold work. He had about forty minutes before his arms and legs would start seizing up. His legs felt the cold first. The rush of water from under the boat started leg cramps after a few minutes. Soon his hands were blue, as the rain kept falling, and the wind pushed them further along the coast.

After thirty minutes, the good gearbox was ready to remove. Brody's hands were feeling sluggish and tight. The pads on the ends of his blue fingers were white and puckered. He could hardly feel the hexagonal head of the final steel bolt. But the worst was over. Slowly the gearbox eased out over the water. The last few inches were the most difficult to remove. The rope slings were stretched to their maximum, and the stainless-steel shaft seemed to go on forever. To get the last couple of inches, Brody forced his head backwards, pushing his legs out under the boat in front of him and tilting his body in the fast-flowing water, forcing his head under the waves. The cold water rushed over him into his nose and mouth. With a final thrust of his legs to get that last half an inch, the shaft slipped free. He surfaced, shivering and blue, to pass it up to Gumbao. As he handed the heavy, slimy, block of metal up, a wave hit the side of the boat. The precious gearbox, their lifeline to safety, slipped out of Gumbao's hand. Brody realized it an instant too late. The intense cold had slowed their brains down. They had forgotten to put the loop around the prop. Brody grabbed for it and just managed to get a grip of the slippery, stainless-steel shaft. As he lunged, his feet came out of the stirrups. With nothing left to hold him, he slid out of the upper rope. His hand grabbed the gearbox, which weighed about forty pounds, and he was dragged below the waves. With no fins, a swim back to the surface holding a large weight was almost impossible. His choices were very limited. He could let go of the gearbox and fight to the surface. The boat was probably twenty feet away now, but he could get back on board. Or he could fight until his last breath to try to get back the ten feet above him and get a gulp of air.

With a final push, his head momentarily broke through the waves. He was able to gasp a lungful of air before the weight of the gearbox dragged him back under. With full lungs, he knew he could last for four minutes, five at a push. However, he was pumping his arms and legs which would use up the oxygen much, much quicker. Brody was sinking into the water, losing the battle with buoyancy. The darkness was starting to close in around him. Drowning was very quick. All you have to do is let go of the muscles in his neck and take one big lungful of water. Shit, this had gone badly. Gumbao would probably get washed up in Somalia and never be seen again, and he would just disappear out of sight, never to be heard of.

As the blackness crept in, he opened his eyes once more. The final act of defiance before he gave up, his stubborn nature would not let him let go of the gearbox in his arms. Gumbao was in front of him. The stupid fool had jumped off the boat. He would die as well now. But Gumbao snatched the gearbox and looped a rope around it, letting it fall into the deep, then grabbed Brody by the hair and pushed for the surface. Suddenly, they were up again, coughing and gasping for the precious oxygen. The current was pushing the boat along. The rope around Gumbao's waist was dragging the two through the wave-washed ocean. Slowly, Brody got his bearings back.

Gumbao shouted, "Pull yourself along the rope first, then I'll come!"

Hand over hand, totally exhausted, Brody, hardly thinking, pulled himself through the current along the rope. The force against him was about three knots, but it felt like a waterfall, filling his lungs with water. Coughing and choking with only the sheer force of character left, his muscles screaming for him to let go, he pushed on. It felt like an age, but gradually he inched to the stern of the empty speedboat. Gumbao was pulling along behind him, covering the distance together. At last, they hauled themselves back onto the boat. The rain had stopped, and the wind was dying off. They lay on the deck, panting for a few minutes getting their breath back.

Once the two could stand, they hauled the rope with the gearbox back up to the surface and back onto the boat.

Brody said between panting breaths, "Man, you saved me. Thanks. I'll never forget that."

Gumbao answered, "No, Boss, you saved us. If you had dropped that gearbox, we were dead. I just helped. No one I know would have held on that long, Wewe ni samaki," 'You are a fish'.

Hassan was about thirty miles to the south of the speedboat, searching the ocean. He was desperately trying the radio and watching the radar. He knew the current was going north so had started his search to the south, then he could race along the rip current until he found them. He had turned north about an hour ago and was pushing *Shukran* as fast as he could, tacking every hour to keep as straight a course as possible.

Hassan kept going, with the rain pelting the deck, and the wind constantly changing direction. As the squall passed, one second the sail would be full then the next it was flapping in the wind. But the weather was clearing slowly. He would keep on this bearing all the way to Somalia if he had to. If those guys were alive, he would find them. After another two hours, a faint blip appeared on the green screen of the radar. The overlay map showed the small boat was moving with the current and was right up at Kiwayu, nearing the border. He willed *Shukran* on, but there was nothing he could do. She was already at maximum speed. The 120hp Yanmar engine below his feet had been whining and complaining at full revs for over two hours. It would not hold out much longer. This was all he could get out of the poor old girl. He just had to pray and wait.

In the sunshine, Brody's mood lightened very quickly. The heat was slowly thawing them out. The wind had dropped. It was time to fit the gearbox and see if their idea had worked. Slowly, and with everything possible tied to the boat, Brody lowered himself into the water. His legs took the strain on the stirrups under the hull. Gumbao carefully handed him the gearbox with a big loop around the prop. After several attempts with his head underwater and Gumbao leaning far out between the engines to keep everything steady, the team managed to slot the gear selector into the shaft and push it home. Then it was a simple task to tighten the bolts.

Back on board, Gumbao lowered the engine, primed it with fuel, then turned the key. Nothing. It was dead. Brody said with frustration, "Shit, man, what now? We don't deserve this!"

Gumbao fiddled with the cables connected to the battery, then turned the key again. The engine sputtered then roared into life.

Brody shouted, "Thank all the gods! We live to fight another day!"

He high fived Gumbao who was grinning from ear to ear.

Gumbao turned the boat around immediately, heading towards the shore, but also south away from the border. Brody's handheld G.P.S. was showing their position was past Kiwayu. This was a dangerous place. The pirates patrolled the coastline looking for easy targets. The boat was sluggish with only one engine, moving through the water at around four knots. Using the G.P.S., Gumbao set a course back towards Lamu town, a cold beer, and some hot food.

Shukran was about ten miles to the south of them. Hassan, as usual, had guessed their direction as he watched them carefully make a beeline for the mouth of Lamu port. He was so happy. *Shukran* could intercept the boat about five miles off the entrance. Only then he would know for sure it was his friends, and Allah was on their side.

Gumbao shouted. "Boss, look, out to sea! Can you see our *Shukran*?"

Brody stared. "Gumbao, I can't see anything out there. You are imagining things. Too long in the ocean. It's gone to your head."

"No, Boss. It's *Shukran* with her sails up. You can't see her? Stand up on the gunnel."

Brody climbed up on the side of the boat and stared out to sea. After a few moments, as they rose on the top of a wave, he caught a glimpse of a fat-bellied dhow in full sail heading straight for them.

Brody shouted. "Hove to. Let's go and find Hassan, make sure he's not lost!"

Gumbao swung the boat around in the water and headed off towards his friend. He had stories to tell tonight. In Lamu, he had an old wife and was sure she would greet him well. Mr Brody would give him some money for sure, enough for a bottle and a goat. Fatma, he was pretty sure she was called Fatma. All he could really remember was the bright smile on her lovely brown face and those gorgeous swinging hips hidden beneath her black bui bui, mesmerizing him. He smiled, remembering the first time Fatma had lifted the black robe over her head. That was one hell of a night. Swahilis know how to have fun! He had not been in Lamu for many years. But with a goat and a bottle, a long-lost returning husband would be met like a king, especially with all the stories to tell.

Chapter Four

It was dark by the time they tied up to the small pier in Lamu harbor. Brody had been here before, but Hassan and Gumbao knew the streets like the back of their hands. Both had family and relatives in the town. These Swahili towns were all linked. Old Town Mombasa, Pemba Island, and Lamu Island were just extensions of each other. Arab traders had first visited these places in the 14th Century, introducing new and exciting products and trading them for spices, precious metals, and ivory for the middle eastern markets. The bazaars became so large and wealthy, and Arabs intermarried with the local coastal tribes, thus creating the Swahilis, a hybrid of Arabian and African.

Gumbao asked slyly. "Boss, I have a good friend I want to meet here. Give me some cash so I can arrive in style."

Brody replied, "No worries. I hope she is worth it!"

Brody had a deal with the British Army, as he was an unofficial lookout for them on the coast. If he saw something unusual, he would make a call and pass the information on. For this, he received a salary for him and the crew. Gumbao knew this, but never wanted anything to do with a salary. He only wanted folding money and no paperwork. It would all be spent by the morning anyway, however much he was given.

Gumbao said, "Thanks, Boss. See you tomorrow," then wandered off into the night.

Hassan asked, "Boss, I have an uncle in the village. He knows about engines and spares. Let me go and see him, then tomorrow we can fix up the speed boat. I'll send his youngest son back to watch *Shukran* tonight. What'll you do, Boss?"

Brody replied, "I need a drink first, a long cold drink, then some food. After that, I'll have a hot shower and a very long sleep. We start tomorrow around 10:00, OK?"

"Sure, Boss, sounds good. See you later." Then Hassan also wandered off into the dark streets of Lamu.

Brody slung his seabag over his shoulder and headed off along the quiet seafront. Lamu was a coastal town set on a small island, protected from the ravages of the ocean by a long peninsula covered in sand dunes. Then, after a stretch of calm water, there was a reef before you entered the Indian Ocean. The town had no cars. The only form of transport were donkeys which seemed to wander all over the place with no owners. The second-largest group of denizens were the goats. There were hundreds of them, just walking around up and down the narrow alleyways that made the back streets of Lamu. The town was old, some of it dating back to the first trading in the area in the 1300s. There was even talk of the Chinese coming to Lamu in the 7th Century and of buried treasure off the coast. The town was perched on the edge of the creek between the water and the sand dunes surrounding it. The buildings were old, or looked old, built one on top of the other, tightly packed, leaving only a small space for the narrow-cobbled pathways between them, like an old Victorian town. The houses all had multi-colored wooden window shutters. Brody wandered around the village marketplace which was full of early evening residents chatting and drinking tea while shopping. Inside the large square were open-air meat and fish stalls, thronging with chattering people, all laughing and arguing over prices. The meat was not set into cuts as he had seen in the west. To choose your piece, you just picked up a long stick the butcher had put on the counter and used the pointer to touch the bit of the animal you were after. A lengthy discussion on price would follow. Then the butcher would slice off the chosen cut, wrap it in newspaper and hand it over.

Brody wandered through the market, listening to the sounds of the people hawking everything you could need around him. He stopped at one stall run by an old Swahili lady, dressed in a brightly covered cloth, wrapped around her body with another for her head. He had seen these in old town Mombasa. The wraps were called kangas. On the edge, as usual, was an old Swahili saying. She was sat on the floor among piles of second-hand clothes, a big business in East Africa called Mitumba, which meant bundles, as the clothes arrived in large bales from Europe and America. As he knelt down, she gave him a huge toothless smile, splitting her wrinkled brown face in half.

Then the old crone pushed a little boy off a low, three-legged stool next to her stall and passed it to Brody. "Heh Muzungu, take some tea it's fresh." She handed him a small glass of black sweet tea called 'Rungi'.

Brody said, "Asante," thanks, as he sat on the stool. He was getting used to these ways. Shopping was a social affair here!

"Grandma, what does the saying on your kanga mean?"

She cackled. "Eh 'Muzungu,' you are no tourist; I will be careful with you. This says, 'Ndovu hashindwi na pembe zake', 'An elephant can never be defeated by its tusks'."

She took a swig of her tea and winked wickedly at Brody. "Everyone has problems, but you must carry them along as part of your life. Do not let them defeat you. They are part of you."

The old women looked deep into his eyes, then spoke to him like his grandma used to back in Ireland. "I can see you have been to places and seen things that you carry. Remember, the elephant cannot remove his tusks. They are part of him."

Brody looked into the middle distance, remembering the screams, smoke, and death of the battlefield. "True enough, Grandma." He paused for a long moment. "Listen, my clothes are old. I need some new things for my stay on your island."

She smiled again, pleased the Muzungu was a polite one. "Boy, you don't just need clothes, you need a warm body to keep you busy at night too!" She let out another long cackling laugh as Brody blushed in the gloom of the oil lantern.

"Grandma, not tonight. I've just arrived. I need to see the sights before I settle on a woman."

The old lady smiled a wicked smile, "OK, my Muzungu. today I'll sell you some clothes, then tomorrow you can meet my daughters."

Brody laughed. He knew this was just the banter of the Swahili marketplace, but the idea did not seem so bad.

"OK, Grandma. You give me a good deal on the shirts, then I'll know you are honest and I can trust your daughters."

The old lady feigned she was upset. "My daughters are as honest as Allah. If they cheat you, then you send them back to me, and I will beat some sense into them." She giggled like a small girl, then started sorting through the clothes.

Brody smiled. "Grandma, I need five shirts, four shorts, and some shoes. What do you have?"

After some translation issues of style and color, the old lady wanted to sell him the brightest most colorful clothes she had. He just wanted army drab. Then came a negotiation on price. Brody managed to get some clothes for the next couple of weeks. He paid less than five dollars for the lot. Some were even designer. The old lady smirked as she took the cash. Brody thought, "She's done well!"

Then as he was leaving, she said, "So, don't forget my daughters are all waiting for you. Come back, and we can all have a party where you can meet them!" Brody laughed as he walked off into the back streets.

Now he had clothes, Brody wanted a drink. After wandering around for a while along the main pier, he spotted a lone, brightly-lit bar at the end of the street. This place was Muslim. Alcohol was not readily available. The only bar in town was at the far end away from the main drag.

The place was called Petleys probably after some long-lost hippy that had come in the '60s to live a life in paradise. The place was set on two floors. The ground floor had a long wooden bar running the full length, which was about twenty-five feet. The rest of the room was open, with low tables and chairs scattered around. Brody went straight for the bar. A tall African ambled over. He had long dreadlocks hanging down to his shoulders. Around his wrists were hundreds of thin bead bracelets, all in the colors of the Kenyan flag red, black, and green. The bartender looked Brody up and down. "Hi, man. I'm Satan, your barman. What can I get you?"

Brody said, "Satan?"

"Yeah man, Satan. My mum thought I was a little devil, and as you can see I offer temptation to the weak, so she was right!" He stood looking at Brody. "So, man. What can I get you?"

Brody said, "An ice-cold Tusker, plus a whisky chaser to start with."

"Man, you have come to the right place."

Within seconds, Brody was enjoying the cold beer. He had already felt the burn of the whisky.

He settled in to enjoy the ambience of Petleys. Satan looked like a throwback to the sixties, when Lamu had been a hippy commune. He stood about six feet tall with a square, muscular body, long black dreadlocks, and a hand-rolled cigarette hanging out of his mouth that smelled very suspicious. In his hand was a tall glass full of a multicolored liquid. He kept the drink topped up from a cocktail shaker set in a red plastic bucket of ice on top of the freezer. This was Brody's kind of place, relaxed and easy-going, a bit run-down, but friendly, a place that could easily become your local.

He sat and enjoyed several more beers followed by the whisky chasers. After a while, Satan approached him. "Man, do you want food? We got some great fish, just brought in today, or octopus, calamari, goat. We got plenty of fresh goat!"

Brody said, "How do you make the octopus?"

Satan shouted. "Hey, Minor, come out here. We have an order for you. The guy wants to know what you do with da food!"

Minor came ambling out of the kitchen. Nothing here went quickly. "Man, how you want your food? I can do whatever you need. You just sit and enjoy your drinks."

Minor was a skinny, taller version of Satan. He stooped down as he walked through the doorway to the kitchen, then strode across to the bar. Brody noticed he walked with a limp. The white cook's apron tightly wrapped around his thin waist had seen better days. It looked like he had just slaughtered a cow with his bare hands or had not thought to wash it since the day it was purchased. His dreadlocks hung to his shoulders, and a long, slim, hand-rolled cigarette protruded from his ample lips. When Minor arrived, he immediately offered his hand to Brody. They shook, as is the custom of this part of Africa.

Brody looked up at the friendly, smiling face. "Jambo, Minor. I want the octopus, how'll you cook it?"

Minor said, "Jambo, man. Me, I use the grill, I light me charcoal, then I cook your food, no problem. I can tell you, I'll put some fine herbs in it for you, make you forget all your troubles."

Brody answered. "OK, sounds great, but forget the magic herbs. Just the octopus and salad."

Minor looked at him as if he had just been offended. "What? You don't want me famous herbs!" He grinned, and his whole face lit up. "No problem, my friend. You just sit and enjoy your drink. I'll light the fire now, in as short as an hour, I'll prepare a feast for you."

Brody was used to no one caring about time. An hour was probably an understatement, more like two if Minor was just going to light the fire. He grinned back at Minor. "Asante Sana. I'll wait here for you with your friend."

Brody passed the time away chatting to Satan. He did not mention his near-miss with death during the night and the day on the ocean. For all he knew, these people might even be connected to the smuggling operation. It was well over two hours before the fresh grilled octopus with a tomato, chili, and onion salad appeared, locally known as Kachumbari. The meal was delicious. Brody was starving. He had not eaten since the night before, and now it was past 23:00. As he was finishing, Satan asked, "Man, do you need a place to crash?"

Brody looked up from his meal, slowly wiping his hands on the napkin. "I need a hot shower, and a good bed. Where around here can I find a nice clean place?"

"Man, my sister runs a cool hotel down the road called Lamu State House. You'll love it. The rooms are clean and safe with loads of hot water."

"Sold. Let's go. I'm knackered."

They wandered down the deserted street, heading east back towards the ocean. The place was fast asleep. Even the donkeys and goats were scattered around the streets like carcasses in the darkness. It only took five minutes to reach Lamu State House. It did not look very presidential, but would suit the purpose. Satan knocked on the locked door. "Hey, sis, it's me. I've a friend who needs a bed for da night."

After a few minutes, the door creaked open, and a pretty young girl stood blinking into the night. "Satan, what you doin, wandering around at night? Who's this?"

Satan smiled. "This is my new friend Brody. He arrived today. We fed him at Petleys. Now he wants a good bed." Then he said, "Brody, this here is my younger sis, Chiro. She's the clever one, a business lady of Lamu."

Brody replied, "Good evening. Sorry, we are so late. The food took a while to arrive. I need a bed for a few nights, and I hope a hot shower."

Chiro said, "Cool, man, that's easy. It's what we do. Come on in. Satan, you can go home now to mum. Say hi from me."

Satan nodded as he turned to leave. "OK, sis. Good night, Brody, we do a good breakfast in da morning, coffee and everything."

Brody entered the small foyer of the hotel. Chiro gave him a key and said, "It's late now. Here's your room key, number 24, up the stairs and along the hall to the front. You can book in tomorrow. I'm going back to bed."

He wandered up the stairs and found his room, took a long shower, then hit the bed. Within seconds he was sound asleep.

At 04:30, the local mosque started its first call for prayer, the lone cleric singing the haunting words of the Koran, reminding the faithful the day was beginning and the first thing to do was come and pay your respects to Allah.

Brody rolled out of bed, put on his new running shoes, shorts and a Calvin Kline T-Shirt, then headed out for a morning jog. Running was a passion, more of a ritual than an exercise. As long as he was on land, five miles had to be covered every morning. His body was so used to the rhythm that there was no need to measure the distance. He ran along the edge of the beach, heading east towards the large sand dunes that protected the small island from the strong winds off the ocean, then climbed up the long soft dunes. The muscles in his legs began to burn. He knew from his Special Boat Service days he could keep this up for about another twenty minutes. Then the lactic acid would start to build up in his muscles, causing cramps. It felt good though: the blood coursing through his veins, his feet sinking into the sand as he climbed higher and higher.

Finally, he reached the summit. The view was stunning. To the west was the town of Lamu, stretching out into the distance, a real Arabic town. He could easily be in Cairo or Old Town Dubai. The whitewashed houses all reflected the early morning sun. There were dark cobbled alleyways between the houses which were no more than eight feet wide. Lamu started at the harbor then moved uphill towards him, climbing the sand dunes. The buildings all seemed to interlink, joined here and there with corridors, one on top of the other. It seemed planning was not much of an issue. The houses grew in all different directions, with a new floor being added as cash was available or a new child arrived.

To the east, the ocean layout before him. The sun was climbing into the sky. It spread a golden glow over the still, quiet waters. Beams of white light shot up into the clouds above, tinting them with silver as the sun made its way up over the horizon for the new day.

Brody turned for the home run: back down the dunes, through the town to the Lamu State House and another shower.

After a long relaxing breakfast with Satan, he wandered back along the old quay to *Shukran* and the broken speed boat. Gumbao and Hassan had already arrived. The stern of the boat was up on a small wooden platform keeping the engines out of the mud. Gumbao was stripping it down with a friend of his. Hassan's uncle was on site, he had sourced a spare engine block from a hotel on the mainland. He said it would arrive later in the day or at latest the following morning. The gearbox was easy. There was a supply of them on the island, as boats were always running afoul of rocks and tree trunks floating in the water.

The back of the boat had taken several hits from the machine gun rounds, but none had penetrated the thick fiberglass hull. With some patches and repairs, they would be ready to head off again in a day or so none the worse for their adventure.

A small crowd of interested onlookers surrounded the boat asking Gumbao questions about the trip. The night before he had been busy in the illicit coffee houses all the old men used. The story had been recounted to anyone who would buy him a coffee with a tote. Each time he told the tale, the adventure grew and grew.

Brody had an agreement with the British Army. A Lieutenant Colonel John Briggs had made him an offer a year or so ago. Brody and his crew had been staying in a small town on the Kenyan Coast called Mtwappa, and accidentally helped thwart a bombing of a hotel. After recovering from the injuries sustained in the bombing, John Briggs had approached him, asking if he would keep an eye out for anything suspicious, then call on the satellite phone and report directly to Lieutenant Colonel Briggs. Brody thought now was the time to call in what he had witnessed.

Seeing everything was going well on the dockside, and realizing there was very little he could do, Brody headed back to Petleys for a drink. Sitting at the bar alone nursing a cold beer, he dug the satellite phone out of his seaman bag. Once it was on and had found the signal, he went to the memory. There was only one number. He pressed the dial button and waited. After a few rings, Lieutenant Colonel John Briggs answered. "Major Brody, long time. How are you? How is Lamu?"

Brody was shocked these people were keeping tabs. "I'm good, Colonel. Thanks. Been living the dream as promised. And it's just Brody. My military rank was a long time ago."

The Lieutenant Colonel replied, "That's good. Some people get hung up on the rank. You can call me John. It will be a lot easier and quicker."

Brody said, "As promised, I've been keeping an eye out for anything untoward. But this place is quiet. Usually, I see nothing at all to mention to you. However, as you know I'm up in Lamu. We were sailing around Ziwayu, a small island just off the coast, and I'm pretty sure I saw some serious ivory smugglers. They were aggressive as hell, shot up my boat and left us adrift. We got back to Lamu last night and are fixing up the speed boat now. No one was hurt, it just got me pretty mad, that's all."

The Lieutenant was quiet for a moment. "That sounds terrible, Brody. There have been whispers from our informants of some serious poaching going on inland. We have no idea where the tusks go, then they turn up in Hong Kong and Shanghai. When they're there, we are helpless, even to prove where the ivory originated from."

Brody listened as he drank his beer. "So, John, what shall we do? Should I report to someone or will you handle it?"

The Lieutenant replied, "Brody, it's a bit difficult right now. We are stretched, and as bad as it sounds ivory is not our main concern. Our task force is more orientated towards terrorists and drugs that have a direct effect on the U.K."

Brody was annoyed at this. "But John, when I was in Somalia we proved that the Al-Shabab use everything to generate income: drugs, human traffic, prostitution, anything that makes a buck. I'm sure this has some kind of links, even indirectly."

John Briggs replied, "Listen, I agree. But I can't authorize any operation on this intel. You know that. Have a snoop around. Be careful though, and don't get close. See if you can track their boat movements on your radar or something. Once you get more to go on, then I might be able to arrange for a group of your old friends to turn up. The Americans are there all the way up to Somalia. Maybe if you could find out when they move the stuff out to the ships, we could set up a sting."

Brody was disappointed but knew the Army, their rules, and protocols. "OK, John, let me have a think about it and see if we can get some better information for you."

John replied, "Be careful, Brody. Those guys take no prisoners."

Then he hung up. Brody sat brooding over his beer. Satan wandered over. "Man, that's a cool phone you got."

Brody looked at the gadget. "Yeah, it's special for sailing. I was just calling my Mum back home telling her I was safe."

Satan said, "Good man. You should always keep in touch with family. You want another cold one?"

Brody felt angry about the call. He knew the systems in the army were long and protracted. Getting someone to do something always took an age. If he came across the Chinese who had fired the machine gun, then left them for dead drifting in the ocean, he would pay dearly. Letting this pass was not an option. Plus, killing those animals was just wrong. His internal justice system could not let it lie. After a few more beers, and some deep-fried calamari, the decision was made. The crew of *Shukran* would head back out and have a nose around. He would find the route and times the boats came and went. Then John Briggs could send in a patrol of Special Forces for a sting operation and put the smugglers out of business for good.

Brody spent the afternoon sitting in the bar. He knew the boats were in good hands. Hassan and Gumbao would argue all day long, but finally, get the boat back and ready. The negotiations and conversations, which always had to be completed before any work got underway, was very frustrating for a person of action like him. It was better he just sat here considering his next move and waiting. Besides, the company was good. Satan chatted all day long. Minor turned up around noon with a big wicker basket full of fish. Brody ordered a whole white snapper cooked with whatever Minor could find, as long as it was legal!

The following day, the long, sleek speed boat had two fully functioning engines and the fiberglass was patched up like new. Gumbao was happy he had his boat back and had decided to kill a goat and name her. This was traditional among Muslims. Gumbao was not that religious, but it meant roast goat from the Muslim side and plenty of alcohol from his wharf rat friends along the pier, so he was in. The ceremony did not take long. The cleric arrived and blessed the goat. It was now Halal meat. It was strung from the canopy of the boat by its hind legs. The cleric stood by reading a prayer as Gumbao slit the animal's throat. The goat's heart pumped blood out into a bucket placed on the deck. When the bleating had stopped and the goat hung still and limp, the religious leader took a cup of dripping red fluid. He proceeded to walk to all four corners of the craft, tipping spots all along the deck, over the engines and the steering, even onto the anchor. Once the blood had been placed all over the boat, he announced she was cleansed of her old life and now could be renamed. The cleric then announced from this day onwards, the boat was to be called *Aminika*, which meant reliable or trustworthy. Brody thought, *"after the last few days the boat had really proved that point."*

The ceremony continued on the beach. Unbeknown to the revelers. out in the wide creek that led from Lamu port to the ocean, a long, wide, shallow-draft boat was chugging slowly towards the main harbor. No one noticed it pass in the general traffic that was always plying this busy thoroughfare. The two people on deck looked ordinary enough. One was called Captain Faraj. He was a local guy from the coast who had worked on many different contracts. A couple of years ago, he had been left on an island called Kiwayu and watched as his boat was sunk. That day had been the worst of his life. He had sworn then that the Muzungu who had destroyed his boat and set free the slaves he was planning on selling in Puntland in northern Somalia would pay. The other person was a thin, wiry Chinese guy called Fu Yee. The Captain and his new friend had met in Malindi, a town further south. Yee had made Captain Faraj an offer he could not refuse. The Captain had no love or knowledge of elephants. He was a man of the ocean. If they all disappeared, he could not care. In fact, good riddance. They were big and dangerous. The best part of the deal, however, was the money. The Chinese paid huge amounts of it for his services, piloting the boats along the Tana River.

Fu Yee noticed the speed boat in the middle of the ceremony and immediately knew they had failed. This was bad news. Nobody could know about their current work. If people started shoving their noses in where they were not wanted, they would be chopped off.

William Brody African Ivory

Chapter Five

Naydia Mathews stood up slowly, pulling strands of long blond hair away from her face. She spat on the dark red earth at her feet, then took a long slow swallow of plastic-tasting warm water from the bottle in her hand. It was immediately spat out too, taking the foul taste of bile with it. Standing at a respectful distance was Naipanoi. His mother had cursed as he had come out and immediately named him, "the big one." He was a full Maasai warrior, having finally passed the test of killing a lion in the Mara. He stood six feet five inches tall, with broad shoulders which had long, thick, bulging scar tissue across both the front and the back. The lion had rolled him through the bush, raking him with its talons until, in a last-ditch effort to survive, Naipanoi had managed to slide his fourteen-inch blade between the monster's ribs, silencing the animal forever. That had been ten long years ago. Now he was a proud ranger in the Wildlife Service of Kenya. He had been given the special duty of watching Ms Naydia Mathews like a hawk, making sure she came to no harm. He was worried. She had been throwing her guts up behind the small bush for a full ten minutes.

Naydia was embarrassed showing such weakness in front of these men. She had seen it all before, but the shock never went away, the awful brutality of the unnecessary slaughter.

She had been in Africa for six months as a volunteer veterinary surgeon on a special mission: to try to find ways to stop or at least slow the massive poaching problem in the area. Over the last few years, it had more than tripled. The whispers in the wind said it had risen so rapidly after the first road-building contracts were given to the Chinese. But there was no proof for this.

Naydia had started her life in sunny California. Her father was an investment banker, so life was pretty good. She excelled at math, which made her father even prouder. He could not have asked for more. Naydia would join him in the firm and climb the ranks. A perfect scenario. However, his daughter had different ideas. She could not help herself, she just loved animals all shapes and sizes. Every sick or crippled creature from a frog to a large golden retriever had found its way to her house. Each creature was lovingly tended to until it was ready to face life again. Sometimes there were seven or eight different animals racing around the family home, much to the chagrin of her parents. When Naydia announced on her sixteenth birthday that she was becoming a vet and would devote her life to the animal kingdom, her father was not very pleased, to say the least. He cajoled her, threatened her, told her terrible stories of the diseases she could get, anything he could think of to stop this lunacy. After her first two years of college, Naydia was given a place in the Early Acceptance Program at Cornell University of Veterinary Medicine. This was almost the end for her poor father. His dream had slipped away. He finally submitted, giving his blessing, and now was an ardent supporter of her many causes.

Naydia graduated from Cornell with honors, then decided she needed a broader experience and chose Africa as the place to get some with the larger animals. After a short stint working for the Sheldrick Elephant Trust, she had transferred to the Kenya Wildlife Service Anti-Poaching Team, a special unit set up by the president in conjunction with the World Wild Life Fund. Their remit was simple: the rise in poaching was unprecedented, a real growth industry to the detriment of the country. The President of Kenya had visited their offices and spoken to them personally. "This team is in the front line. Together, we must eradicate this terrible business once and for all. You are all entrusted with our most valuable assets. These magnificent creatures must be here for our children, and children's children, to see and enjoy." The speech had made a powerful impression on her. The president of the country was behind them.

Now she was here, in the middle of Tsavo East National Park, the oldest in Kenya, covering 5300 Sq. Mi. of wilderness, throwing up behind a bush. The shock of what she had just seen never went away. They had smelled the carcasses from well over two miles away. The sickly-sweet smell of rotting flesh under the hot African sun is unforgettable. The band of eight wildlife rangers had trudged on, preparing themselves for the carcass of the poor creature. When they finally found the small copse of acacia trees in the bush, it was more than the rangers had expected. The large old bull was laying on the ground in a small clearing. This was terrible, but he was old and would probably have died in the next couple of years anyway. Everyone was relieved it was not as dreadful as the team had thought.

Naipanoi pointed to the bloated stomach of the old bull. "Look, Madam. The old man did some good damage."

Naydia looked where he was pointing. There were two safari boots with legs disappearing below the massive creature. "He got what he deserved, the evil bastard!"

Naipanoi said, "True, Madam. At least the old man got something in return. But he was very old and sick by the looks of him."

"True. He must have been sixty years old. But there is still no need to just shoot him and butcher him like this. There is no dignity."

Naipanoi did not really understand the dignity of an elephant, but he nodded in agreement.

A shout came up from another ranger. "Madam. Boss, come over here, this is bad!"

Naipanoi and Naydia ran through the thicket to be presented with the devastating site of three young mothers mowed down with heavy gunfire and smaller automatic weapons. The three females had charged towards an acacia tree. It was only as they walked around the dead, stinking corpses that the two very young calves came into view. The death and slaughter combined with the stench of blood and intestines had been just too much for Naydia. Her stomach had lurched. It was uncontrollable. She loved these animals.

Naipanoi said, "Madam. We have to catalogue this find and estimate the size and amount of ivory taken."

Another ranger appeared wearing new boots. "Boss, I will measure the old bull. We can get an idea of his tusk size from the diameter of the stump."

Naipanoi replied, "Make sure you take photos, plenty. Cut the feet off that are sticking out, and see if you can find a hand to cut too. We might get prints or D.N.A."

The ranger said, "No worries, Boss," As he pulled a long glinting panga, a razor-sharp knife, from its scabbard at his side.

Naipanoi turned to Naydia. "You deal with the ladies here. I will make sure the old bull is treated properly."

Naydia unpacked her bag and started recording all of the data required for the base. Then she took extensive photos of the bloody scene. Even the feet had been taken. Some fat Chinese businessman would be stubbing out his cigarette in those feet for the next twenty years. Naydia hoped he died painfully of cancer.

After an hour, they heard the sound of the light aircraft approaching.

Naipanoi held the radio. "Sky one, this is ground search twelve, do you read? Over."

"We read you. Put the smoke out for the landing site."

"Sawa, it's starting now. Three, two, one. Do you see us? Over."

Sky one replied, "We have visual. Coming in now. What have you got for us?"

"Mostly measurements and photos. A couple of hands and feet for testing and prints."

"Good news. Do we pick the passenger?"

Naipanoi replied, "Affirmative. We will follow the poachers and try to apprehend. Get you some more hands to print."

Sky one, "Sawa, coming in now. Get ready. We don't want to be down long."

The drab brown Piper Super Cub was just a dot in the pale blue, cloudless afternoon sky. It circled three more times as if it was looking for any danger, like a dik dik at a watering hole, then came in at a steep angle to land on the dusty savannah. The 150 hp engine raced as the plane hit the dirt, bounced back up about twelve feet, then came back to ground and settled onto the bumpy surface. The rag and tube framework rattled in the wind as the airplane twisted on impact. The Piper Super Cub braked hard, then skidded in a tight turn to get back to the rangers waiting for her. The small plane pulled up in front of the troop, about forty yards from the acacia copse, and cut the engines.

Captain Herman Wachalla jumped out. "Jambo, Naipanoi. How's the going?"

Naipanoi shook his hand. "We're fine. Do you have our supplies and ammo? We'll follow these guys; my tracker says it'll be easy. One member ran off to the west back towards the main road."

Captain Wachalla said, "We'll go back towards the road then follow it back to Wilson Airport. If we see a lone guy, we'll report to the rangers."

Naipanoi said, "OK, you'll take Madam Mathews with you as agreed?"

"Yes, all set. I have no co-pilot today, so there's room. Do you have the bag of remains?"

Naydia had been listening to the conversation, it was in Swahili, so she only grasped parts of it, but when her name was mentioned her ears pricked up. "What's this about me Naipanoi?"

"Madam, you will go with the Captain back to Wilson. We will track these guys to their base."

Naydia was still feeling the anger and pain of seeing her beloved elephants slaughtered. She replied, "No way. I'm here to stay. I'm part of the group here to stop this bloody massacre of the elephants. I need to see what these people do. Then I can figure out a way to reduce the poaching."

"No, Madam. It's dangerous. They have automatic weapons and are very organized. We need to move fast like soldiers."

Naydia said, "I can keep up with you. That's no excuse. I was commissioned to be here. I'll not sit in an air-conditioned office with a computer while this is happening."

Naipanoi said, "But Madam, your safety is my concern. I cannot guarantee that if we are ambushed by these guys."

Naydia replied, "Look, my friend, I understand, but unless you are going to tie me up and bundle me on the plane, I'm coming with you." She knew this was not possible. The African men would never manhandle her; the repercussions would be more than their job was worth. Although it was unfair to the team, she truly believed her help would be useful in stopping the poachers in their bloody work.

Naipanoi said, "Look, I can't stop you, but remember this is your decision."

He spoke to the captain with a desperate look on his face and said in Swahili. "Captain, Unaweza kurudi wakati yeye amechoka sana?" 'Can you come back when she is tired?'

The Captain smiled. He could see this was a no win. "No problem," he said. "Just call and I'll come running."

Naipanoi looked at Naydia. "OK, Madam, it is agreed. But you keep up with us, and you do what I say, when I say it!"

Naydia said with a cheeky grin. "Agreed. No problem."

The small group of eight rangers marched out at a fast pace into the late afternoon sun. The trail was easy to follow. The tusks all together must have weighed nearly a ton. With no vehicles in the area, the poachers had left heavy footmarks in the dry dirt heading east. Naipanoi sent two scouts out on either side of the trail to watch for any tricks or turns. The main group followed the almost straight path through the bush.

The team knew the animals had been dead for about seven or eight days. But in the bush at this time of year, a trail this easy to follow stayed for over a month. The problem was how far would they have to go. Once outside the game park, the place was even more lawless. All the tribes in this area carried Kalashnikovs and would shoot a ranger on site just because they did not like the government. There was no real law. Everyone poached what they called game meat: occasional zebras, the smaller antelopes, and buffalo. It was a way of life. The locals used the meat as a subsidy for their diet. The rangers were not interested in the occasional animal going missing, but the locals did not know this and would shoot them out of fear.

Naipanoi knew the poachers would be on a river or a road in as remote an area as possible. There were some large rivers here. The Tana river led to the ocean some two hundred miles to the east. It was notoriously difficult to navigate with shifting sandbars and shallows and rough rapids over rocks, then the fourteen-foot crocodiles and, even more dangerous, the families of hippos living in the deeper sections. This was the African bush though. There were always unscrupulous or just plain poor people looking for an extra buck. Getting help navigating the river or finding a suitable place to hide was only a matter of dollars.

The team trudged on through the bush. On the third day, the park was left behind them. Now the troop were in unmapped territory. The trail seemed to be heading towards the river, but the scouts were not sure yet.

On the fourth day, the team of rangers woke to dark, heavy skies. After trudging for three hours through the pre-dawn, they stopped for a break. The first drops hit the ground like buckets being thrown at a car windscreen. Then the deluge came, massive amounts of water just pouring out of the sky. Visibility dropped to a couple of feet. It was like a solid wall. There was no escape. Everyone was soaked from head to foot, trudging through the sodden earth. Small rivers formed immediately in front of their eyes, turning to torrents all flowing towards the river. The troop struggled miserably through this strange storm. There was no wind, the water just fell out of the sky in sheets bouncing some four inches off the muddy soil.

The rangers were suddenly pulled up short. One of the trackers had raced back and was shouting over the noise of the downpour to Naipanoi. "Boss, stop! Go back at least a hundred yards."

"Why, Gatimu?"

"There's a massive herd moving towards the river. They'll cross our path. Maybe ten thousand buffalo."

As Naipanoi turned to give the order, a massive bull buffalo stumbled out of the torrent of water in front of them, his three-ton black body steaming in the rain. The animal snorted, as surprised as the two rangers. It turned and disappeared into the storm.

Naipanoi said, "Quick, everyone back! Move, move!"

As the Rangers ran back the way they had come, more of the enormous, satanic creatures started appearing out of the gloom like steaming apparitions, with massive curled black horns. The animals started bellowing and pawing at the mud, heads down, ready to charge.

Out of breath, the group sloshed through the new rivers and pools to a small copse. Naydia sat dripping in the rain, listening to the cacophony of well over ten thousand large land animals passing them by, all grunting, bellowing and shuffling, hidden behind the wall of water.

All traces of the poachers were trampled into the wet mud. The rangers stood listening from the trees as the huge herd walked past in the downpour, knowing any chance of tracks being left were long gone.

They camped in the rain that night. The herd took four hours to wander past. Naipanoi asked the head tracker. "What to do Lankenau? These animals have ruined any chances we had."

Lankenau was an old tracker from the Mara. He too had killed his own lion some thirty years ago. He stood six feet tall. His slim, scar-covered, wiry body had seen many adventures in the bush. He replied with a deep sigh. "Yes. There'll be nothing left. The herd was over a mile wide. We'll never pick-up the trail on the other side. It could be anywhere."

Naipanoi asked, "Any ideas at all? What can we try? You are an old Masaai man. You must have seen this before?"

Lankenau said, "Boss, my heart tells me we walk to the river and continue east towards the rising sun. When I was a boy out here, people used the river like a road. It is the only thing I can think of."

The following morning, the rangers made a B-line for the river, a deep cut in the landscape running from the west to the east, then into the ocean. The plan was to hit the Tana, then move along it towards the ocean, asking anyone they found if they had seen any strangers. The area was so sparsely populated anyone new would be seen immediately, especially a foreigner.

Chapter Six

The engines of *Aminika* had been fully tested. The water and fuel tanks for *Shukran* were topped off, ready for a long stay off the mouth of the Tana river delta. Brody was still a bit annoyed at the ocean clash and being left to die, but it was fading. He had decided the best idea was to hang around the mouth of the river near the small island of Ziwayu. While he waited, there was plenty of diving, fishing, and spearfishing in the crystal-clear waters. Not such a bad situation. Hopefully, they could sit it out and get some good intel on the times and dates the boats moved around, then report back to Lieutenant Colonel John Briggs and get something done.

Shukran would set off on the outgoing tide first thing in the morning. Gumbao had sloped off early to see Fatma; the smile had not left his face since the dhow had arrived in the town. Hassan was doing some business with his uncle and his father over in Pemba. He always seemed to have a deal going on. Swahilis loved to chat and make these long-protracted arrangements, usually involving fish or boats. The current one was selling a beautiful 36ft Zanzibar dhow to a luxury hotel in Lamu.

Brody headed for Petleys, his new local, and a chat with Satan. After sinking a few ice-cold Tuskers and eating fresh, thinly, sliced, raw sailfish with chilies and soy sauce, he was feeling good. This was a nice place to stay. After the recon, he would come back and maybe spend a month just sitting in this bar. Life was good. The afternoon turned into evening as the sun slid down behind the golden sand dunes. Brody was feeling the effects of the beer and whisky. Satan was always on hand with a fresh shot and a full beer bottle, along with good company.

Satan was sat on the bar with his cigarette burning between his lips and the long glass full of the cocktail of the day in his hand. "You see, Brody, I'm not from here. My parents were from inland. They had never seen the sea. Then when you guys, the English, left, our new president wanted to spread us out. We had lost our farms and land to you, and he didn't know how to give it all back to the right person. Plus, he wanted loads of it for himself!"

Brody was vaguely listening. "So why did you come here then?"

"Well, my mum and dad didn't have much choice. They were put in lorries upcountry in the Rift Valley and shipped wherever the President said. Some came here, others went to all corners of Kenya. The President gave us some spare land and settled us."

Brody said, "Bloody hell, mate, that must have been a bit of a shocker for your mum and dad."

"They never got used to it. My dad was a farmer, not a fisherman. He could not get anything to grow in this shitty sandy soil. My mum was a market girl, selling vegetables and fruits. The markets here are OK if you sell fish, but, not what my mum was used to. And they were not from the local tribe, so considered outsiders."

Brody asked, "What happened?"

"Well, they could not go home. Their land was gone. My dad became a drunk, and my mum left him and married a Swahili. They have a house up the hill, where I still crash now."

Brody looked up from his beer. "Sorry, mate, that sounds like a shit upbringing."

Satan laughed. "This is Africa, my friend. If your stomach is full and you are alive, life is good. Anyway, look at this place. I'm a very lucky man. My sis is lucky too with her job."

Brody agreed and ordered another drink.

It was past midnight when they finally shut up the bar. Brody set out on the short walk back along the ancient harbor towards Lamu State House. The evening was sultry and hot. Even sitting still seemed like hard work. The crescent moon was glowing above, looking like a slice of lemon, dark craters on its surface clearly visible, bathing the old cobbles of the harbor in a golden hue. It was like a black and white Western movie when the directors shot the night scenes during the day. Long shadows formed in all directions. The alcohol in his system was giving him a slight buzz, the warm feeling when you are on the edge of being drunk, but not quite. Life was good, and they were back in the ocean tomorrow, Living the Dream.

He passed the market entrance and continued into the darkness of the streets, heading along the final quiet stretch towards Lamu State House. Suddenly, his neck prickled, and the hairs stood on end. During his Special Forces days, he had been trained by the best trackers in the world, in the jungles of Sumatra, then the Sahara Desert, and once in the frozen wastelands of Patagonia. There was one thing all the trackers agreed on and planted in your brain on the first day. *'Always listen to your gut feelings'.*

When Brody felt the hairs on his neck go stiff, he knew there was something wrong and immediately slowed his pace. Looking like you were spooked was a dead giveaway, and moving at an even, measured pace gave him time to scan ahead for danger. Stumbling a few times and talking to himself gave the impression he was very drunk. He noticed out of the corner of his eye three men walking intently towards him. Quickly glancing to the other side, there was one more. He was sure there was a fifth in the alley he had just passed, but was hiding. Probably the head of the gang, waiting for the spoils without the risk.

The three men blocked the alley. The fourth was behind him stopping any escape. The narrow streets of Lamu were only about six to eight feet wide. Brody had solid stone walls on either side. The largest guy stepped a foot further forward. "Hey, you drunk? What you doing here? We don't like drunks."

Brody looked up slightly bleary-eyed playing his role to the full. "What? I just met my friend. We had a few, that's all. No law against that."

The big guy said, "No law? You are joking. We are the law. A friend of ours says you need to stop breathing and sent us to help you."

Brody said, "What? I'm just a tourist. I don't know anyone from here. You got the wrong guy. Look, if you want money, no problem. I spent most of it in the bar, but you can have what's left. I don't want any trouble." He offered the guy some screwed up notes from his pocket.

Brody knew he could take these guys in a second. Close quarter combat was his stock and trade. The big guy would go down first, then the one to the right, before the one behind knew what was going on. If the last two did not run, then they would follow their friends. But the better part of valor was to retreat. It was only a few dollars. It did not matter.

The big guy said, "We don't want your money. We'll take it from your dead hand and empty your pockets before we chuck you in the harbor. Your little friends will follow you too."

Brody realized this was no mugging. It was different. Why kill a guy over less than thirty bucks? "OK, guys, calm down. We can all be friends here." He was staggering, getting closer to the big guy. Another step and he was within striking distance.

Brody sensed the guy behind was coming in closer, probably to get the first blow in. Well, that was not going to happen. The words of his sergeant major came into his head. "Lad, in a brawl. He who strikes first gets to walk away. Remember: fast, hard, no mercy."

Brody took one last staggering step forward. His right fist, which had been relaxed at his side, suddenly spit out, like a striking cobra, so fast it was just a blur. The punch landed on the solar plexus of the big guy. He let out a rush of air, staggering backwards. Then Brody took a knee and moved to the right as the blow from the rear went over his head. The guy behind was set off balance as his long two by four had totally missed his target. Brody took the opportunity, stood up, taking a pace backwards, and elbowed him squarely in the nose. He felt the bones and cartilage shatter under the immense blow, then heard the scream.

The second guy came forward with a six-foot-long, hawser-laid rope. On the end was a massive Turk's head knot about eight inches in diameter. He was swinging it in fast semicircles in front of him, pushing Brody back towards the wall in the narrow passageway. Brody ducked under a close swing, feeling the air from the knot rush across his head. He ducked again as the knot sliced through the air and rolled across the narrow alleyway. As he was rolling, he grabbed the two by four. Now it was even. They both had a weapon. The knot rushed passed his face again, then thudded onto the rough cobblestones of the pavement. Before the rope could be pulled back, Brody lashed out with the flat end of the two by four, like a lance, hitting the guy squarely in the stomach with more force than a solid left uppercut. The guy doubled over. Brody did not want anyone dead, but he had to stop them, so brought the two by four down onto the crown of the attacker's head with just enough force to knock him out. He went down. Headfirst onto the floor.

The first and second guys were getting their senses back and charged towards him. Brody thought, *"This is easy. Why would they do that?"* He dodged the first one, slipping past him, then took the second one. Using his momentum, he grabbed the guy's head and slammed it against the hard stone wall of the alley. There was a loud, sickening crack. Brody thought, *"Shit, I might have underestimated the guy's skull strength."* The thug went down, crumpling into the gutter beside the pavement.

The guy with the broken nose took out a long, thin, black stiletto knife. Brody ripped off his T-Shirt and wrapped it around his arm. The guy lunged once, then swung around, whipping the knife in front of him left and right. He was grinning, enjoying teasing his new prey.

Brody dodged and backed up along the narrow street. The guy was not proficient, but this was a lethal weapon which had to be dealt with. Brody kept backing up, watching the attacker's feet as he became bolder and bolder. The guy was concentrating on Brody's torso, trying to slice it with the knife. His right foot stepped forward as he swung the blade to the left. When the knife was at its furthest point, Brody took a step forward and used a Jujitsu kick to take the attackers right knee out. He stumbled from the hard kick and fell forward. Using the man's forward momentum and the continuation step of his kick, he right hooked him in the jaw. The attacker's head flew back, and the knife bounced on the floor as he slumped unconscious to the ground.

Brody spun as the last guy came for him, swinging a long timing chain from an old diesel engine. Brody thought, *"What the hell!"* The chain hit the floor beside him, then lashed back, coming out a second later for his head. Brody ducked and spun around. The chain was flashing this way and that. The guy was like a samurai warrior, slashing left and right up and down. Brody was backing away. The guy was smiling. He had seen they were heading for a dead end. Brody would have to take a chance here and lunge in between the slashes of the chain, if it hit him, he would be seriously hurt. His left foot touched the back wall. No more retreat; this was it. He was going to have to time it just right. One more swing and the guy would have him completely cornered and at his mercy. If the chain hit him even with a glancing blow, that would be it. Brody would be disabled, and the guy could do what he wanted after that.

The thug swung the chain back. The target could not move, this was going to be easy. He would be a real tough guy now. Then the two by four came out of the night like a silver sword and caved his head in. Brody was almost as shocked as the guy, whose knees buckled as he crumpled to the floor. Brody smelled the hand-rolled tobacco with the suspicious substance, and saw the long dreadlocks of his new friend Satan. "Hey, man. Nothing like a nice piece of hickory."

Brody stood stunned, "What the fuck!"

Satan said, "This isn't hickory I know, but I always wanted to say that. You know Clint Eastwood, western, he was my hero when we got T.V. here. I watched the V.H.S. videos, got the lot!"

Brody said, "Thanks, that guy had me."

Satan smiled his usual relaxed smile. "Man, I was just walking along and heard the ruckus. Thought it might be a party. Saw you just in time I think. Glad to be of service. Did I kill him?"

Brody said, "I think so. People's heads don't usually have a groove in them."

Satan said, "Shit, man. We better leave. That's not good, shit. Hope no one saw us. Shit, man, not good shit this is. Bad for the vibes and all that. I'm a peaceful dude."

Captain Faraj had watched the whole thing from the safety of a rooftop above the alley. His plan was to wait for the Muzungu to be dying in the dirt alley, then come down and look into his eyes. The white man would remember him from before and realize it was Captain Faraj that was killing him. He would slowly slit his throat and watch him choke on his own blood, then present the head of the Muzungu to his Chinese business partner. That had all failed this time, but he was learning. After cleaning up this mess and disposing of the fools laying in the road, he would find another way to get the white man once and for all.

Chapter Seven

Shukran pulled away from the dockside well before dawn. The crew were all a bit bleary-eyed after their boss's early wake-up call, but no one complained.

Hassan asked, "Boss, we're leaving well before first light. What's the rush? Yesterday you said we were just going to sit at Ziwayu and watch the traffic?"

"Things changed last night. When those guys attacked me, they were not after my cash. They wanted me, actually us, dead. I'm sure it has something to do with the run-in we had in the ocean. I don't think those guys like having witnesses."

"OK. So, what's the plan?"

"First, we run away with our tails between our legs. Set a course on the G.P.S. directly east. Once *Shukran* is eight miles out, no one will be able to see us from the beach. We'll hang around just out of site, panning the entrance with the radar. I'm pretty sure whoever attacked me last night will head off back towards Ziwayu as soon as it's light. We'll find them in some quiet spot and sort this out once and for all!"

Hassan replied, "Sawa, Boss. Do you want coffee?"

Brody laughed. "I never say no to a coffee."

The two boats slowly made their way down the long creek, past the sand dunes, then out to the reef and into the Indian Ocean. Once they were safely underway, *Aminika* was tied off behind them, and Gumbao came on board for breakfast. *Shukran*'s boom was hauled to the top of the mast and the sail let out, then trimmed carefully until it was pulling her through the water at a good six knots. The engine was turned off and baited lines were dropped behind them in the wake for fishing. Hassan monitored the radar, Brody watched the lures bouncing in the blue water, and Gumbao, as always, took the tiller.

After two hours, *Shukran* was sitting at the eight-mile mark, directly off the entrance to the creek, waiting and watching. Several boats came out as the sun rose into the sky, but nothing headed south. Brody had just pulled in his fifth skipjack tuna for their lunch. Gumbao kept the boat moving through the water at a slow pace. It was an idyllic scene, if it weren't for the deadly mission, Brody was contemplating.

He was mad as hell and had decided enough was enough. These guys had come in and threatened his crew and tried to kill him. He would find out who was behind this and sort it himself. John Briggs did not seem that interested anyway. This was a wild and deserted place. Accidents happened, and people disappeared.

Hassan yelled, "Boss, come see. This looks like our guys!" The boat came out and turned south as soon as they passed the reef.

Brody looked over Hassan's shoulder. "Cool, let's stay out here and shadow them, see where they go. Gumbao, head south, but keep this distance from the shore. Hassan, make sure you keep them on the radar. We can't afford to lose their signal in the clutter from the mainland."

Shukran made a gentle turn in the water and slowly headed south on a dead run. Gumbao trimmed the sails to keep her at an easy four knots. The dolphins loved the bow of *Shukran* as she creased through the azure blue waters. The wind was light but steady, keeping the bright white sail full. The waves were long, slow, moving lines, marching through the ocean. Pods came and went, leaping out of the water just in front of the bow, then reappearing and jumping over the white wake following the boat.

Hassan kept a close eye on the small craft heading south. She moved along at about five knots through the water so was not a fast boat. That was about all the radar could tell them. When the green blip reached Ziwayu two hours later, it turned almost west heading for the shoreline. *Shukran* moved up as close to the horizon as possible. Brody climbed the thirty feet to the top of the mast, then stood on the solid boom. From there, he could just see over the horizon when *Shukran* rose on a wave. With binoculars, the craft could be seen out in the swells some seven miles off. She seemed to be moving in a purposeful direction towards the shoreline.

Brody shouted down to the deck. "Hassan, if that boat maintains course, where will she hit land?"

"Boss, that's where the boats came out the other night, when you got shot at. I think it's one of the small rivers heading inland."

"Shit. If she goes inland, we'll lose her and the crew. They might not come back for weeks. Gumbao, alter course for Ziwayu. Stay just south of the island. We don't want to lose sight of that boat."

Shukran slowly altered course again, coming around to a broad reach, heading for Ziwayu Island.

Brody stayed in his crow's nest at the top of the mast as the sail billowed out below him, the boom wriggling under his bare feet and bouncing against the mast as *Shukran* settled into her new course.

The smaller craft was moving faster now. She was out of the current, heading towards the town of Kipini. Maybe it was just a supply boat for the small town. Hassan watched as the small green blob on the screen approached the landmass. He knew as soon as it was under the lee of the land it would disappear. The electronic blob blipped a few more times, then melded into the African Continent, disappearing altogether. Hassan clicked to mark the point on the radar, so they could navigate to the exact location.

He shouted, "Boss, it's gone! Maybe to Kipini or down a river. We'll have to go and look."

Brody had the glasses to his eyes. "I can just see it. I don't think it's stopping. We can't follow that boat up the river in *Shukran*."

Hassan yelled back from the deck. "We can leave *Shukran* with the shark fishermen on Ziwayu. One is an uncle of mine. Then we can follow in *Aminika*. She can handle the shallow water."

Two hours later, *Shukran* had moored just off the beach at Ziwayu Island. Hassan was in deep conversation with one of the shark fishermen. "Uncle, we need you to watch the boat. We have to go into Kipini and have a look around."

The old man replied, "There is nothing to see there, boy, not even any women! I went. It's rubbish. Your Muzungu will not enjoy it."

Hassan went on, "OK, Uncle, but we still must go. We will be a couple of days. Can you sit on *Shukran* and watch her for us?"

The old man smiled. "Do I get food? And I need something warm for the evenings. I'm not used to sitting on cold boats anymore."

Hassan reached into the storage locker behind him. "Uncle, you are a good Muslim. Only use this for medicine, nothing more."

The old man smiled at the bottle of Red Label whisky Hassan was holding. "OK, cousin, I will only take a drop when the wind bites me."

Hassan looked at him doubtfully. "Sawa, Uncle, but you must keep a keen eye on our beautiful boat, and you must stay on her day and night."

The old man said, "It's fine, cousin. I was sitting on these boats before you were born. She will be safe with me."

Brody and Gumbao had taken everything they could off *Shukran*. The weapons which they had picked up over their time on the coast amounted to one old Kalashnikov AK-47, this was the ubiquitous assault rifle of the African Continent. These guns were everywhere. The one Brody had was a fold-out metal stock. It was brilliant, a real industrial tool. You cleaned it, and it worked. Water, dust, mud, or dirt, nothing would stop it spitting bullets. The second and favorite of Brody's weapons was an Ithaca Defense M37, five-round, lower ejection, pump-action shotgun with an eighteen-inch barrel and adjustable plastic stock. The last items were two Glock 17's with ten-round magazines. These guns were ideal for on-board life as they were made from polymer, not metal. They were very easy to clean and reliable in a firefight. *Shukran* had made a few stops over the years in less than friendly places. Each time, as the occasion arose, the crew collected as much ammo as they could find, so that was not a problem. Brody also added a couple of dive tanks and equipment along with his heavy stainless-steel dive knives. All they had for navigation on the *Aminika* was a handheld Garmin G.P.S., which would have to do.

Hassan packed enough food and water for a week while Gumbao loaded as much petrol as he could fit on the boat. When he was finished, they were sat on a floating molotov cocktail. If anyone shot at them, they would go up like a firework on the Fourth of July. Gumbao explained. "There are no shops, Boss. We need to carry everything except meat. Plenty of game to kill."

Brody was not worried about supplies. He had traveled for weeks in the bush in his army days with just his Bergen on his back. This was luxury. They had a boat to carry everything.

At 16:00, *Aminika* set off towards the mainland fully laden for a trip up-river. The speedboat raced for the beach. On the final approach, Gumbao had to slow down. The river was crowded with a crash of hippos. The group must have been forty strong and had come down the tidal river to play and forage in the surf along the reef line just off the beach. *Aminika* cautiously maneuvered between the huge grey animals. Most were on the surface, but a hippo can stay underwater for up to six minutes. If one came up from below, it would capsize them immediately. The large cows gazed at the passing boat, and some roared a warning, opening their mouths exposing a long pink tongue and enormous canine teeth. Hippos were normally quiet animals, but if they had young or were pissed off, they could tear the small boat to pieces.

Aminika carefully maneuvered around them, some weighing much more than a ton. Once she was clear of the main group, they motored towards the river mouth.

Hassan said, "This is one of the biggest rivers around. My uncle in Lamu said it goes for hundreds of miles inland. But near the ocean, it has many branches where it's easy to get lost."

Brody said, "I guess we will have to stay to the bigger waterways. I'm sure that boat would do the same."

Gumbao looked up from the controls. "We'll see some people. There are always nosey people around. Us Swahilis are their brothers and sisters."

Hassan answered, "Yeah, these are the Pokomo Tribe the people who made the Swahilis. We can ask them what they have seen."

Brody looked at his two friends quizzically. "What does that mean 'Made the Swahilis?'"

Gumbao explained, "Pokomo are one of the oldest coastal tribes. The Arabs met them when they came before even you 'Muzungus' had heard of Africa. The Arabs fell in love with the beautiful tribal women. That's how Swahili came, it is a mixture of Pokomo and Arab. Even the Kenyan National Anthem is one of their songs."

Aminika pushed further against the tan-coloured freshwater flowing from the highlands into the ocean. The channel widened until it was about one hundred and eighty feet across. Sluggish water pushed against the hull, slowing their progress as the speed boat moved further into the delta. Gumbao was navigating, keeping to the largest tributaries and deepest water. As the team moved upstream, the sandy, mangrove-covered banks slowly changed to a deep red, covered in long green reeds with bright yellow flowers. Cicadas scratched their long back legs together, like a thousand bad violinists at practice. Frogs croaked, looking for a mate, creating a combined cacophony that was almost deafening. *Aminika*'s forward motion was the only respite from the heat and sweat of the oppressive, heavy atmosphere. It felt like a weight on your shoulders, air full of water, the molten globe above burning with fierce intensity. The broad flat delta spread out in front of the boat, narrow tributaries on all sides. Tall verdant grasses swayed in the current, covered in iridescent, blue, crested finches, bright yellow love birds, and arguing weaver birds all fighting for a place. It seemed this was the centre for birds in East Africa. Hidden among this natural beauty, lethal crocodiles and hippos lazed in the shallows, enjoying the late afternoon sun.

This was wild Africa, an area still largely unmapped. Only the Pokomo and crocodile egg hunters came along this river. *Aminika* cruised against the stream, keeping a close lookout for sand bars, staying as near to the center of the river as possible. Hassan was at the bow with a long stick continually prodding it down into the brown water. The afternoon wore on into the evening. As the sun went down in front of them, Brody said, "I think we make camp around here tonight. We'll only hit stuff in the dark. I'm sure the boat ahead is doing the same."

Gumbao edged closer to the marshy, mosquito-ridden bank, looking for a place to stop. The deep, ominous, impenetrable forest was just meters away. Huge betel nuts hung from a palm left by Arabs hundreds of years ago. "This place is no good, Boss. We can't stop here. It's too wet, and the air is bad."

Brody was thinking the same. "Yeah, we'll have to anchor in the river tonight. It probably gets dryer upstream. We are right in the middle of the delta now."

Hassan threw the anchor overboard. It immediately stuck in the soft muddy bottom of the river. The bugs just kept coming. The air was thick with hungry mosquitos the size of small birds. Hassan cleared a space at the bow of the speed boat as far from the petrol as possible and lit the gas stove to make coffee for the crew. As they settled in for an uncomfortable night, the sun finally left, throwing them into pitch black. The stars came out one by one, and even the planet Jupiter was visible in the eastern sky, far away over their beloved ocean. All around them, small red, beady eyes started to emerge from the gloom. Hundreds of crocodiles were sitting on the banks or partially hidden among the reed beds. In the ever-growing darkness, these beasts started moving around looking for food. As the air-cooled, it was their time to hunt. *Aminika* lay at anchor, gently swaying in the current. Hassan had set some lights with baited hooks to attract fish for breakfast. Unexpectedly, the water started churning as larger river predators fought over this easy meal.

Brody sat listening to groans and splashes coming from every direction. Sporadically, one of the larger crocs bumped into the boat with a bang, pushing it through the water. There was no sleeping, just drinking coffee and waiting for the dawn when the mosquitos would stop biting and the light would allow them to continue upstream. He was starting to have second thoughts. This was not such a good idea. They were sat in a crocodile-infested river in the middle of nowhere. The only backup was really no backup. If he called Briggs on the satellite phone, he could never get to them in time. His crew were not prepared for this. Maybe he should turn around in the morning and head back to the mouth of the river, then wait for the smugglers to come back out. If he did this though, it could take weeks. Not knowing what was going on was gnawing at his gut, and being shot at and having an attempt made on his life was enough to really piss him off. As the long grey strings of dawn were slowly pushing up into the sky in the east, he had decided one more day. If they did not come across anything by the evening, he would tell the crew to turn around and head back along the river to sit and wait at the entrance.

As soon as there was enough light to see, the small boat started heading upstream, slowly at first in the wide, shallow river. After an hour when the heat of the day was settling on their heads, the river began to close in on them. It was becoming much narrower and faster with lots of twists and turns. The water was deeper as they moved out of the delta and into the major river system heading inland. Gumbao was able to increase the speed, making better time. The edges of the river were still marshy, but it was becoming less so as the land around them turned into the savannah of the high plains and bush.

As the burning hot sun hit its zenith, the craft rounded a corner in the river and was presented with a long stretch of flat, calm, open water. On the right-hand side, about three hundred yards ahead, was a steep muddy beach running along the bank. Small dugout canoes were lined up in a neat row. A faint smoky odor hung in the air, combined with the sharp hint of cordite. Brody immediately felt something was wrong. The oppressive atmosphere of so many firefights he had been in over the years hit him like a punch to the gut.

He urgently grabbed Gumbao's arm. "Slow down. This doesn't look good!"

Gumbao immediately slowed the engines to a crawl, just holding them steady against the current. Brody opened his green seaman bag and removed the Ithaca shotgun. Five shells were in the magazine. He pumped one home, then took another ten and stuffed them in his pockets. "Gumbao, land me here at the end of the beach. I'll take a look around. You stay right back until you see me."

Gumbao nodded his agreement. Hassan reached for the bag and took the Kalashnikov out, cocked it, and sat at the bow.

Everything was quiet. No movement on the beach, just the rush of the water against the bows of the boat and the wind whistling gently through the trees. Brody jumped onto the mud at the furthest end of the open bank, ran up to the edge of the bush, and disappeared instantly.

He walked slowly and noiselessly through the rough undergrowth. The smell of burning was getting stronger as he made his way west towards the center of the beach. After several minutes of struggling through the thickly-thorned trees, the first clearing appeared. In the center were the remains of a burnt-out thatched hut. The roof had collapsed into the small building. The brown mud and wattle walls were cracked and stained with black soot. Laying in front of the house, on top of some narrow wooden burnt beams from the roof, was a dead, bloated brown mongrel dog. It was covered in a thick layer of flies humming in the bright afternoon glare. Brody stood in the cover of the trees and watched for a few minutes. Usually, a village would have the natural sounds of babies crying, dogs barking, and children playing, but everything was still. Gradually, he entered the clearing. Flies came up off the dog like a black, annoyed rain cloud, then buzzed angrily around his head. He nudged the dead dog with his toe, and more flies came out of a huge gaping hole that used to be the top of the poor animal's head. It had been shot with a high caliber revolver or rifle. Most of the cranium had been blown away. Off to the right, a glint caught his eye. A few feet away in the dust was a massive brass cartridge. It was as fat as his thumb and twice as long. This was the wrong size for a sniper round. The caliber was huge, built to pack a short-range punch, a hard-hitting round with no accuracy at any distance. One thing was for sure, it was way overkill for a small creature. Whoever did this was high on his own firepower.

    The thatched hut was empty, no bodies. Brody stealthily moved on through the deserted village, passing three more burnt huts. Each one had the forlorn belongings of the owners scattered on the ground, like an orgy of violence: thrown clothes, furniture, stored food, pots and pans all over the place. Ahead was a narrow path leading towards the beach. He followed carefully, the Ithaca held ready, watching for any signs of life. The pathway had trees and bushes on either side. The river could be heard burbling away in the near distance. He idly wondered if Hassan and Gumbao had done what he had asked. This was a peaceful, beautiful place to be quiet, calm, with the sound of running water nearby. A real Garden of Eden, apart from the dead dog!

As the path came to an end, it broadened into what was the center of the village. In front of him stood a large burnt-out, round house. It must have stood some twenty feet high at its center with solid mud and buffalo dung walls. The villagers had probably spent their days working here mending nets, running the livestock, and doing all of the other daily routines a community needed to survive in the remote bush.

Now it was the scene of carnage. Scorched and mutilated bodies lay across the entrance to the burnt-out building, as if the people were trying to escape. The roof had collapsed into the center. The walls were pockmarked with automatic rounds which had been fired into the blaze. As Brody got closer, he could see the people in the doorway had been shot at point-blank range. Small entry wounds and gaping exit wounds covered their bodies. The poor villagers had been defenseless against these attackers and now lay in the dirt, the wounds full of flies as the flesh rotted under the broiling African sun. Brody almost gagged and took a step back. Sitting in the middle of the massacre was a huge African fish eagle, buried up to its shoulders inside a stomach. He shouted. The disturbed bird slid its head out of the sloppy mess, looking at him with a large evil eye. The beautiful white plumage of its neck was stained red, gristle dripping off a pointed orange beak. He could not help himself and fired the shotgun into the air, scaring all the birds from the trees. The fish eagle expanded its five-foot, black and white wings and took off into the air with a long screech of anger at being disturbed from a hearty meal.

He just stood and stared at the poor innocent villagers. Women and children in the wrong place at the wrong time. Who had done this and why? It was recent, not more than a day or so. He turned to head for the beach. They would bury all of these people before moving on. As he did so, there was a thud, and something hit him on the back of the head, then everything went black.

Brody's mouth felt dry and full of dust. His eyes would not open, and there was a dull throbbing pain in the back of his head. Slowly, so as not to attract attention, he tried to move his hands to feel the wound. It was useless. They were tied tightly behind his back. As the senses gradually came back, it was clear he had been trussed up like a forest animal. His legs were crossed in front of him, then a pole had been slid between his thighs. He felt like a sitting Buddha facing the pole. Escape was the priority. The guys who had done all the killing could still be around. From the look of the massacre, he would not last long. He strained his thighs trying to stand up, but all the forces worked against him. It felt like his ankles would snap like a twig. His arms were tied tightly together and high up on his back, which made it impossible to stand.

Brody's first reaction was to shout for help. The boat was only meters away in the river. Before making such a foolish mistake, he stopped. This had been an ambush, which could easily happen to his crew. They could be trussed up like him now, or unconscious. He looked around whoever had done this had dragged him a few feet from the dead bodies and trussed him up like a pig for the barbeque. He wiggled his arms and legs, but whichever way he moved was painful. There was no way to get enough purchase to push up onto his feet.

After a few minutes, two skinny, tall teenage boys came out of the dense bush to his left. Their skin was so black it looked blue, and their shaved heads shone in the sun. The kids were almost naked, just a small loincloth around their waists. Each was carrying a long thin bow with a quiver strung over his shoulder. The taller of the two had a leather thong in his hand with a cup in the center. In the other hand, he had a large round pebble from the river. Hung around their waists were long blades. They stood staring, holding his Ithaca and pointing it directly at his stomach. Brody said, "Look, I'm a friend. I didn't do this. I was passing and wanted to help."

The first youth said, "You're a white! Whites did this to our family. Why do you come back?"

Brody said, "No. No, I didn't do this. I'm traveling upriver. I mean you no harm."

The second boy spoke to the first in a language Brody had never heard before.

Then the first youth said, "We'll kill you. You're white it repays the debt."

Suddenly, from the other side of the muddy bank, a calm voice could be heard. It was speaking in the same language as the youngsters. It chatted on for a while, the young kids looked around trying to tell where the voice was coming from. After a couple of seconds, Gumbao appeared over the ridge leading to the river. He was unarmed and smiling, walking in a slow leisurely pace, like he was out on an afternoon stroll in a city park.

Brody felt a mixture of relief and anger. His orders had been disobeyed. However, he was tied to a post after being knocked out easily and had lost his weapon in less than two minutes!

Gumbao kept talking to the youngsters until he was level with Brody. He spoke in Pokomo. "Salaam Alekum. Listen, this man is not your enemy. He is a good man. We will help you bury your family, then we will catch the whites who did this to you."

The youngsters looked at Gumbao. He looked like the Gasa, the old man their father went to for advice with his white curly hair cropped close to his head, two front teeth missing, a real elder. The teenage boys were unsure. The shotgun hung heavy in their young hands. They had never killed a person before.

Gumbao said, "I will help you. Don't worry. Give me the 'bunduki' and we can sort all of this out. You do not want the blood of a white on your hands. Maseha will not be pleased." Gumbao edged closer to the lads.

They were unsure and could see this old man knew their language and their ways. He was probably someone to trust, and right now they were so scared. They had seen their whole family slaughtered from their hiding place in the bush.

Gumbao took the shotgun off the boys and walked over to Brody.

Brody said through gritted teeth. "You should not have come. I told you to stay on the boat. I had this. They would have let me go. Who the hell is Maseha?"

Gumbao said with a broad toothless smile. "Yeah, Boss, I can see that. I heard the gunshot and thought I would take a look. Maseha is their bad goddess. You don't want to make her mad!"

He cut the ropes binding Brody and pulled him up by the shoulders to straighten his legs.

As he walked off the stiffness in his joints, he said, "Let's go down to the river and get something to drink. We can ask them what happened."

Aminika was beached on the long muddy bank next to the dugouts. Hassan still had the Kalashnikov over his shoulder and was ready for anything. Gumbao sat with the boys on the bank and started chatting. Brody came to the boat. "Hassan, pass me some water and a beer, will you?"

"OK, Boss. What happened?"

"Those poor bastards have had their family murdered. Gumbao is talking to them to find out what happened."

Gumbao approached after thirty minutes. "Those kids have had it shit, Boss. A group of maybe ten or twelve guys came through last night. It was after dark; the boys were already in their hut on the far side of the village. These lower Pokomo are very superstitious. There is a devil for everything. The men surprised them. Some came from the river and others came from either side. The boys say suddenly there was gunfire from the edges of the village. It was total panic. The Lower Pokomo are a friendly, peaceful tribe, not like their cousins upriver. Each house was emptied by the men, and all the villagers had to come to the main square. The kids broke the back wall of their hut and escaped into the bush. Their mother and father were not so lucky and got dragged out. The boys hid in the trees for a while, then carefully walked around the edge of the village until they could see the main hut. The men were inside, laughing and joking, then shouting and shooting guns into the air. The boat they were on was pulled up onto the bank. It was big and wide, not like a canoe. The men had taken bottles from the boat and were drinking in the round house. All the villagers were inside sitting on the floor. One by one, the big white and brown men came out of the hut with a woman and took her into the bushes. All they heard were screams. Then the main guy, a small thin white man, came out and shouted at them all. The village men were tied up and pushed to the water, then loaded on the boats. The men set fire to the main house and all the others in the village. When the old men, women, and children tried to escape, the white men shot them. That's it, Boss. Tana Delta is a wild place. Things like this happen here."

Brody almost felt ashamed to be white. "OK, Gumbao, what can we do for the kids? We can't take them with us."

Gumbao said, "Further upstream there is a branch that leads south-west. There's another village about ten miles further along. We can take them there to be looked after."

Brody frowned. "That takes us out of our way. We need to catch these guys before they do any more damage. But I guess it's the least we can do."

It took another four hours before all the dead were buried. *Aminika* pulled back out into the river as the sun was slipping below the horizon, and continued west. The channel was wide and deep enough for the boat to continue travelling at night. With a three-quarter moon giving them some light and the boys to guide them at midnight, the youngsters spotted the tributary to the village. After another hour, small lights could be seen in the distance. The bank broadened again, and a few thatched huts came into view under the moonlight. The boys started shouting a greeting to make sure the men of the village did not come out firing bows and arrows. People didn't travel these waters at night. The hippos and crocodiles were out hunting and could tip a canoe in a second. It was also the time when Maseha walked and could take your heart forever.

After a very brief greeting, Gumbao jumped back on the boat. "They'll be OK here. I told the head elder what had happened. His brother was living in the village. He's frightened for him now."

As the boat was pulling away from the shore, Brody asked, "Have they heard anything?"

"Yes, there is a gang of people no one wants to go near. The gang stays well beyond a canoe's journey for two days. The boat passes the head of the tributary sometimes, carrying many heavy things."

Brody said, "Let's go. We've time to make up. If we can keep a steady pace, it won't take more than a day or so to get to that part of the river."

Chapter Eight

Naydia had never walked so far or so fast in her life. As a college undergrad, fitness had been a major part of her life, running, badminton, tennis and cycling. Until now, if anyone would have asked, she would have told them nothing could defeat her.

This was different. The men in the squad led by Naipanoi were all either Masaai or other clans from the plains of Africa. Running and walking was a part of life. These men were tough, and stopping before the sun went down was not really something they understood. Just march and jog the whole day through. Naydia wore a small day pack containing enough water and snacks to last until the sunset. The Rangers carried a full pack and a Kalashnikov semi-automatic rifle with ammo, but they still had to wait for her sometimes.

The team woke at dawn, quickly ate cold rations, then started walking. Before the sun came up, Naipanoi always wanted to cover some good distance. The routine was grueling. For the first three hours before sunrise, the team walked for thirty minutes, then jogged for another thirty, then back to walking. Once the heat of the day hit, they took a small break for one hour. Then the slog began, a full nine hours walking under the blazing sun. It was relentless. The other members of the team did not seem to notice. But Naydia almost instantly got a headache and had finished her daily water ration by lunchtime. Naipanoi would find her, while the rangers sat in the shade for the twenty-minute lunch break, and refill her bottle. Then during the day, whenever she was lagging behind, he would say. "Madam, if you are tired, we can call the plane. It will come for you."

This only made Naydia angrier. She would stubbornly shake her head. "Naipanoi, for the hundredth time, I'm here to stay. You can't get rid of me with this macho display."

The head ranger always smiled his toothy smile and nodded, like he was talking to a petulant child. "OK, Madam. Your feet, not mine. But just let me know if it gets too hard."

This was how Naydia had spent the last five days trekking through the African bush. It was not really a luxury safari. But on the bright side, she had lost some weight, and her legs were starting to look really toned and firm. When she got home, her college mates would be so jealous.

Today, as usual, the soldiers moved through the bush in a rhythmic line, everyone keeping pace, with Naydia trailing at the rear. The drab brown savannah was slowly turning a vivid green. Trees had lush green leaves with heavy fruits hanging from their branches. Brightly colored birds flitted between them, twitting in excitement as the troop filed below. Monkeys in the trees screeched warning to each other, dancing from tree to tree high above their heads. In this new environment, the air even tasted better. Gone was the dry, dusty feeling at the back of her throat which had nagged for days.

The game increased as well. The rangers had surprised a large family of zebra about an hour ago. The lead scout had managed to divert the rangers just before they blundered into them. There were so many more birds- white egrets and saddle beak storks with their long black and orange beaks. Some stood three feet high. This area was altogether a better environment than the hot, dry plains behind them.

Naipanoi was walking behind her. "Madam, you notice we are nearing the river. You've done well. I didn't expect you to survive this walk."

Naydia replied, "We women are not all soft to be left at home. What's the plan now we're here?"

"We'll track about a mile off the river where the ground is still hard. Hopefully, we'll come across some prints or, if we are lucky, a path to a camp. These poachers will probably use the river for most of their supplies and taking the ivory out."

Naydia said, "So, we just keep going and looking?"

"No. I'll set up a base camp in an hour, then send small groups out along the river looking for any signs. They'll report back every three or four hours."

Naydia was still angry at the poachers. She could not understand why someone would murder such a magnificent animal just for a statue or cigarette holder. "OK, I'm in. I can help you find these bastards, then we can stop some of this killing for a while."

At dusk, the troop halted and made a permanent camp about four hundred yards from the river. The rangers had been told they would be there for at least a couple of days. Like any soldiers, the guys made it as comfortable as possible. Naydia was the only one with a tent to sleep in, but the soldiers soon built small wooden beds and cots to lay on. After just a few hours, the camp was as comfortable as any manyatta on the Mara.

The following day when Naydia woke, the camp was almost empty. There was just one guard sat smoking a cigarette by the smoldering embers of the fire. Naydia demanded. "What happened here? Where's everyone?"

The ranger replied, "Ah, Madam, they're on patrol. They left before the dawn came. You were snoring, so the boss left you to sleep."

Naydia stormed off to the river bank to get a wash and some peace. She was even more annoyed now. At the bank, she stripped down to her bra and pants. There was a small pool of quieter water just off the mainstream. First, she washed her sweat-stained clothes. Then after a quick dip, she sat on the river bank as her clothes dried in the morning sun. Naydia looked around at her surroundings. Africa was a truly beautiful place. She was at least one hundred miles from any civilization, sat beside a rushing river. Life was all around her. Small birds sat in the trees chirruping and squawking to each other. On the other side of the river, a troupe of baboons were busy foraging. The mothers with the babies holding on tightly to their bellies. In the distance, she could see the heads of seven or eight giraffes chewing on the higher leaves of the acacia trees. After sitting and contemplating her position, she felt much better, even, privileged to be part of this landscape, helping it to survive. She stood up, got dressed, and headed back to camp feeling much better, ready to take on anything.

As she arrived, there was a frenzy of activity. Two groups of rangers had arrived back, very excited. The recon group had found a small path leading into the bush towards the river. The soldiers had followed the path carefully until they smelled cooking fires and heard voices. At that point, they decided to return and report.

Naipanoi came back an hour later. The rangers quickly reported their findings and pointed in the general direction of the camp.

Naydia watched them prepare. "Naipanoi, I'm coming with you. I'll need to document any tusks we find there."

"No, Madam, this is seriously dangerous. We need to scout it out and then come back and make a plan."

Naydia was quick. "I can help you scout it out. You're not going to attack or anything, just have a look. Well, I can be as quiet as anyone. I need to survey any tusks to give us an idea. Then we can call the plane in to bring reinforcements and take these guys."

"That's a bit simplistic, but yes, basically the idea. If you come, you stay with me and do exactly what I say. Is that clear!"

Naydia agreed, "Crystal. Scout's honor, or ranger's honor."

Naipanoi didn't know what she was talking about. He would rather have her behind him than wandering around getting into trouble. Anyway, this was just a reconnoiter, no contact at all.

The small team of rangers prepared, then headed out into the bush. The journey to the entrance of the pathway took nearly two hours. Naydia was sweating in the late afternoon sun, but kept up as they slowly marched through the dense bush. The three lead scouts kept about fifty yards in front walking slowly, watching and listening for any sound. The poachers could approach from any direction. They were continually out finding more tusks, wandering all over the savannah hunting for their grisly cargo.

The path was about nine feet wide, no vehicle marks at all, just bare and booted footprints. The lush green bush had been hacked down to allow the porters to carry the cargo down to the river. Luckily, the path was not straight. Large trees grew near the river's edge. The path wound around them. Naipanoi said, "The river's about six hundred yards south of here. I expect their camp is right on the banks to get some breeze."

Naydia said, "What's the plan?"

"You stay with me." He pointed at the rest of the men and continued, "You two go east for about one hundred yards, and you two return west. We'll move slowly and silently through the bush to the perimeter of the camp. Remember, no contact. Our party is too small. We look and report only. Then get reinforcements to take the lot of them."

Naipanoi waited for about ten minutes, then motioned for his group to move forward, holding his fingers to his lips. "No noise."

The teams slowly crept through the dense bush next to the river. As they got closer, the ground became very wet and boggy, slowing them even further. About a hundred yards from the camp, familiar sounds started to be heard: cooking pots clanking together, small talk, and laughter, even some shouting.

At fifty yards, they could smell the food cooking, plus stale sweat and cheap cigarettes. The place had a pall of death hanging over it, like a storm cloud on a summer's day. The guys in the camp did not seem to worry about noise. There was even a radio blaring weird music; lots of drums and plucking of a guitar type instrument. Naydia felt strange creeping up on these people. It was almost as if she was a peeping Tom abusing their privacy.

The three teams reached the edge of the clearing at almost the same time. The group to the east had come out behind some light-weight wooden shacks; the western group behind the latrines. Naydia and Naipanoi were at the end of the long track in the bush, surveying the whole camp.

Naydia nudged Naipanoi. "On the left, those tents look like sleeping quarters?"

Naipanoi nodded. "Yes, this place is the biggest camp I've seen so far. It has space for maybe forty people."

The camp stretched out to the left of them past the green canvas sleeping quarters until it hit the dense bush about eighty feet away.

Naydia said, "There's smoke and music coming from over the far side near the river. That must be the cook tent."

"Yes, and to our right looks like the ablutions area. It's set aside from the rest. No one is over there."

The tent sat on its own was a good forty feet passed the little track to their right.

Naydia said in a whisper as she crouched in the bushes next to Naipanoi. "My God, that's awful. I just can't take my eyes off it. It stinks. It's terrible. How can these men live with this?"

In the centre of the clearing just in front of the river bank was a huge pile of tusks. It was at least ten feet high and twenty feet long. These were not the white tusks you see in the newspapers, with the proud African President standing in front, declaring a win against the poaching industry. This was different. It was a pile of bloody, stinking tusks, all shapes and sizes, covered in flies and dried blood, the cut marks still visible in the rotting flesh where the poachers had hacked the long beautiful lengths of ivory off the elephants, rhinos, and buffaloes. It was disgusting. Forlorn elephant feet sat around the edge of the pile, put out in the sun to dry, just standing there in a row as if they were waiting patiently for their owners to return.

Naydia felt the bile rising from her stomach. She desperately swallowed to keep from throwing up. "There must be more than five tons of the stuff." She whispered in between swallows.

Naipanoi looked at her. "Are you alright? Don't make any noise. They'll kill us without a thought. This camp has been here a long time. These guys have been busy. It must be a major part of the supply chain to get this stuff out of the country, and we didn't even know about it. I am sure there is a boat to take it downriver to the ocean, then to a waiting freighter offshore."

Naipanoi shifted his head to one side. He had heard a distinct bird call. The guide on the east had some information. He moved back ten yards, leaving Naydia at the forest edge, and waited. A few moments later a ranger appeared next to him. Naipanoi asked, "What did you find?"

The guide replied, "Boss, we have surveyed our section. It is mostly sleeping quarters. But we just heard an engine. Something is approaching from the east, we think on the river. It's a couple of miles out, but coming steadily."

Naipanoi crept back to his position. "We must be quiet; a boat is coming."

They sat waiting in the bush for another half an hour, not moving a muscle. The mosquitoes had found them. Naydia sat motionlessly as she was slowly sucked dry, hundreds of bites on her exposed arms and legs. She so wanted to move and squash the damned creatures, but it would mean certain exposure to these terrible men.

The boat gradually hove into view, moving against the current, slowly creeping up the river until it was abreast of the main camp. Then the captain put on a spurt of speed and raced for the shore. The flat-bottomed craft rammed the soft mud, sliding its length about two thirds out of the water onto the bank. As the engines were cut, a group of guys came out of the mess tent to greet the new arrivals.

At the head of the group was a skinny almost white guy. Naydia said, "He's Oriental, maybe Chinese or Korean."

The other seven guys were a mixture of whites and blacks, they crowded over to the river bank.

The Oriental guy shouted, "Fu, you're late. What kept you? Was Lamu too interesting for you, eh! We've a business to run here. You can't just lounge around leaving us to do all the work."

Fu Yee jumped off the boat. "We ran into some trouble offshore, then we went for supplies and collected some more labor along the route."

"I hope the labor is better this time. The last lot were rubbish. They hardly lasted three weeks. Those savages are so weak, dropping in the bush like flies. Took us an extra five days to get this haul in."

The Oriental from the boat said, "Listen, you do your work, I'll do mine. It's hard to find these people. They run away now before we even get close."

"How many did you bring?"

"I have twenty-five men; the females were no good. We got rid of them."

"Good. No witnesses?"

"Ah, my friend, you think I'm an amateur. These savages are always fighting amongst themselves. The village was burnt to the ground."

"Come inside. We have tea and rice. Did you bring me some whisky?"

"Ah, don't worry, Wai, I always think about you. You two, get the savages off the boat, then chain them by the load. Make sure you chain them properly. Anyone escapes and it comes out of your share."

Two guys broke off from the team and started shouting and waving their arms at the poor wretches remaining on the dirty boat. The villagers were dragged and kicked off the long fiberglass craft, then taken over to the stinking pile of tusks and elephant feet and chained to posts.

Once the villagers had been secured, the whole gang retreated to the mess tent, leaving only one guard on duty.

The eastern team of rangers had moved slowly along the edge of the camp, careful to stay out of sight. After painstakingly creeping through the dense jungle, the two rangers had managed to get behind the mess hut and sat listening. Goko the larger of the two, said quietly. "Kairu, you are small and quiet. Move closer so we can find out what those 'Muzungus' are saying."

Kairu nodded, then slowly inched forward until he was within a yard of the back of the tent. The gang were chatting, mostly too quickly for him to understand. These people were talking in a strange language. It was only when the few African's spoke he understood.

Kairu had decided to return to the safety of the bush. Suddenly, directly in front of him, a flap in the tent swept open, and a man exited, pulling on the fly of his trousers.

Kairu looked at him for a split second, then slipped his blade from its scabbard and stabbed him in the throat. The blade was honed to perfection. It went straight into the thug's neck and voice box, stopping him from screaming. The problem was the man fell backwards against the canvas and through the flap he had come out of. There was silence from inside. Before Kairu could move, ten automatic weapons were pointing in his direction. He stood and stared. The guy gurgled on the floor as he bled out.

Goko was still hidden about ten feet further back in the bush, too far away to help. And anyway, what could he do against ten automatic weapons? He slowly and very carefully lowered himself to the jungle floor, hoping and praying to all of his gods that the thugs would not search the undergrowth, as they would surely find him in seconds.

Kairu was dragged through the mess tent and thrown out the other side into the open compound. Three of the larger men started brutally kicking him. Kairu rolled, trying his best to protect himself, then curled up in a ball on the dirt floor. One of the thugs was larger than the rest and seemed to relish in handing out violence. The tall, strong African had a long, thin, highly-polished length of what looked like a tree branch, about two feet six inches long, with a heavy round knot at the end, as hard as steel. This weapon of choice for many of the coastal and central tribes was called a 'Rungu'. He beat Kairu showing no mercy, with the hard tree knot on his arms and legs as the others continued to kick him.

The oriental man came out of the tent and shouted. "Stop, Stop!"

He drew a long-barreled pistol from a holster on his hip. The gun was his prized possession, a 'Magnum 45' one of the most powerful handguns ever made. It looked massive in the small, wiry man's hand. "Who are you?" he demanded.

Kairu laid still as if he was unconscious.

The oriental man said in a high-pitched crescendo of a voice. "Listen, my name is Wai Chan Quai. I will get answers from you, or my men will tear you to pieces!"

Another tall, slim Swahili pushed through the crowd. It was obvious from his poise that he had authority in the gang. His burnished copper-colored skin shone under the sun. He was dressed in a bright white Kanzu, the traditional long, one-piece dress of the Swahili people. On his head was a small round hat with a flat top called a 'Kofir', covered in intricate needlework. "Quai, this is a Park Ranger, but we are not on parkland, he's outside his jurisdiction."

Quai said, "Faraj what does that mean, jurisdiction?"

Faraj answered patiently. "These soldiers protect the park. They only have control within the boundaries. But we are over fifty miles outside of any game reserves here."

Quai shouted again in his squealing pitch. "What are you doing here? Pick him up and tie him to a post."

Naipanoi had seen the problem unfold in front of him. "Shit. Now we have trouble. I told those guys to stay hidden, just watch."

Naydia whispered urgently. "What will they do to him?"

"It won't be good I can tell you. We have little jurisdiction outside of the parks. We need a special order to arrest these guys."

"That seems like the least of our problems right now. Those guys are mean as hell. They'll take pleasure in killing him."

Naipanoi retreated into the bush and waited. Goko crawled through the undergrowth and joined him a few minutes later. "Boss. Kairu was listening at the tent. One of the guys came out and saw him. Kairu slit his throat, but there were too many he had no time to escape. I could not help or I would be out there too by now"

Naipanoi thought for a second. "Go back to your post. Sit and watch. We'll see what they do."

In the centre of the camp, Kairu was tied to a post with his arms pulled high above him. He stood on the tips of his toes, moaning. The beating had taken its toll.

Quai shouted, "You have friends here. Where's your team?"

Kairu tried to feign unconsciousness and kept his eyes closed.

Quai nodded to the guy holding the Rungu. He flashed an evil grin, then lashed out at Kairu's stomach, smashing the wind out of him.

Quai said, "You will talk or die as you hang there. The parks are miles away. You have no rights here. I'll kill you and feed your body to the crocodiles."

Naipanoi touched Naydia's arm. "He won't be able to hold up for long. We'll have to get help or rescue him."

"How can we get help quickly?"

Naipanoi looked at his trooper in the middle of the clearing. "Dusk is coming. We can try to rescue him when it gets dark, if he is still alive."

Quai returned to the mess tent. "Captain Faraj, I don't like this. We have never had visitors before. We'll push up our schedule. How long will it take to load the boats and get out of here?"

Captain Faraj said, "About a day to load the boats with the next shipment. But listen, there are a least two more loads before we clear the beach of all the tusks. Then we can finish here, maybe shut down for a while or move camp."

Quai was furious. "We pay good money for this not to happen. I spent months in Nairobi greasing palms and paying bribes. My business partners were assured no one would bother us out here. A free-range to take what we wanted. What has happened? Heads will roll for this!"

Quai stalked off as Faraj started shouting. "You guys, untie the locals. We need to load the boat and get out of here."

The sun was setting on the camp. The Rangers remained in the forest, watching their comrade hang from a pole. All around him people were running, carrying the macabre cargo and loading it carefully onto the boat.

Naipanoi said, "We'll sneak in after dark, when it goes quiet. Once we get Kairu, we'll make a run for it and get help."

The ranger team backed off out of the forest, then headed for a small clearing a couple of miles away to wait until it was dark. The team were very subdued, sitting quietly in the gloom. Naipanoi sat brooding at the edge of the clearing. He felt he had let his guys down. He had known these were dangerous men, and the rangers were well outside the game reserve. It was his fault Kairu had been caught. Being in charge meant the ultimate responsibility fell solely on his shoulders. This had left his men exposed. Deciding to chase after these poachers was just looking for glory. Now the team had been put in a precarious position, with a lost man and a stupid woman. The situation would be impossible to explain to head office back in Nairobi. He would definitely lose his command if either the girl got hurt or Kairu was lost. After working ten long years, all the training and walking the bush, it would be a sad end to an otherwise exemplary career. As head ranger, he could retire with a decent pension in another seven or eight years. Maybe even get a job in headquarters before that. He decided calling base had to wait until this mess was over. If the Rangers could get Kairu clear, they would all become heroes. Maybe he'd even get that job in head office earlier than expected.

The eight rangers and Naydia sat in the clearing until the moon was high in the night sky. Naipanoi cursed. It was almost a full moon. That meant loads of light, making it even more difficult. He hoped the poachers had drunk themselves stupid.

The men prepared for the sortie. Everyone was subdued. This might be their last night on earth, it was dangerous work: poachers were killers. All weapons had been checked and rechecked, locked and loaded. Anything that might make a noise was removed and left behind.

When the moon was high, and Naipanoi thought the poachers would have started drinking, they crept back to the long pathway into the camp. This time Naipanoi only set the teams a few yards apart to allow them to give covering fire if needed. He prayed it would be a simple in and out.

Naydia had been allowed to come along, but stayed at the head of the track. Naipanoi whispered, "Don't argue. Stay here out of sight, if you hear anything or see anything, fire this gun. Do you know how to use it?"

"Yes, I'm American. We know guns."

Naipanoi just nodded and disappeared into the darkness of the jungle.

Naydia hid at the edge of the pathway, sitting with her back against a tree. The full moon shining above seemed so close you could almost reach out and touch it. The stars were large and plentiful. There was no natural light for miles around, but because of the moon, it was as bright as an early morning back home in California, when she would jog along the beach before college. Naydia was brought back from her reverie with a start. Something was moving towards her. There was rustling in the undergrowth to her left, then to her right. Every shadow seemed to be holding a gun. Something let out a long, high-pitched screech from above. A huge owl tumbled out of a tree and flew out towards the savannah. The rustling around her got louder. She held the pistol with shaking hands. She had said she could shoot a gun, but killing someone? Could she do that?

Sweat trickled down between her breasts. Her white knuckles clenched the heavy shaking gun stretched out in front. In her mind, she was ready for anything. The surrounding jungle was alive with sound and movement.

She spun left and right, pointing the gun at shadows, certain each one was a poacher come to kidnap her. The Glock Naipanoi had left felt heavy in her hands. Cramps started crisscrossing through her shoulders. This could not go on much longer. The shuffling stopped, and Naydia spun round to face the threat. Whatever it was she, would go down fighting. There was silence for a moment, then a large scaly black and brown snout appeared, followed by an armored body and a long, wide, flat tail. The ground pangolin marched out into the clearing with its short stubby legs. Ignoring her completely, it made its way into the moonlight, then headed off to a nearby termite's mound to feast. Naydia almost laughed out loud, letting out a long sigh of relief as the creature carried on its way. It was a privileged as a lover of animals to have seen such an endangered species.

Naipanoi and his team slowly crept to the beginning of the path. The camp spread out in front of them. Everything looked quiet. Kairu was hanging from the post, his bloodied wrists had metal cuffs secured to a long chain wrapped around the top. The troop spread out left and right, cautiously moving from cover to cover across the camp, Kalashnikovs set on auto. If the shit hit the fan, they would just light the whole place up and kill anything that moved.

Naipanoi was the first to get to Kairu. He whispered, "Kairu, are you awake? Can you move?"

Kairu looked up. "Boss, I'm sorry. I should have moved quicker. They beat me bad, Boss."

"Can you walk? We need to get you out of here."

"Boss, I'll try."

Naipanoi grabbed the chains. They were tight on Kairu's wrists, then knotted and fixed at the top of the post. He could not loosen or untie them. He pulled at the chains which made them rattle in the night. It sounded like a church bell ringing for Sunday service.

The head ranger had a problem: he could not release the chains. The only option was to shoot the link with his rifle, bundle up Kairu, and run like hell. He signaled to the other six troopers guarding their perimeter, motioning what he had to do. After glancing around in the darkness to check all was quiet, he raised the rifle, set on single shot, and aimed at the top link, ready to fire, then grab his trooper and race for the cover of the bush some thirty yards away.

The team were poised and ready. Kairu looked up at his boss and saw his head jerk, then felt a rush of warm moist air on his face as a 9mm hollow-point bullet entered the back of Naipanoi's skull and left through the right eye. The soft-nosed lead pellet took most of his boss's face with it. The blood and brains splattered into Kairu's gaping mouth as he stared in shock. Naipanoi slumped over Kairu, sliding slowly to the floor. The other troopers opened fire immediately into the darkness. The first two fell where they stood, taken out as bullets stitched up across their bodies and into their faces from machine gunfire. Two more started firing and running towards the pathway and safety, but more poachers stepped out of the entrance and mowed them down. The last two saw what was happening and threw their guns away, holding up their hands in surrender. The tall, dark Swahili captain walked slowly out of the gloom. He was smiling as he pulled the Glock 17 from the holster on his hip. Captain

Faraj looked at them for a second with his cold dark eyes, then shot them both in the head in quick succession.

Naydia heard the gunfire and jumped to her feet. Suddenly there was noise all around her, animals frightened and running. She was confused. Was it better to stay put or run? But run where? Certainly not towards the gunfire. Naipanoi would be coming soon and needed to find her so they could escape. Anyway, she had no idea where she was. There was no way to get to civilization without the help of the rangers. They had the satellite phone. Naydia stood. Her whole body was screaming run, but her brain could not decide where to run too! She was frozen to the spot. Up ahead, people were running along the track. It must be the Rangers and Naipanoi. She stepped out of her hiding place and was grabbed by rough hands, then hauled along the track like a sack of potatoes, her feet not touching the ground.

Naydia was dragged into the clearing kicking and screaming. Strong hands pulled her to the centre and threw her roughly onto the dirt floor. Her nose was immediately filled with the stench of dead and rotting flesh. She almost gagged. Then a boot came out of the darkness and slammed into her stomach. She retched onto the pile of tusks beside her and curled into a ball, panic and now dread filling her body. She lay for a few minutes in the fetal position, almost giving up hope. This was surely the end. The poachers would rape and kill her, then throw the body into the river where it would disappear into a crocodile's stomach. She would never be heard of again, another stupid white do-gooder lost in the depths of Africa. Naydia slowly opened her eyes and peered around the camp. She was next to the tusks and elephants' feet with a group of poachers stood in a circle leering at her.

Kairu was tied to his post about two yards away. His body was limp. He looked unconscious or maybe dead. Her blurred vision from the tears of pain and anger slowly cleared. At Kairu's feet was another body. Her jaw dropped as the one staring eye of what had become her very good friend looked up into the night sky. Naydia had never seen human death before. This was all too much. She collapsed back into a heap on the floor in a dead faint.

Chapter Nine

Brody looked up as he heard gunshots in the distance. "Gumbao, are you watching out for the bloody crocs?"

"Yes, Boss, you are clear right now."

Since dropping the young boys on the river bank *Aminika* had made good time running upriver. The current against them was about five knots and the width had grown to over one hundred feet, giving them plenty of room to avoid the sand bars and tree trunks that littered the shallow water. The crew had taken shifts at driving. Brody was at the wheel, running the boat at half speed. They were just rounding a long easy bend in the river when a hippo surfaced in front of them. He instinctively swerved the boat, missing the animal by inches. *Aminika* raced across the current, almost hitting a branch jutting out of the water. As Brody turned the wheel again to avoid the second collision, he rammed a sandbar just under the water. The sudden reduction in speed sent the crew tumbling forward as the boat rode up on the sand, leaving her high and dry. Brody quickly cut the engines as Hassan and Gumbao staggered back from the bow.

With a schoolboy smile he said, "Shit, that was a hard one. I didn't even see it. Must be completely underwater. Switch the light on and keep an eye out for crocs."

He jumped over the side into the knee-deep river. Hassan switched the light on, and Gumbao searched the fast-moving water for beady eyes, which were the last thing most people saw before the massive jaws snapped your legs, spun viciously, then submerged, taking you to the depths.

Brody waded to the front of the boat. If the crew stood right at the back, he could rock it back and forth, moving it slowly along the sandbar and into deeper water.

Gumbao shouted, "Boss, back on the boat!"

Brody looked over his shoulder just in time. The one and a half-ton, gray-skinned, pissed-off hippopotamus lumbered out of the water with surprising speed. The animal lunged, swinging its enormous wide mouth, trying to knock him into the river, the huge white canine teeth flashing within inches of his chest. He ducked under its chin, falling into shallows next to the sand bar. Gumbao blinded the hippo with the light. Hassan reached for the Glock. Brody shouted, "No, don't fire! You will only make it mad!"

The bright light hid him from the creature for a few seconds. He took the opportunity and scrambled along the boat, half expecting his legs to be caught in a crocodile's mouth at any minute. Once clear of the jaws of the hippopotamus, he lunged over the gunnel, landing in a heap on the deck. Gumbao kept the huge brute blinded with the torch beam. The hippo roared at them again, exposing the eight-inch-long canine teeth.

Brody said, "Man, that was close. Those things are bloody massive!"

Gumbao kept shining the light until the animal got fed up with the game and slowly turned, walking along the sandbar and then disappearing into the river.

As soon as the coast was clear, Brody jumped out and started rocking the boat back and forth, again and again, slowly edging the craft along the bank. Everyone was wary of the dangers. Gumbao kept swinging the light from left to right. The boat groaned and slowly slipped backwards inch by inch. It was then that the gunfire erupted in the distance.

Brody stopped pushing to listen. It sounded like a one-sided firefight: One single shot from a revolver, then some rat a tat tat from the familiar Kalashnikovs, then silence. A few moments later, another two shots rang out, probably a Glock.

Brody looked up at his friends. "What do you think that was?"

Gumbao said, "I hope those bastards are not having more fun."

Brody gave a long hard push on the bow of the boat and felt her stern raise as it got enough depth to float. Then the whole boat gracefully slid back into the current. He ran after *Aminika,* not wanting to be left on the bank with the hippo.

Brody said, "Hassan, we have to be careful, we don't know what we are dealing with here. They sound well-armed and seem to know what they are doing."

Hassan said, "So. Boss, what'll we do?"

"Same as before. You drop me upstream, I'll go in and have a look around."

"But Boss that didn't work out so well last time."

Brody said, "OK, fair point. Gumbao can come with me. Hassan, you stay way back in the river, out in the middle so you can escape easily."

Aminika nosed its way along the river on the northern bank, moving in the shadows. It wasn't long before a faint glow appeared above the trees in front of them.

Brody said, "That looks like a camp up ahead. We'll get out here. Hassan, go back at least three hundred yards and wait."

Hassan slowed the boat, taking it into the bank. "Sawa Boss."

Gumbao with his Kalashnikov and Brody with the Ithaca set off through the dense jungle. The going was tough, although the moon was full, giving plenty of light. The bush was verdant and full, a mass of tangled, wet undergrowth. Gumbao said, "We have to move inland a bit. Close to the river is dangerous. Too many snakes."

Brody agreed and headed inland to get clear of the boggy area. Once the ground was firm underfoot, he signaled to Gumbao, then turned west towards where the camp should be. They cautiously moved through the bush, wary of snakes and other night creatures out finding a meal. Away from the breeze along the river, he soon started to feel the heat descend onto his shoulders. His shirt was sodden after only minutes, trickles of sweat kept dripping into his eyes and making them sting.

Brody was in front, Gumbao about five yards behind, moving pace by pace through the dense bush, not wanting to alert anyone of their presence. The ground was hard underfoot with dry sticks and twigs scattered among the undergrowth. This was like the days in Borneo for Brody, long, sweat, filled hours slowly and silently moving through the jungle, systematically watching for tripwires and booby traps, ever alert for the next ambush. The camp suddenly appeared as a clearing. Brody signaled Gumbao with his fist to take a knee. He crouched at the edge of the undergrowth, listening to the normal camp sounds and smelling the coffee being brewed, mixed with stale cabbage and sweat. Still strong in the air was a heavy scent of cordite. Brody moved back to Gumbao and whispered, "You're my back up. Stay here. If it goes to shit, come out firing."

Gumbao nodded. He knew Brody could look after himself. They had been through a few scrapes over the last couple of years. The last time, Brody had ended up on a sinking boat after chasing some terrorist into the ocean. Gumbao had found him unconscious in the craft up to his waist in water with a bullet wound in his shoulder.

Brody disappeared into the darkness of the bush and was gone, like a ghost.

The camp was busy. A guy was hanging from a post in the centre with some sort of uniform on. Over by the river bank, there were bright lights shining on a huge pile of tusks and workers slowly moving them over to a large wide riverboat moored in the water by the bank. To his left, the mess tent, then further to his right were sleeping quarters and far off on the other side were the heads. This was a basic, standard military operation. All armies used this design for short and midterm occupation. Brody had stayed in places like this all over the world.

Just next to the guy hanging on the post was what looked like a pile of clothes chucked on the ground. As Brody's eyes became accustomed to the changes in light around the camp, he realized it was a pile of bodies, arms and legs stuck out at weird angles. The corpses had been flung in a heap carelessly, dark stains looking suspiciously like bullet wounds and glassy eyes stared up into the moonlight.

The main noise was coming from the mess tent. A small, wiry guy came out waving his arms about. He strode towards the bank and shouted. "Men, we have to get this loaded before dawn. I want to leave early and get back down the river. Faraj, what is happening? Why are you so slow?"

A taller Swahili guy stepped out of the gloom. Brody's blood ran like ice in his veins. He saw him standing in the clearing-- Captain Faraj. The Captain had visited Pemba years ago and kidnapped Hassan's sister along with some other girls. Then he headed for Somalia and the slave markets of the Horn of Africa. Brody had caught up with them and rescued the girls, but Faraj had escaped over the side and swam to safety. This guy was a very dangerous pirate who had a lot of deaths to answer for, and now he was working for the Chinese who had tried to kill him and Gumbao in the ocean.

The guy hanging from the post looked in a bad way. His face was black and blue and covered in blood both eyes were swollen shut. His shirt had been torn off his back, exposing huge red and purple welts. The poor guy could be dead already.

Then Brody saw the villagers. There were over twenty of them dressed in a simple 'kikoy', a cloth used by

Swahili men, wrapped around their waists, and a grubby turban on their heads. The group looked pitiful and frightened. It was obvious from the steel shackles on their ankles this was not paid employment. The macabre pile of tusks stood about twenty yards from the boat. Two of the villagers were standing next to it. They heaved one of the large tusks, which weighed over one hundred pounds, up and onto the head of one of the villagers. He staggered across the dirt, then into the thick, sticky mud of the beach with this huge weight pushing down on his tired, slumped shoulders.

The poachers were watching over them, shouting to keep them moving. One had a bullwhip and used it without mercy. As Brody watched, the villager stumbled at the water's edge, dropping the tusk onto the mud and collapsing alongside it. The man with the bullwhip lashed at him, shouting for him to get up, then kicked him several times. The poor old guy just rolled further into the river, as Brody watched and gripped the shotgun until his knuckles were bright white under the moon. The old guy had obviously been knocked out and started floating off down the river face down. The current tugged at the body, pulling it away from the bank. A sudden swell of water erupted, like a Tsunami hitting the beach. Huge jaws with long white teeth appeared for less than a second. Then the body was gone, and the river was quiet once again.

To his left, there was a sudden scream. A person was bodily thrown out of what seemed to be the mess tent. There was a solid thump as the unfortunate person landed face down in the dirt. Brody thought one of the poachers must have upset the boss man and was now paying for it. Justice was tough out here. As he watched, a pretty face emerged from the dirt, surrounded by an unruly mass of long blond hair. The girl looked as if she was in her mid-twenties. With long, muscled, sun-burnt legs. Brody was taken aback. He had not seen a Western girl in a while. Gradually, and with what looked like considerable pain, she stood up. Her tan safari shirt was stained and torn open to the waist, but her eyes were still defiant as she stared at the two men emerging from the tent. Brody thought to himself, *"Well this has just become more interesting"*.

She shouted, "I'm an American citizen! You won't get away with this. People will be looking for me right now!"

Straightening up and gathering her shirt around her bare chest, she glared at the Chinese man.

He seemed to smile. "You will never be found where we are taking you. A blond will fetch a good price in Hong Kong."

She looked bewildered. "You can't take me away from here. I have family in the states, and I work for the Park Rangers."

The Chinese pointed at the pile of bodies. "The brave rangers did not help you much. They ended up very dead. We found this lovely new telephone. I will keep it now, maybe sell it when I get home."

He laughed and looked at her, then spoke to Captain Faraj. "I don't want her spoilt. Nobody messes with her. She will fetch at least ten thousand dollars, but if she is ruined, then we get nothing. Do you hear me, Faraj? Ten thousand, and you get a good cut."

The Captain nodded in the moonlight. "No problem. She'll be fine." He led the girl across the compound to the hanging ranger and tied her arms next to his. As he did this, he leered as her shirt was once again torn open, exposing her to everyone in the camp.

Brody crept back into the bush and walked away, staying alert to any sounds he might make. His mind was on killing these people. He had to stay focused, but one thing was certain, they would die. He could not think of anything else the gang could actually do which would do more harm to the country he had started to love and make his own. It was more than personal now. He reached Gumbao. "This is serious. We have to do something. There are tons of tusks up there being loaded onto the riverboat we saw in the ocean. These guys have done loads of bad shit. I'm going to stop them once and for all."

Gumbao followed him silently back through the thick undergrowth. When they arrived at the riverbank, Hassan saw them and came alongside.

Brody said, "Let's head down river about a mile or so. We have to plan."

The sun was starting to show itself again on another beautiful African day when they found a small inlet to hold up and make a plan. Hassan set about sorting out some coffee. Brody had hit the whisky as soon as he had got back on board.

Gumbao tied off *Aminika* alongside a small muddy bank. Brody started the conversation. "I saw over twenty poachers in the camp. The worst thing is our old friend Captain Faraj seems to be in charge of the boat, and the Chinese we met in the ocean has a friend who runs the camp. The Pokomo villagers are being used for loaders. Twenty heavily armed men are too many for us. We would get mowed down before we got half of them."

Gumbao thought for a moment. "If they are loading the boat, they will set off soon back down the river."

Brody answered, "Yes, that's what I was thinking too. They'll split up at least four or five on the river. That cuts our odds a bit. I saw a strange blonde American girl tied to a post. I don't know who she is, but we need to get her out too."

Hassan chipped in, "If she's a prisoner, the poachers will ship her out with the ivory. They won't want her around the camp causing trouble."

Brody replied, "Good point. They're heavily armed and will shoot without warning. To get them we'll have to set up an ambush."

Hassan asked, "Even if we get the tusks and the girl, what about the villagers? They are slaves now and won't last long. You said the poachers were beating them."

Gumbao looked out across the river. "Boss, those are our cousins. We can't leave them behind. The Pokomo are good people."

Brody took a swig of whisky. "You're right. We'll have to sort the boat, then get your friends to safety. How far back to that village? Do you think they would help us?"

Gumbao nodded. "Yes, Boss, but they are not very brave. These people live in the bush with no real contact. The Pokomo just grow rice and catch big catfish."

Brody said, "But we will need them to set up an ambush. I'll need bodies to help me in the river."

Hassan chipped in, "Boss, we just go and ask. It's downriver. We can get there in less than a day if we leave now. We must rush. The boat will probably leave tonight and will travel quickly downriver. We'll only have a few hours."

"OK, Hassan, let's get moving!"

Chapter Ten

Gumbao introduced Brody to the village elder, or 'Kijo', on the steep-sided, muddy bank of the Tana. The 'Kijo' was a small thin man, about five feet four inches tall, with polished ebony skin, in his late fifties or early sixties. His completely bald head and broad flat nose complemented the large, friendly, dark brown eyes. When he smiled, there were only a couple of brown teeth remaining in his mouth. Around his neck and across his chest hung a bamboo lattice covered in red, white, and green beads. The old man's only piece of clothing was a wrap around his waist of what looked like the soft brown hide of a hirola antelope. His hard-working hands, with skin like leather and fingers that were permanently curled, the nails broken and missing, held a small strung bow. Over his left shoulder was a quiver full of arrows and dangling across his right was a lethal-looking slingshot. This man had seen work pulling nets on the river and working in the paddy fields for many years. He stood expectantly on the river bank, his wide, absolutely flat feet with broken toenails sinking slowly into the soft mud.

Brody introduced himself, "Salaam Alekum. My name is Brody. We passed by here the other night. How are the two young lads?"

The 'Kijo' said, "Mr Brody, we thank you for bringing us our boys. They were lost and you found them. We are most grateful. My name is Yuda Hiribai. I'm the 'Kijo'. I make the decisions for the village."

Brody said, "Listen, there are some evil people around here right now. They're taking your elephants and killing your people."

Yuda listened and replied, "I understand. I walked all the way to Garsen three days away from here to tell the Chief of Police. That was two months ago. He said he would help, but I've seen nothing."

"I think it's time we did this ourselves. I'm here to help. All I need is a little assistance from you, then I can make these men go away."

The Kijo looked shocked. "Ah, Mr Brody, we are peaceful fishermen. All we do is grow rice on the riverside and eat the catfish in the water. We are not like the Masaai, ready for a fight."

"I understand you. It's not nice to have to stand up to these people, but your men are being taken for slaves. I saw at least twenty in the camp. They were chained and beaten."

Yuda thought for a moment. "Then I must go back to Garsen and plead with the chief of police to make him send soldiers."

"That will take too long. We need to stop the poachers moving along the river. The only way to do that is to destroy their boat."

Yuda looked at Brody, then at Gumbao. "Mzee, what do you think?"

Gumbao said, "Mzee Yuda, you are a wise man, I can see that. And you have many wives, so you know the ways of discussion." The old man smiled. "I was here many years ago as a young soldier when you had problems with the Upper Pokomo. I saw then you are brave. We fought together to bring peace to this region. Now you must stand again to stop the destruction of your tribes. We'll not ask you to endanger yourselves. All we need is some of your men hidden in the jungle on the side of the river. We'll do the rest."

Yuda looked at Gumbao thoughtfully. "Mzee, you know us, that's true. I'll ask the men. If they want to go they can, but I'll not force anyone."

The old village elder turned on his heels and walked up the beach towards the thatched huts, leaving them alone. Several women immediately took his place, setting large bright red, handmade, earthenware bowls fired in locally built kilns on green banana leaves covering the dry mud. Wooden spoons carved from tree branches were laid beside a large pot full of stew for all to enjoy. Gumbao said, "Hassan, eat. These people have good food, catfish they call 'mpunzi' and if we are lucky 'matoke'!"

Gumbao sat and started eating. Brody and Hassan soon joined him. The meal smelled delicious. The chili catfish soup was mixed with cooking banana, 'matoke', and a large helping of brown rice was piled on another banana leaf. A second brightly-painted, orange gourd and four carved wooden drinking bowls were brought by giggling children that immediately ran shyly away.

Gumbao laughed. "Now Mnazi." He gulped down a large bowl of the fermented baby coconut juice before handing the rest to Brody.

After their meal, Brody sat on the boat with his beer, thinking about the plan. It was risky, but they had no real choice. As a military strategist, he knew the group had to be attacked separately for any chance of success. With a larger force, it would have been easy to surround the camp and take them all in one go. However, he only had Gumbao and Hassan plus whoever would help from the village. Gumbao had explained the Pokomo were not fighters. They loved their Tana river and shunned modern society. Life was simple: no TV or radios, just the sound of the bush and whatever they could get from it to live off.

He took the satellite telephone from his green sea bag. It was time to report to John Briggs. After three rings, John picked up. "Hi, Brody, I hope you are still alive and kicking? It seems you've strayed from the original plan."

"What do you mean, John?"

"Well, you are now a good two hundred miles up the Tana river. What have you been up to?"

"The poachers decided to make this personal. Then they went on a killing spree on their way upriver."

"What!"

"Yes, it's shit. These guys need to be stopped. Not only are the elephants being murdered, but they've also decided to go into the slave business."

"Listen, Brody, we can't get involved yet. We need some real concrete evidence. The Chinese have a lot of political clout in this country at the moment. The Chinese State Bank funds most of the roads and major developments on long-term government loans."

"What the hell has that got to do with murder, mayhem, slavery, and poaching!"

"You were a major in the Special Boat Service. You know exactly what this is. If we charge in and kill or arrest a Chinese national or attack a Chinese boat, we could get kicked out of the country altogether. The contraband will be disappeared before we can do anything."

Brody said, "Well, I won't let this lie. If I get any more intel, I'll let you know."

"Brody, I'm warning you. Do not get involved. Head back to Kipini, sit offshore on your island, watch and wait. We will get something done in the end."

Brody said, "OK, I can see where you're coming from."

John hung up, leaving Brody with just the sounds of the river flowing past and the occasional screams of the red colobus monkeys in the trees above. He was well pissed off. This was wrong on so many levels. It was above politics. People were dying.

As darkness fell across the river, Yuda reappeared on the muddy bank. Behind him were ten young men, most of them barely at the end of their teens. The group all had slingshots draped over their shoulders and bows with identical quivers on the other.

Yuda introduced the group, then pulled Brody aside. "Mr Brody, these men have come forward to help. They are our bravest and youngest. Do not let any harm come to them."

"Don't worry, your boys will be hidden in the jungle. No one will even know they're there."

Everyone climbed onto *Aminika* as she pulled away from the bank and headed back towards the head of the tributary. Brody hoped the boat had not passed while they had been sitting on the beach enjoying the hospitality of this friendly tribe.

Early the next morning, he sat in *Aminika* sweating, as usual. She was tucked away under the dense bush in a short, narrow offshoot from the main river. The vantage point allowed one hundred and eighty degrees of vision, stretching some nine hundred yards upstream to the next bend. Now all they had to do was wait.

Gumbao came out of the tangled bush. "Boss, it's all set. You give the signal, and the Pokomo will do as you asked."

"Great. You told them as soon as they are done to hide and meet us at the rendezvous point downstream?"

"Yes, Boss, all done. The Pokomo are good people. We have nothing to worry about."

"OK. We just sit and wait then. Hassan, are you sure they haven't passed."

Hassan answered, "Yes, Boss, that boat is slow and heavy. Even with the current, the crew have to be careful. Do you think the Captain'll be on board?"

Brody looked at Hassan. He had hatred in his eyes for Faraj. "I hope so. We have some scores to settle with him."

The sun was almost overhead when Hassan heard the deep-throated chug of a diesel engine coming downstream. He shook Brody. "Boss, wake up. It's coming!"

Brody was immediately alert, "Good. Gumbao, send the signal to the Pokomo." Gumbao stood on the bow of *Aminika* and let out a long low bird whistle. A few seconds later a reply came from further downstream.

Brody picked up his binoculars and stared at the bend in the river some nine hundred yards away. The large, flat- bottomed fiberglass boat came slowly into view. It had a beam of about sixteen feet and a length of well over thirty. Smoke was belching from a stack on the top of the pilothouse. Dirty black stains streaked along the sides, and old car tires hung at intervals acting as fenders. The original bright blue paint of the hull was dirty and chipped. Brody had only seen the boat in the darkness and was surprised at the size. The younger Chinese guy from the camp was standing on the prow with what looked like a shotgun cradled in his arms. He seemed relaxed, even bored. A cigarette hung from his lips. Brody scanned the length of the boat, counting. Nine armed guys sat smoking along the low gunnels of the craft. At the rear was the pilothouse with enough room for two people. One guy was on the wheel. He saw Captain Faraj standing in the stern of the boat. He looked smug. Business must be good. Brody scanned back up the starboard side. There were some Pokomo tied to the gunnels. In front of them about two-thirds of the way along the boat was a metal cage.

The cage was balanced between the starboard gunnel and the tusks. Inside was what looked like a badly beaten man. He was slumped on the bars at the bottom. Standing in the sun next to him was the blond girl. She had obviously been tied to the metal bars with something. This changed the current plan, which was to slow the boat and spray it with loads of bullets. Now they had up to eleven innocents.

Brody passed Gumbao the binos. "What do you think, Mzee?"

Gumbao surveyed the boat. "We have to be careful. Those Pokomo are tied to the gunnel. We can't sink it, and the cage has someone in it."

Brody thought for a second. "We carry on as planned, but leave it later. We come at them at the last minute. Gumbao, you take the wheelhouse and anyone on the stern. I'll deal with the bow and the prisoners. Hassan, you have to come out like an arrow from a bow. Then get as close as possible to give me a chance to board, OK?"

His two friends nodded in agreement. Gumbao picked up the Ithaca, ratcheting the bolt, loading the first cartridge. Brody took his Glock from the waistband of his shorts and slid the action back, putting a bullet in the chamber. This was going to have to be fast and dirty. As a last-minute thought, he tied the heavy, razor-sharp, stainless-steel dive knife to his calf. Hassan had the Kalashnikov on the seat beside him. The driving would be dangerous and exposed to fire from the poachers. To maneuver across the current of this fast-flowing river was no mean feat. It would take all of his concentration just to get close to the other boat without sinking their own.

The poacher's craft approached the ambush. As it passed *Aminika* hidden in the small inlet, Gumbao let out another long low whistle. He waited for a few seconds, then nodded as a reply came back on the breeze. The tribesman had pulled the anchor rope from *Aminika* tight just under the water at the top of the bend. Brody crouched on the bow of his boat, watching as the long fiberglass craft ran over the submerged line. This was a simple tried and tested method to stop any propeller-driven craft. Simply tangle the prop and the whole thing came to a standstill. The one-inch nylon rope easily slid unnoticed along the hull of the vessel. It popped over the sea gland where the shaft left the boat and entered the water. This was not enough to tangle as it was so smooth. But when it reached the propeller, spinning one thousand five hundred times a minute, it was grabbed. The rope was sliced, one end wrapping itself around the blades of the prop and then twisting along the shaft back towards the hull. As it entangled itself, the friction became too great, forcing the engine to overheat. Finally, the motor could take no more and came to a stop with a loud bang. The eight-foot stainless steel connecting shaft twisted and buckled through the hull, pushing against the sea gland, finally twisting it free and leaving a baseball size hole in the bottom of the boat. Water immediately started rushing in. The twisted rope was securely tied to a stout tree on the northern bank which was now taught and drawing the poachers towards the dense, tangled roots. Pokomo tribesmen quickly pulled in their loose end. A valuable resource such as rope could not be wasted.

The sudden pull from the underwater line jerked the craft in the river, throwing the Chinese guard ten feet through space. He landed with a yell in the flowing waters and was carried off downstream.

Brody dropped his arm, signaling to Hassan to start moving forward. *Aminika* roared into life. Hassan slammed both throttles into forward gear. She shot out of the inlet, racing towards the now drifting river boat about fifty yards away.

The poachers were all yelling. The lost guard was drifting further away, shouting and waving his arms. He fired off two rounds from the shotgun as a large wave started moving towards him. Huge jaws opened as the croc surfaced. They slammed shut on the guy's torso. He beat the animal with the stock of the shotgun and yelled for help. But the fight was over before it had begun. As quickly as it had appeared, the animal and its prey were gone.

Aminika was like a stone from a slingshot racing across the water. As she came alongside, Gumbao blasted the wheelhouse with three rounds from the Ithaca, blowing the small wooden house to pieces.

Hassan expertly controlled *Aminika*, judging the river flow to speed up or slow down. With a final turn of the wheel, she brushed gently along the side of the tires for just a second. Brody waited, holding his breath, judging the distance, then leapt, landing on the narrow deck between a pile of bloody tusks and the gunnel. The poachers had been completely surprised and were slow to react. Gumbao's shotgun blasts had sent them racing for cover, giving Brody an opportunity to board. But they recovered quickly. *Aminika* raced away in a tight circle, followed by the rat a tat tat of automatic gunfire.

Brody landed on his feet about amidships. The Pokomo were staring at him in fear. He was like 'Maseha', the evil spirit of the forest, come to avenge their bad deeds. The villagers cowered from this white avenging angel. Brody slipped his dive knife out of the scabbard on his calf and cut the ropes of the poor tribesmen. They immediately knew what to do and dived over the side. Brody glanced out of the corner of his eye and saw three canoes leaving the beach, heading towards the stricken boat.

One guard appeared on the opposite side of the craft, but could not get across the tusks. In one fluid action, Brody slipped the Glock from his waistband and put two rounds into the guy's chest. Without stopping, he moved forward to the man in the cage. The gang were regrouping, but were not sure who to shoot at first. Captain Faraj had ducked for cover and started shouting orders. Gumbao pumped more shots into the rear of the boat. Hassan drove in ever-closer circles, weaving left and right, trying to occupy the poachers and draw the fire, giving Brody much needed seconds.

Most of the villagers were in the river, swimming as fast as they could downstream, heading for their friends in the canoes.

Brody grabbed the cage and shook it, looking for the door to get the ranger out. It had some sort of pin and lock system. As he was pulling at the pin to unlock the door, he was hit from behind with a huge elephant tusk. One of the poachers had made his way along the edge of the boat. The blow stunned him for a second. As he turned to face the attack, the tusk flashed out in a straight thrust, trying to impale him. Brody managed to dodge, but the tusk hit his hand, knocking the Glock to the floor. Brody parried another blow and picked a horn from the pile. The two were thrusting and parrying blows from each other, like ancient knights with macabre bloody broad swords.

The guy managed to get a long swing which hit Brody in the upper arm. The blow was hard, knocking him off balance. But he recovered and swung his elephant tusk around in a wide arc, hitting the poacher on the side of the head and knocking him into the pile of bloody stinking tusks.

Brody tried the cage again, loosening the pin. The ranger was almost unconscious from his ordeal so could not help. The blond girl was cowering as the bullets started to fly towards the front of the boat. Brody grabbed the Glock off the deck and sent six more shots into the stern of the boat. One poacher screamed in agony as a bullet went through his thigh. The pin was almost out now. With one final pull, the cage door opened. As it did, the poacher who had been sword fighting with Brody grabbed him and threw him onto the tusks. Brody rolled and came up, then swung a roundhouse kick into the side of his head. The poacher staggered. Brody came back to get the girl free, as he did, another of the thugs grabbed him. Brody lashed out with a lightening right hook, slamming the guy in the jaw. This gave the first guy an opportunity. He shoved Brody hard in the chest sending him sprawling back along the gunnel and crashing into the cage, which then toppled into the water, taking the ranger and the blond girl with it. Brody saw what was happening and followed it over the side, diving deep into the water.

The turgid brown river had zero visibility. Brody just hoped he had hit the water right and was following the cage down. At about eight feet, he felt the metal bars with his fingers. Pulling himself to within an inch of the cage, he quickly felt around the edges. Then a kick hit him in the side of the head. He turned to face the threat. It came again. A small barefoot hit him square in the nose. He grabbed it and followed the leg to the blond struggling in the water. Sliding his knife out once again, he cut the plastic cable ties attaching her to the cage. Then he reached inside and grabbed the ranger under his arms, pulling him out. The blond girl helped, holding the unconscious man as they pushed off the deep mud of the bottom.

The three of them broke the surface, taking huge lungsful of air, holding the unconscious man between them. They were about thirty feet downstream. The riverboat was being pulled into the northern bank away from them as planned. The poachers had more to worry about trying to stop their boat from crashing into the tree branches, which could easily pierce the hull fatally. Brody glanced over his shoulder and saw *Aminika* heading to pick them up. Gumbao was shouting and waving his arms above his head. Brody did not know what was going on. The noise of the engine and the roar of the river made it impossible to hear Gumbao's shouts. He spun around in the deep water, not knowing what to expect. Then he saw it. A wave about two feet high, heading directly for him at about twenty knots. The sixteen-foot crocodile was powering through the water with its long muscular tail, only the top of its head showing. Life on the river was full of competition. If the crocodile did not grab its prey fast, other predators would charge in and snatch this meal away.

The blond girl started screaming as the animal raced in their direction. Gumbao jumped up to the bow of the boat as it roared towards them, then passed them in a tight circle. Brody heard Hassan ram the engines in reverse, pulling the boat back between Brody and the crocodile. Gumbao let loose four rapid blasts into the beast's head. As he was firing, Hassan had his arms over the side of *Aminika*, pulling the unconscious ranger onto the boat. Brody grabbed the gunnel and threw the blond girl up and over, she landed in a heap on the deck. Then Brody launched himself out of the water and onto the boat.

Hassan grabbed the steering wheel and turned the boat as he rammed the throttles into forward gear, sending them off down the river and away from the stranded poachers.

Chapter Eleven

Aminika raced off around the bend and out of sight of the now stricken riverboat laying alongside the muddy, tangled bush on the northern side of the river. Brody laid on the deck of the speedboat gasping for breath. The blond girl just lay in a daze as if she had fainted. Gumbao grabbed Brody as the boat turned a sharp bend into a small tributary heading towards the meeting point.

"Boss, you OK?"

Brody patted himself down. All he could think of was the giant crocodile racing towards him. Even with all of his training, there was no way he would have got himself out of that one. "I'm good, no injuries. Thanks for the rescue."

Hassan shouted, "No problem, Boss. We got to keep you alive."

Next Brody looked over to the blond, semi-naked girl laying on the deck of the boat. He quickly pulled off his T-Shirt and shouted over the engine noise. "Hey. Take this. Put it on, my friends are shy!"

The girl woke from her daze with a start and took the shirt, pulling it over her head. "Who the hell are you? We are in the middle of Africa. Where did you come from?"

Brody heard the American accent. "I'm William Brody, and this is my crew. We are on holiday on the Tana river and thought you might like our sightseeing tour."

She just stared at him with her mouth open. Brody passed her a bottle of water. "So, what's your name? And what's the story?"

The blond said, "Where is Kairu?"

"Is that the guy in the cage?"

"Yes, what happened to him? Is he alive?"

Gumbao had picked the unconscious guy up and propped him against the gunnel of the speed boat. "Boss, he's taken a good beating, but he's breathing, I think he'll be OK."

Brody said, "There, Kairu'll be fine. What's your name?"

The blond girl replied, "Naydia. I work with the National Park Rangers in the game reserves."

"What the hell are you doing on the Tana river with a bunch of cutthroat poachers?"

"I could ask you the same question?"

"That's true. Those guys pissed me and some of my friends off. We have a score to settle."

Naydia was still in shock. "OK. I was taken prisoner. They killed the other rangers I was with. Kairu is the only survivor, we were trying to rescue him when they ambushed us and killed everyone."

Brody said, "Shit, sorry, that sounds awful. We will take you to safety. I am sure the Pokomo can lead you out to Garsen, then you can get back to your people."

Naydia just sat quietly and stared at the water racing past. Brody figured she was in shock and needed some time to process what had happened. He stood up as they approached the meeting place.

Everyone had made it without injury. The canoes had quickly picked the men up from the river before any of the crocodiles had realized what was happening. The poachers had been too busy with Brody and *Aminika* to bother with them. Everyone was jumping around singing and chanting, all full of adrenaline, congratulating each other on their escape from certain death. The villagers had never done anything so daring and were full of stories of the adventure. Gumbao chatted with them until Yuda came out of the jungle and walked over. As he approached, everything went quiet.

Yuda said, "Mr Brody, you seem to have had a success. I'm very happy for you. Now, will these bad people come back? I need your word on this."

Brody looked serious. "That was just the first round, Yuda. I'll sort this out. Now, at least we have two groups. One is marooned on the northern side of the river. The other is still in the camp. I will go back in a while and check the poachers stuck in the riverboat. But don't worry, I'll finish this!"

Naydia was slowly coming to her senses. She had been saved from certain death. The poachers were hard, callous people. She was sure her death would have come before reaching Hong Kong. This tall, strong stranger had come out of nowhere, rescuing everyone. She didn't really know what to make of it.

Brody came over to the boat. "Are you feeling better?"

"A bit, I've had a crazy week. I don't really know what has happened. It's all a blur. Where did you come from?"

"We followed the poachers upriver after we met them in the ocean about a week ago. Those guys are not so friendly. The more I get to know them, the more I want them to stop existing."

"I was with Kairu and the rest of the platoon. We tracked them across the savannah after we came across some of their handiwork: one old bull, three females and a couple of calves. It was terrible, the sight of those poor animals. Then Naipanoi, that was our platoon leader, he died in the rescue." Naydia put her head down and sniffled for a few minutes.

Brody said, "Hey, I understand you have been through a lot. You don't have to tell me now."

"It's OK. I think having someone to talk to in my own language is good for me. We found the poacher's camp and were watching them; the plan was to call in support and arrest them all."

"So, what happened?"

"Poor Kairu got close so he could listen, then they caught him and beat the poor man. The platoon went in at night to rescue him, and it all went wrong. All of them got shot. The poachers grabbed me and kept me prisoner. They said I was going to be sold in Hong Kong."

"Real nice guys, this bunch. Not only poaching, but kidnap and slavery too!"

"Yes, I really don't know how I would have gotten away, and Kairu would have been killed too. I'm sure it was only a matter of time."

"We'll take you downstream later. Then you can get to Garsen and find your people again. You'll be fine now."

"What are you going to do?"

"I've made a promise to the Pokomo. I will finish this once and for all. There are a couple of personal scores I need to settle too."

"What's your next step?"

"Once these guys calm down, I will head back upstream and pay a visit to the riverboat."

Naydia said nothing. This man was as dangerous as the poachers, but he had a decency about him. It seemed there was not much between the good guys and the bad, just some small shred of decency that kept them apart.

Brody shouted to Gumbao and Hassan. "Guys, come on. I have to go and see our friends upriver. Naydia, you stay here with Kairu and the Pokomo."

Aminika set off quietly upstream. The day was almost over, and the sounds of the night river creatures had already started. There were red colobus monkeys jumping from tree to tree, screeching a warning to each other as the boat slowly cruised up the northern bank. About two miles short of where Brody had last seen the riverboat, he jumped onto the shore. This was a solo mission. During his time with the Special Forces, he had spent months in the jungles of Borneo, training to move silently through the undergrowth, sneaking up on unsuspecting prey.

By the time he could smell the poachers camp, it was pitch dark. It had not been too difficult to find; the poachers were noisy and the smell from their cooking pots wafted through the air like a storm cloud. That combined with the stench of the rotting tusks on the bank was like setting off distress flares giving away their locations.

Brody approached downwind, just in case they had any dogs. The camp had been set up right next to the river bank. Some of the guys were still on the boat. Others had made a clearing and lit a small fire. A pot was hanging from a metal tripod over the flames, heating some stew. Brody counted six poachers altogether, but could not see Captain Faraj. He must still be on the boat in the battered wheelhouse. The men seemed a bit wary, but not overly. Brody figured they must have thought it was all about rescuing the villagers.

When the moon was high overhead, all he could hear from the camp was deep snoring. One guard was posted on the bow of the boat, where there was a good view of the river and the camp. The guard was holding his Kalashnikov loosely in his arms, lazily smoking a cigarette. He would be hard to get at, as he had a commanding position which was easily defendable. A frontal attack would be suicide. The guard would have plenty of time to see him and fire at his leisure. Brody moved back along the river bank about twenty yards. He took a full ten minutes surveying the area for the bright red eyes of the crocs. The camp would have scared most creatures away. He hoped that included the sixteen-foot long crocodiles he had seen basking on the mud banks earlier. After checking for the fiftieth time, he gingerly slipped his whole body into the shallow water.

Using only his hands to pull himself through the tangled undergrowth silently, he slithered forward until the boat was only five yards in front. The guard seemed to think the main threat would be from the bush or figured he would hear an engine approaching along the river so was facing inland. Brody took a deep breath, submerged, and pulled himself along the bottom, moving from branch to branch until his outstretched fingers touched the fiberglass of the hull. He sat motionless in the murky river, 12 inches under the surface, for two more minutes, then surfaced just beside the boat. The guard's foot was two feet above him, and his stale sweat and rancid breath filled the air. Brody sat in the water, just his eyes showing, then glided stealthily back towards the wheelhouse, listening for any movement. Every few feet, he placed his ear to the side of the boat. Nothing. No talking, just silence. The stern of the beached craft hung lower in the water. He held the rear transom and pulled himself up, scanning the length of the boat. It was empty. Where was Captain Faraj? Brody slipped silently out of the river and crouched on the deck, water dripping off his body. The moon was bright overhead, but he was hidden in the shadows created by the canopy above. Cautiously, he moved along the narrow deck towards his dozing target. It was the most dangerous part of the plan. If the target sensed his approach, he was dead. The man sat leaning against a crate, his chest gently lifting and falling, almost asleep. Brody managed to get within striking distance before the guy sensed something and spun. But it was too late, the stainless-steel knife raced across in a tight curve between them. The guard's throat became a long red gash, slicing his voice box, silencing him. Brody twisted the man around. As he did so, he slipped the knife in again between the third and fourth rib, penetrating his heart. Stopping him forever. The poacher of ivory was dead before he knew it, slumped in Brody's arms like a sleeping child.

He lay him on the deck and took the automatic rifle from his lifeless hands. The AK was a Chinese knockoff called a Norinco. It had probably been made in the Sudan on license. It was as good as the original, just cheaper. He checked the load. It was time to move on to the next target.

Brody found the first sleeper wrapped in a blanket to keep the mosquitos off, slightly away from the fire. He remembered the guys face. The last time he had seen him was when the poor old villager on the beach was whipped and kicked, then taken by the croc. Before the poacher even woke up, he was dead, a knife straight into his neck severing the spinal cord. The next four went in the same way.

Brody stood up and walked over to the last sleeping guy and kicked him hard in the stomach. He woke with a start, reaching for his gut and his gun, but his hand came up empty. The poacher then felt excruciating pain in his groin as another kick landed. He rolled, but got tangled in his blanket. Thankfully no more pain came. He lay on the ground moaning, wondering what would happen next. After a few minutes of recovery, inquisitiveness overcame fear, and he opened one eye. Two yards away, sitting on a rock, was a soaking wet, well-built guy about five feet nine with dark hair and an automatic rifle pointed at his midsection.

The poacher said, "What the fuck do you want? My boss will kill you for this."

Brody replied, "Doesn't look much like that from where I'm sitting."

"Fuck off! You're a dead man."

"Well, right now I'm holding the gun, and you're in pain. You tell me what I want to know, and you might just live to see the sun."

"You can't do this. We have protection. No one is allowed to come look for us."

Brody said, "Where is Faraj?"

The poacher laughed. "Yes, the captain said he recognized you. Some trumped-up fucking hero who goes around saving people. Fuck, man, you are in so much trouble. You won't know whether to shit or have a haircut when they get hold of you!"

Brody smiled a mean, mirthless smile. "Well, it's only over when it's over. Where did you say Faraj was?"

"Tell me why the fuck I should tell you anything? What you going to do?"

Brody pointed to the man's teammates. "Pretty much that, actually. But I want answers; so I'll gag you and cut your fingers off one at a time first. Then we might go and wash them off in the river, see who's passing by."

The guy had not noticed he was laying among five dead bodies. He glanced up at the boat where it was easy to see the slumped guard laying in a dark pool of sticky fluid. "Shit, man, you did that? You're fucking mad!"

"Yep, and you're next or you tell me what I want to know. Now, where is captain Faraj? Last time!"

"OK. OK, he left heading inland then back to the camp. He took one guy with him. We were meant to sit tight here to guard the tusks."

"Good. You see, that was not so bad. Now, let me tell you something: you were chosen at random to live, so it was your lucky day. However, this gives me a dilemma. What to do with you."

"Man, just let me live. You'll never see me again. I'll untie the boat from the bank and float downriver. When it gets stuck on a sandbar, I'll walk all the way to Kipini. These guys aren't any friends of mine."

Brody said, "OK, sounds good to me. I'll be watching you. One wrong move and an arrow will come at you when you least expect it. You sit there until daybreak, then leave. Are we clear?"

The poacher said, "Crystal. I'm out of here at daybreak. You are fucking mad. You will never see me again."

When he had finished talking, Brody had disappeared silently into the jungle. The guy did not know what had happened. All he did know was he was scared and did not want that lunatic coming back. For the rest of the night, the poacher sat amongst his dead comrades, jumping at every sound. Every creak or groan of the jungle surrounding him sounded like a deadly arrow, stone, or bullet flying out of the darkness.

Brody slipped out of the forest and onto *Aminika*. "Let's head back to the meeting point. That's one problem solved."

Hassan said, "Sawa, Boss." He started the engines, pulling the boat out into the river.

Captain Faraj had been walking through the bush for many hours. First, he had headed north to move away from the river, where the ground was boggy underfoot with dense undergrowth snagging at your boots. The jungle turned to forest, then bush with scattered trees and hard ground. Here he turned west, heading towards the now setting moon and back towards the main camp, some 30 miles upriver. Captain Faraj and the guy he had chosen were walking as quickly as they could. He knew that leaving the valuable hoard on the riverbank for any length of time could prove to be very dangerous. You never knew who was coming along. The tusks on the open market, even in this unfinished state, could easily fetch over half a million dollars.

The Captain was angry and annoyed, that damn man had come back into his life to ruin it all over again. The last time he had seen Mr William Brody, the captain had been swimming for his life, heading towards the shore away from his beloved dhow. That had been the end of the deal of a lifetime. All he had to do was take the six girls to Somalia, get them to the slave dealer, and he would have been set for several years. Then this white man arrived and stole the girls back, killed some of his crew, beat him to within an inch of his life, and sank his lovely boat.

Faraj stamped his way angrily through the open bush. Blisters were already appearing on his soft feet. He was a seafaring man, who only felt at home when his feet were on a wooden deck feeling the swells through his soles, not trudging through the savannah. Sweat soaked his white kanzu and the insects incessantly bit, reminding him this was somewhere he was not happy to be. And it was all the fault of one man. He wanted it over with, and most of all he wanted this white man dead.

It would take a good six or seven hours to get back to the camp. Faraj's brain was racing. Wai would want an explanation about his early return. What could he say to maintain face against the Chinese overlord? The Captain's team of cutthroats had been so easily ambushed and almost lost the craft along with the precious ivory. And most of the slaves had jumped ship. The Chinese would not be happy. This was the first time something had gone wrong, and with the biggest load. Faraj knew he was able to repair the shaft of the engine of the boat and get the propeller spinning again so they could head off downriver. However, he did not trust the people he had left with the tusks. But leaving them was the best idea he could come up with at the time. This meant he had to rush to get to the camp and collect the spares, some tools, and more men, then head directly back to the boat to get it fixed so they could continue downriver to the waiting freighter.

After seven hours of hard walking through the bush, the captain finally reached the junction of the little track leading down to the main compound. He reached the mess tent and took a long drink of water, followed by a long drink of whisky. Wai Qui Chan strode into the tent. "Where have you been? What has happened?"

The Captain wasn't sure whether, to tell the truth, and face the anger of the Chinese or tell a lie and find an easy way out later. He had a personal vendetta against

Brody and wanted to get the man on his own and kill him slowly. This was the second time this Muzungu had ruined one of his projects.

Faraj glared at Wai Quai Chan. Slamming his whisky glass down on the table, he said through gritted teeth. "The boat ground on a sandbar and twisted the propeller shaft. Your stupid Chinese mate fell in the water and disappeared. I need some tools and the new shaft from the store. I can have the boat going in a couple of hours, and we can get back on schedule."

The Chinese said, "I employed you as the captain. You're meant to know these rivers; how can you possibly have hit a sandbar? Do you know how much that shipment is worth?"

The Captain replied, "Look, I know exactly how much it's worth. It's my money too. If I don't deliver, I don't get paid! The sandbars on the river change all the time. All it needs is a tree to fall. The current changes, and a new one appears. It was just below the surface and caught us by surprise."

Wai Qui Chan said, "That's no excuse. We need to get this finished. I'm on a tight schedule. Those tusks need to be out on the ship within the next 48 hours and in Hong Kong in three weeks."

Faraj replied, "Don't worry, I'll get them there, and finish the job. You better pay me on time, or you will see a side of me you did not believe existed."

The captain strode out of the tent heading for the supplies area where he could pick up the new shaft to repair the boat and the tools. He quickly loaded them onto a small fiberglass canoe with a 15 hp engine, along with two men to come back with him. They pushed the boat into the muddy river and headed downstream. The little engine started on the first pull and pushed the boat through the water quickly. With the current in their favor, it would not take more than a couple of hours to reach the stranded boat. Fixing it would be another four hours. Then they would hold up close to the ocean and wait for his phone to ring with the signal.

Brody and his crew headed back down the river and then down the tributary to get to the Pokomo village. They arrived as the day was breaking. The sun rose in the east, turning the river to molten glass. *Aminika* reached the muddy sand bar, and the crew wearily climbed out of the boat. Naydia came down the beach to meet them. She looked more refreshed and rested. It appeared she was getting over her ordeal of being kidnapped and chained up, then dumped in a crocodile invested river. Kairu was also looking a bit better. He could now stand up straight. His face was less swollen, and he seemed to be getting his strength back.

Naydia asked, "How did it go? Did you find the boat?"

Brody said, "Yes, don't worry. I found it. We'll not have any more problems from them."

"So, what's the plan? What do we do next? Where do we go from here?"

"Well, what we do with you is send you to the nearest village with the chief, so that you can head back to Nairobi and civilization. Kairu needs to see a doctor; he could have some broken ribs or internal bleeding. You and the chief can head off right away."

Kairu stepped forward. "You cannot do this to me. Those bastards hung me from a pole and beat me. My tribesmen were murdered in front of my eyes. Their lives need to be avenged!"

Brody looked at the poor beaten man. He knew that he would do exactly the same. They were fellow soldiers. A debt like this could not be left unpaid as long as there was breath left in Kairu's body. Brody knew in his heart that there was nothing he could do to stop this man coming with them to avenge the deaths of his fellow tribesman. Being a soldier was just like being in a tribe. Everyone looked out for each other. It was an unwritten rule that everyone got back alive, or if the worst came to the worst, you went back and avenged your comrade's deaths.

He took a long look at the defiant man standing in front of him. "I understand, Kairu. I was a soldier once. As long as you can keep up, then you can stick with us, but if you lag behind you are on your own"

Kairu nodded. He knew they were kindred spirits and would drive himself until his last breath to avenge the deaths of his fellow tribesmen.

Naydia said, "That's settled then. We'll go back together, deal with this Chinese smuggler, and finish it once and for all."

Brody looked at her in astonishment. "Why the hell would you want to go back into this bush and go meet the people who kidnapped you, tied you to a post, ripped your clothes off, and then were gonna sell you in Hong Kong as a sex slave?"

Naydia shouted, "That's exactly why I do want to go! These people need to be stopped. I cannot go back to Nairobi now without finishing this for good. Those guys are evil. Not only are they killing my lovely elephants, but they are willing to do anything to make money. Even the Pokomo are suffering because of their evil ways. They're enslaving them and killing the women and children. There will be none left soon. If I don't do something, then who will?!"

Brody was angry. This was stupid. "Look, I've already agreed to take Kairu. He's gonna slow us down. With you tagging along as well. It'll be like a herd of elephants marching through the bush. We'll be heard from miles away. Why can't you just go back to Nairobi and report this and then bring in reinforcements to get rid of these gangs for good?"

"By the time I get to the village and someone comes to pick me up and take me back to Nairobi, these people will be gone. The camp will be closed down. The Chinese will have escaped, the tusks will have left the country loaded on a boat, and they'll be heading for Hong Kong. We will never be able to chase them once they leave Kenya. We'll have failed. The captain will have disappeared into Lamu, the Chinese on the boat heading for Hong Kong. We'll have nothing, and the poaching will continue. In three months' time, it'll all start again. In exactly the same place. The elephants will start dying. It's final. I'll go with you or go alone, but I'm going back to that camp, and I'm going to make sure this ends here." She was red-faced and out of breath when her speech was finished.

Brody looked over his shoulder at his crew. Hassan and Gumbao shrugged their shoulders. He knew he was beaten. He also knew that she was right. If they didn't sort this out here and now, by the time the reinforcements arrived the place would be empty. Everybody would have left and disappeared either into the bush or onto a freighter heading back to Hong Kong. Then, in time, when it had all cooled off, it would begin again, the elephants would start to die, and the Pokomo would be enslaved again, until there were no elephants left.

Brody said, "Fair enough. It's your funeral. But don't expect me to save your ass again. If you get into trouble, you're on your own."

Naydia replied, "Don't worry about me. I can look after myself, and keep up with you no problem. I marched halfway across Tsavo to get here."

Brody left them on the beach and wandered off back to the boat and his crew. The problem here was the plan. He had to come up with a clever way of surprising the camp, then release the rest of the local Pokomo slaves, at the same time making sure he was able to grab the Chinese, so Naydia could take him back to Nairobi and have him charged properly. Then finally, he had a debt to settle with Captain Faraj.

Chapter Twelve

The sun was already hot, with the humidity quickly reaching the nineties down by the turgid river. Brody sat in *Aminika* under the shade of the canopy, thinking about his next move. He had a limited amount of supplies and ammunition with no possibility of getting any more. He knew the camp was well guarded, and the poachers were very well armed and not afraid to use violence at a moment's notice. All this was swirling around his head as he tried to formulate a suitable plan. Time was not on their side. After the ambush, the poachers would be keen to get the tusks out of the country as soon as they could. The head man would have guessed that Naydia was free and would raise the alarm, bringing the vengeful rangers down on top of them.

Brody and his crew had to strike quickly. With a small team and a good plan, it was possible to surprise the camp, take the Chinese prisoner, and disable the rest without too much trouble. The germ of an idea was slowly forming. He would need a diversion first to get inside the camp, then grab the Chinese guy and bundle him into the jungle before anyone knew. With the headman out of the way, the rest might just either give in or make a run for it. He knew he was skating on thin ice. There were so many variables, so many things that could go wrong. If only one did, then the shit would hit the fan. Brody decided he would ask the chief for any information he might have about these guys.

The Kijo was sat outside a large, round, mud-walled house, the centre of the village. The rondavel had a roof made of dried grasses and reeds. Inside it was remarkably cool. Scattered around the hut were seven large mats which had been woven from coconut palm leaves. The mats were covered in piles of rice stalks which had been harvested from the flood plains of the Tana river, waiting for the husks to be removed.

Brody approached the old chief. "Habari a leo, Mzee?" 'What is the news, sir?'

The old man looked up from his work weaving more mats for the floor. "Karibu, chukuwa kiti." 'You are welcome. Take a seat.'

Brody sat on a three-legged stool. He had to fold his knees almost up to his chest. "Sir, I have come for some advice."

The old man looked up. He had deep, brown, friendly eyes, the kind that had lived a life away from war and trouble. His ebony skin was blemish-free, and the few teeth left showed as he grinned. "What advice can I give you, my friend? You are from another place. A place where they have everything and know so much."

Brody laughed quietly, if this old man only knew how many people longed for his trouble-free existence. No T.V. or mobile phone. It was one of the reasons Brody had left Europe and his army life behind. Too many distractions. 24-hour news bulletins covering stuff he could do nothing about, but it left its indelible mark on his soul. Everyone was worried for one reason or another. This old man had the clothes on his back and the food from the rivers or the delta, fruit in the trees. Who needed anything more? Who had everything!

Brody said, "Sir, I do come from outside, you are right. I don't think it is better than your life. I was a soldier once and fought against men like the ones who have stolen your fellow village people. If I don't step in and stop them, they will continue to come and change your home. These people are wicked and will only cause more problems as they steal more people and ivory from your land."

The old chief replied, "But if we leave them alone, they will not bother us so much. The white Muzungus are strong. We are just fishermen and farmers. We cannot do anything against them. If they come again, we will move into the bush and hide away until they leave. Inside the jungle, we are much better than them."

"But these guys will not give up. The money that's made from the tusks is so big, when it gets to their country, it's worth millions. As long as there are elephants left, the poachers will keep coming and taking it along with your villagers for labor. This can't be left to continue."

The old chief looked at Brody. "We have been living along this river for so many generations. The Tana floods every year so we can grow our rice, '*Mtonzo*', or if we are lucky the '*Mpunzi*' swim in waters close to the bank so we can catch them. Matoke grows in the bush. We are happy. The Pokomo were the first to talk to the Arabs and Portuguese when they arrived so long ago. Each has come, and each has gone again. We carry on."

"This is different, these poachers have come with greed in their hearts. They just want to steal what they can and do not care if you live or die. Running into the jungle will not save you this time. These people have high-powered guns and will shoot you down. You have already seen with the villages that have been lost. When you complained to the Police Chief he ignored you because he has been paid to look the other way. I'll do something, as I cannot stand by. What I am asking is can you help me with advice and maybe some men?"

The Kijo looked up into Brody's face. He was not happy there was a problem and it was way beyond him. "I can give you some men, the same ones as you had before. These young boys are brash. Some are foolish. They do not stop talking about their adventure with you along the riverbank. I could not stop them coming anyway." He shrugged his shoulders in defeat and looked even sadder.

Brody felt awful, as if he was taking this man's life away. "I understand. It's difficult when you are faced with these terrible people. I'll look after your men and make sure that no harm comes to them. The brave Pokomo will not face the bullets on this mission. I have to set a diversion. Once this is done, your boys'll wait in the bush."

The Kijo smiled his toothless smile. "We will see. Life is what you have and what you make of it. We have to face the poachers or all my people will surely die. I trust you, Mr Brody, and your crew. You'll do your best, and what will happen will happen. If 'Maseha' arrives and takes my young men, then so be it."

Brody stood up, straightening his cramped legs. The old man knew he couldn't really do anything more. Brody would have to step in against these people. The Pokomo were peaceful. They did not want war. They knew nothing of elephants and ivory or the markets of Hong Kong. All they knew was the Tana river, the fish that swam in it, the rice that came from the floodplains, and the bananas that grew in the trees.

Brody walked back to the boat. It was time to make a move, or they would miss the Chinese and the camp would be empty. Waiting at *Aminika* were Kairu, Hassan, and Gumbao. Naydia walked up to him. She had a question in her eyes. He knew it was coming. "So how are we gonna do all of this?"

"I have the basis of a plan. We'll wait here until the Pokomo arrive, then try to take everyone upriver. The camp is about 40 miles further upstream. It'll take some time. I just hope that they haven't cleared out and left by now. We'll also have to sneak past the marooned boat with the tusks."

"OK, but we have to move quickly. Let's hope the Pokomo arrive soon."

After forty minutes, twelve of the brave Pokomo warriors arrived, dressed as before with their slingshots and bows and arrows. It would be a very tight squeeze on the boat. The extra weight would make headway even slower. The odds were stacking up against them.

Brody asked the Pokomo, "We need to get past the craft on the river, the one we stopped the other day. Is there a way we can sneak through without being seen?"

The head Pokomo said, "We can take a cut about five miles from here, a small and very narrow tributary. If we take it, we'll come out just beyond the bend in the river well beyond the broken boat."

Brody said, "Hassan, did you hear that?"

Hassan looked up from his controls. "Yes, Boss. I'll keep this guy near me. He can point out the route."

Aminika pulled out into the river. The water was almost up to the gunnels, but the two powerful engines managed to push it against the current at 5 knots. They had a good 40 miles to travel upstream. It would take some time. Brody hoped that the tributary would be navigable. If they were lucky, the smaller stream would not slow their craft as much.

After an hour, *Aminika* turned north into a dark, narrow, overgrown passageway. It was hardly noticeable along the bank, just a small gap in the dense bush. Once the boat had passed the entrance, it became dark and oppressive. Clouds of mosquitoes rose up from the surface to greet them, all hungry for blood. The water was sluggish but shallow, with a width of only twelve feet. There was dense, verdant, impenetrable jungle on either side, pushing against the narrow stream, trying to suffocate it for good. *Aminika* cruised along the new tributary cautiously. The crew were silent, either contemplating the next few hours or just keeping their mouths shut to stop the insects from flying in. Some sections of the river were so shallow that everyone had to get out and push. Others were clogged with thick weed which caught in the propellers. The Pokomo cut long sticks from the bush and punted the craft through.

After what seemed like an age, *Aminika* suddenly broke out of the dark undergrowth back onto the mainstream. The G.P.S. had been offline with the heavy canopy of trees above them, but now beeped back to life as it grabbed new signals from the satellites. Brody could see they had cut off the long meandering bend in the river and were getting close to the camp. The light was starting to fade which fit in perfectly with his plan.

Captain Faraj arrived at the location of the stricken craft only to find nothing but dead bodies. Five of his crew had been killed in the night, leaving one treacherous bastard that had obviously decided sharing was not a good idea and made off down the river with the precious cargo. Minutes later, the captain was racing along the Tana River, intent on catching the traitor and dealing with him. After two hours, the canoe rounded a bend in the river. Just ahead was their craft, driven up on a sand bar. As the poachers approached, it was plain to see the cargo was intact. The fool who ran off must have deserted the boat thinking he could come back later and steal the tusks. This was fine for the Captain. Finding the traitor could wait for another day. Right now, there was work to do and profits to be made. After some pushing and dragging, the long craft was eased back into the water. With their small canoe to give the craft some steerage, the Captain managed to get it to the river bank where he could affect the repairs. This was going to be easy. Once he had fixed the shaft, he would head down river and all would be back on schedule. He didn't feel or see the small figures hiding in the bush just out of sight. The hunting group of Pokomo had seen the long craft floating down the river with one man pushing it along with a stick as fast as he could. When the boat had neared the shore, the desperate man had felt a tremendous blow to the side of his head, as if he had been hit with a baseball bat. Then he had looked down to see four straight wooden arrows sticking out of his chest. His last thought before falling overboard was, *"Shit that was not in the plan!"*

The Captain removed the propeller and shaft, replaced the gland in the hull, then slid the new shaft through, being careful not to damage the waterproof seals. Within two hours, as the sun was going down, the boat was ready to leave. The river during the day was bad enough, especially nearer the ocean, so he decided to moor in the middle of the stream and spend the night. A few more hours would mean nothing, and if they hit a sand bar in the darkness, it would be impossible to get to the rendezvous.

Chapter Thirteen

Brody had explained the plan on the final few miles of their journey upstream. Everyone knew their role and exactly what to do. He had done his best to keep his promise to the Kijo. The Pokomo would not be put in any danger.

During the last visit, the area had imprinted itself on his brain: the river at this point was about eighty yards wide and flowing at around five knots from west to east. The Poachers camp was set directly at the river bank for ease of access. Then a long steep muddy bank led inland, acting like a rampart protecting the camp from prying eyes and giving the poachers the advantage in a firefight coming from that direction. However, the embankment reduced the view of the opposite side of the river.

The camp was built in a semi-circular design with the flat side against the bank. To the east were the mess tents and some sleeping quarters, to the west more sleeping quarters and the heads. Then nearer to the bank, the pile of tusks and the Pokomo chained to posts.

Brody, Gumbao and Kairu had been dropped off about two miles downstream, then made their way to the edge of the camp. Brody kneeled in the dense undergrowth about twenty yards from the lights. He said to Kairu, "You head around the camp towards the heads. We have no spare guns; you'll have to find one yourself. But take this." He unstrapped his lethal, razor-sharp dive knife from his calf and handed it to Kairu.

Kairu nodded as only soldiers could: he knew this might be the last time he would see his new friend. "Thanks for this chance. I'll come in on your signal. Don't worry, I'm sure one of these guys will give me his weapon no problem." With that, he turned and was gone into the undergrowth, silently making his way to the toilets on the other side of the camp.

Brody whispered to Gumbao, "I'll head down to the mess tent. When they all get excited, I'll go in and grab the Chinese guy you watch my back."

Gumbao nodded and looked on with an impassive stare, then smiled his toothless smile. "No problem, Boss. I'll be here waiting."

Brody moved off into the bush, heading south towards the river where he could get into position behind the tent.

Once Hassan had dropped the first party off, he had headed to the far side of the river, then, using the cover of the bush, he had nudged *Aminika* along the far bank in the shadows. The plan was to get about one hundred yards past the camp, then head back across and set the diversion.

The Pokomo and Naydia would jump off *Aminika* and head into the bush to get as close to the camp as possible. At exactly 22:00, the Pokomo would throw the three Molotov cocktails into the two sleeping tents, and Naydia would set off the string of shotgun shells Brody had rigged. It was a crude construction: a large rag had been laid out on the deck and soaked in petrol, then sprinkled with gunpowder from two of the shotgun shells. Once he was satisfied the powder was evenly spread he twisted it into a makeshift, fuse-like device. The remaining shells were tied into the fuse, close to the firing cap. As it burnt, it would, or should, fire the shells one at a time. Naydia was to string it up between two trees, then, light it as the Pokomo ran passed her and run like hell back to the boat. Hassan would then take them upstream and wait for a signal from the camp that all was clear.

It was a perfect plan considering he had no trained men, no equipment, and very few weapons at his disposal.

Brody sat in the bush just behind the tent. His shirt was soaked through. He wiped his eyes for the hundredth time and blinked to keep them from stinging. This was the worst part, waiting for it to begin. The crux of his plan relied on him being able to grab the Chinese and be out of there before anyone knew what was happening. Currently, his target was shouting about something or other just a couple of yards away inside the tent. The air was full of smells from human habitation, cheap whiskey, and clothes rotting from the constant humidity and sweat. He figured there were about four other guys in the tent, two near the target and two a bit further away, probably sitting by the entrance. The plan was simple: walk through the back flap of the tent, shoot anyone that was there, grab the Chinese, and be back in the bush before the last shotgun charge went off.

Wai Chan Quai was happy. He was on his way home. This godforsaken place was like hell on earth. He hated it and all the people here. As far as he was concerned, everyone he worked with was a savage. Although he was forced to live and eat with them in the same place, it did not mean he was one of them. In China, he was a respected businessman, living the good life, travelling between Hong Kong and the mainland as he pleased, with special papers to stop any harassment. The few times Wai Chan Quai had visited Nairobi, he had been amazed at how greedy the politicians were. Delivering money had been part of his job for many years all over the world, but here it was sad. Wai even felt sorry for the poor wretches these politicians supposedly looked after, as they did not care about them at all. The Chinese bureaucrats were awful. They would beat, torture, and imprison people for no reason. But here it was different. The Nairobi politicians really hated their constituents and would happily kill them or starve them for petty cash. It was just money, nothing else. The high-ranking men had given him passes and special clearances from the ports and the game reserves, then ensured no one bothered them. It was so easy. These greedy people had not even bothered to find out how much a kilo of ivory went for in Hong Kong so only received a pittance for their corruption.

Wai was on his way out though. One last load and it was done for this season. He had made so much money over the last few months that he could afford to send some other fool here to sweat next time. He would be at Divinos in Macau, his 23ft Lancer Chris Craft, with those huge Volvo inboards, which could push him at 50 knots if he wanted to, moored at their private jetty. Sat in a deep, dark, air-conditioned, leather booth with a twenty-year-old scotch in his hand and four, no five, foreign white girls stripping just for him.

Kairu had stealthily made his way around the camp and sat on the edge of the bush waiting for his chance. The Ranger was happy. If he died here today, then at least his friends would be avenged. The cold-blooded murder of the whole platoon had left him full of anger and hatred for these poachers. The only option for him right now was to die or kill. It was not long before he had his chance. A tall, skinny Somali came stumbling out of the latrine, obviously drunk, an easy target. Kairu waited for the man to turn to head back towards the workers. He crept up behind him and reached high to get at the Somali's neck. As he was doing this, the razor-sharp blade slid between the last two ribs. The Somali started to cry out, but was dragged back behind the wash tent. Kairu went into a frenzy, releasing all the pent-up rage he felt for these people. He stabbed and stabbed until his arms ached, and the heavy knife dropped to the jungle floor. All that was left was a bloody heap of meat in front of him, and he was covered from head to foot in blood and gore. The rage had passed for the time. It felt better; a release, something for his friends at least. The pile of gristle on the ground would be noticed very quickly. Animals were probably already heading towards it now. Kairu dragged the corpse back into the jungle and took the old Glock 17 out of its leather holster on the dead guy's waist, then unclipped the Kalashnikov from its sling. He would not be carrying this gun far. Now Kairu was armed and ready. As soon as the second signal went up, he would kill as many of these bastards as he could.

Quai was taking another shot of the cheap, awful whisky. There was no ice, which made it even worse. A loud pop and bang shocked everyone in the tent. Quai shouted, "You two, what was that? Take a look!"

The two brawny bodyguards stood up and walked out of the tent. A few seconds later they returned. "There's a fire over by the sleeping tents. Maybe those idiots were cooking there again."

As they were reporting, a string of shotgun blasts went off. Quai shouted, "Go and see! Quickly! I don't want those fools shooting the labor just because they're drunk!"

The two guys rushed off to their duties. At that second, Quai sensed a movement behind him and spun around, reaching for his huge revolver. It was heavy, which slowed his reaction time down. The next thing he knew, a mop of dark hair was rushing towards his head. It connected with an awful crunch, and he felt his nose explode as Brody's head butt made contact with the soft tissue of his face. Quai staggered back, then heard four rapid shots. His eyes were watering so he did not see the other two men in the tent slump over their table. Then there were another two shots as the cook went down into his soup head first. Brody grabbed Quai by the throat, picked him up with one hand, and punched him in the face again with his gun hand. Quai just saw blackness as he fell into unconsciousness. Brody threw him over his shoulder and slipped out the back of the tent and was gone into the jungle before anyone noticed he had been there, leaving the three dead guys laying in their food as if they had fallen asleep.

Brody quickly made his way into the bush. Now they would wait and see what happened. If the poachers did anything stupid to the Pokomo slaves, he would signal a second time. This would be the call to action for Gumbao and Kairu. Between the three of them, they had the camp in a crossfire and could decimate the poachers.

Hassan sat on the river bank waiting for his men to reappear. It had been five long minutes since the explosions. This was too long. Then out of the bush,

Naydia appeared with only one Pokomo. "What happened? Why are you so late? And where are the others?"

"The Pokomo have decided to rescue their friends. They've headed along the river bank to sneak into the camp while everyone is confused."

"But that wasn't the plan!"

"I know, but I couldn't make them listen."

"We have to stop them, or the poachers will just kill all of them."

Naydia and the one remaining Pokomo tribesman jumped into *Aminika* as Hassan pulled away from the shore. He moved as slowly along the river bank as he could, hoping to spot the tribesmen and stop them from this foolish endeavor. The craft reached the edge of the clearing. No one was about. All the poachers had headed off to the tent to watch the spectacle. Naydia said, "Let me off. I'll go and get them back."

Hassan replied in a whisper, which was a waste of time as the engines were running. "No, you stay on board. We can't risk anyone else."

Without another word, Naydia jumped off the side of the boat onto the beach, sinking up to her thighs in the thick mud and water.

Hassan shouted, "You're stupid. Come back. Those guys'll grab you, then we are all done!"

But Naydia didn't even look back. She struggled out of the mud and up the bank, searching for the Pokomo. The tribesmen had lived in the bush alongside the Tana river for their whole lives. Being hidden was most of what you had to do when you wanted to eat. Even catching the catfish, you kept your shadow off the water. Those tasty fish had not managed to get so big and fat by being stupid. So, although the Pokomo had decided to get to their fellow tribesmen, being hidden was a natural part of the plan. Naydia had never fished or hunted in her life so walked through the bush like a herd of buffalo. She stumbled out of the dense forest and up the bank. Thinking that no one could hear her, she crept to the top of the rampart and knelt behind some storage boxes.

Two poachers had seen Naydia come out of the bush right next to the camp, then climb the muddy bank and go to her hiding place.

The men stealthily crept from box to box until they had her in a pincer movement. No escape. When she decided to move closer, one guy sprang out in front. As she turned to run, the other had grabbed her, twisting her arm up behind her back, then grabbing her hair and pushing her forward into the camp. The Pokomo had watched terrified from the cover of the bush. The fat lady was meant to be in the boat. Why was she wandering about making so much noise? The tribesmen melted into the forest, sitting and watching, not sure what to do.

Brody kneeled on the other side of the clearing, watching, wondering what the poachers would do next. He was totally shocked when he saw, for the second time, Naydia being thrown to the ground in the middle of the compound. She lay still on the beaten earth. A big African guy built like a bull elephant stood over her.

It was easy to see this man was mean. He swung a massive wooden 'Rungu'. In his huge hand, it looked like a child's toy. The guy was called Samson. He was from the Luo tribe who lived near Lake Victoria. These people were known for their size. He stood at least six foot seven tall, with a loose-fitting safari shirt covering his massive chest and arms. His head was polished and shone in the moonlight. Samson had never been to the gym in his life. He had grown up fishing in the lake. When he became too big and aggressive for the boats, he wandered around Kisumu, the thriving port town on the edge of Lake Victoria. The fishing business has many tentacles. It was not long before the Pakistani exporters who bought all the fish realized this guy could be of use to them. Samson had no qualms about violence. He enjoyed it, and his size meant he always won. His chosen weapons were knives and his beloved 'Rungu' which he could inflict immense pain within just seconds. Samson had been taken in by the Pakistanis. His sole occupation was to keep the competition quiet. If any Africans dared to start an export business in Kisumu, selling the tilapia fish to Nairobi or Kampala, then Samson would be sent to ensure the poor unfortunate entrepreneur was dissuaded from his current course. This often meant Samson would beat or even kill one of his fellow Luos, but this did not bother him. The money was good. It was while he had been in Nairobi collecting some bad debts that this opportunity had come up. Six months in the bush, then the payoff of a lifetime.

He reached down and grabbed Naydia by her blond hair and hauled her up. She screamed with pain as her feet left the ground. Samson strode across the compound, heading for the mess tent.

Brody took a deep breath, this was not going to be good. It had all gone to hell in a handbasket. One small thing. Just stay on the bloody boat!

Samson was only in the tent for a second, and came back out with a huge toothy smile on his face. As a Luo, his two upper and lower front teeth had been removed when he was sixteen years old, so there was a big black gap as he grinned. Samson held his hand up. "Quiet, everyone, quiet! I know you are out there, you are watching me. This young girl has ten seconds to live, then I will beat her head in with my 'Rungu', right here, right now!"

Brody knew he was asking for him. There was no choice. Gumbao was about ten yards away. Brody signaled to him to take Quai and remain hidden. Then he moved towards the clearing, hoping that this guy would be happy with one sacrifice and had not guessed there were more.

As Brody stepped out into the camp, his mind cleared. This was battle, what he had been trained for. In the Special Forces, you were beaten to nothing, then your sergeant major rebuilt you into something that was much more than you were before. He could hear the man's voice now in his head. "You're dead son. You know you are dead. Get that into your head, then you can win as you have nothing to lose, boy!"

Brody stood and walked calmly out across the clearing. He could hear Naydia sobbing on the floor. His heart was beating a regular sixty-five beats per minute, no stress, just readiness for whatever was coming. The sweat from the poachers surrounding him reached his nostrils. He could even smell what food they had eaten, then the wall of their hatred beating down on him like rays of the sun. Time had slowed down. He could clearly see the branches in the trees swaying in the northeasterly wind. Around him, the fire blazed as the logs crackled in the night. The dirt under his feet felt gritty and hard. The air on his face was hot from the fire, but the humidity had gone. There was not a bead of sweat on his body. This was like a stroll in the park!

Samson stood and waited for his next victim to arrive. This would be fun, his first Muzungu. Slowly, he swung the 'Rungu' in circles, letting it hit the palm of his hand with a thump just to make the white guy shit his pants.

Brody arrived and stood about three yards away from this mammoth of a man. He felt small next to him even though he stood at nearly six feet himself. Samson smiled a cruel, wicked smile. "So, 'Muzungu,' you come here and think you can take my payday away, eh!"

Brody just stood and stared. His mind was calculating the odds, where was this man weak. The guy was enormous and obviously knew how to fight. He had left the Glock behind. It would have been worthless here. Too many of them.

Samson said, "So, white man, you gonna pay me now. My Chinese has gone. Did you take him? Is he dead?"

Brody just looked at Naydia. "Are you OK?"

Naydia was amazed as she looked up into the cool, deep brown eyes of this man. He seemed totally at ease. "I'll be fine. I'm sorry, I was only trying to help."

Samson interrupted, "Muzungu, you know what you have done. No Chinese, no money. That means you pay me or I beat it out of you one dollar at a time."

Brody looked the man up and down. "So, big man, it's just you and me. Let's sort this out like men." He was hoping to get this guy angry. Then he might stand a chance.

Samson smiled. "You must be joking, man," he laughed, "Grab him, men, I'll take him apart piece by piece."

Strong arms came from behind, pinning Brody's shoulders and holding him still.

Samson said, "Take him to the post. This'll be fun!"

Three guys dragged Brody over to the same post Kairu had been tied to. They hung him up, shackling his arms to the top of the long wooden pole with steel cuffs.

Samson grabbed Naydia by the hair again and dragged her over towards the post. "You can watch your hero scream in pain. When he begs me to kill him, I'll slit his throat in front of you, then these men'll take you!"

Naydia looked him in the eye. "You bastard. You'll die for this, I swear it."

The first blow landed just below Brody's solar plexus, forcing all of the wind out of his body. He had seen it coming, the wind-up and the show. At the last minute, he had twisted, trying to deflect the blow, but all the same, it had hurt like hell. Brody knew this was just a warm-up. Samson was enjoying showing off in front of the other poachers. He probably had ideas of taking over the whole macabre business and needed to assert his dominance.

Samson looked at him. "Tough guy, eh? You think that hurt I was just getting my arm in, like those Yankee ballplayers on T.V. I am going to hit one out of the park." He laughed at his own joke. The rest of the gang were enjoying this, all eager to see the white man scream in pain, then they could all have some fun with the white girl.

The second blow was lower, Samson had anticipated Brody twisting, so it laid straight into his stomach. It was like being hit with a sandbag shotgun round at close range. The pain went right through Brody. His eyes almost popped out of his skull. The feeling was like nothing he had ever felt before, beyond normal pain. This was a totally different experience on another level. The ball of wood at the end of the 'Rungu' felt like it had hit his spine. His head exploded with white light, and he felt the vomit rising through his chest. He could not control it and threw up.

Samson laughed. "That's more like it, man. You're feeling me now. That one landed, but I was only at half speed. The next is going for your balls. Did you like them? Cos they ain't gonna work anymore."

Samson took a few steps back. "I need a good run-up for this one, a nice underarm shot. I been practicing this for a while. I know you're gonna appreciate the style!"

Brody looked at Samson then smiled through gritted teeth. He was still getting his breath back from the last blow and needed more time. "You know, big man, I'm going to break those shiny white teeth and shove them down your throat, then I'm going to hit you so hard your head'll explode."

Samson could not believe this guy. "OK, man, from hanging on a pole with me smashing your balls you ain't gonna do nothin. Stop trying to show the whore you're brave, man."

Brody hung in front of him. He knew he was dead. This blow could not land. All sorts of plans were running through his head. A twist and a kick as Samson got near, or maybe he could spin around the pole and break it. He had to get free. All he could think of was taking the smile off this guy, smashing what was left of his teeth into his face, then slamming his nose up through his brain.

Samson started his run-up, Brody tensed for his final escape attempt. A familiar face stepped out of the crowd, but it was different, covered in blood. The eyes were staring and mad, gore was dripping from his jacket. The poachers stepped back in fear as this bloody apparition appeared in front of them. Kairu turned and opened fire with his Kalashnikov directly into them, killing three instantly. The others were diving for cover, racing over towards the edge of the clearing to escape the hail of bullets. As they ran, arrows started falling among them. Men started dropping with shafts of wood in their bodies. Round river pebbles about three inches in diameter rained down from above, breaking skulls and bones as they found their mark.

Brody used all of his strength, swinging his body to the left as Samson charged in. His outstretched foot caught Samson in the jaw, knocking him off his line towards the crackling fire. The momentum took Brody around the post. He wrapped his knees tightly around the wood and shimmied up. The metal cuff was only forced over the top. As he gained height, he could feel it loosen on the end of the wooden stake. Samson came charging out of the darkness and hit the pole, knocking it and Brody over. The shackle flew off the end, and Brody was free. He staggered to his feet, shaking life back into his arms and legs. Samson came swinging the 'Rungu' once again with a knife in his left hand. The manacles had a three-foot length of chain attaching them. Brody used it to parry the 'Rungu' then the knife. His hands were still connected, which reduced movement. He had to get in close to stop this guy. The 'Rungu' came in a long swing. Brody ducked under it and came up with a double blow to Samson's kidney. This was a surprise. He had never been hit before, and it hurt a bit. Samson stepped back. His eyes showed some fear just for a second.

Then he lashed out with the knife. It sliced a line along Brody's bicep. The blood started flowing freely. He knew he had to get this done before he got more injuries.

The knife came in, again and again. Broad swipes, then the 'Rungu' left to right then right to left. Brody ducked and jumped backwards away from the blade, looking for a chance. The 'Rungu' whipped past his face. Samson had overstretched. He was still sure he could win. Brody pushed the arm further, giving it more momentum. When Samson had his back to Brody, he stepped back and to the side then, like a footballer taking a forty-yard penalty, slammed his foot between the huge guy's legs and up into his crotch. Brody knew he had connected well. He felt the soft meat of his balls disintegrate under the force from the kick and the hard-callused cuneiform bones of his foot. Brody had kicked thousands of sandbags for hundreds of hours to perfect the disabling blow. Samson felt it. He knew he was injured very badly. As he recovered and turned to face his foe, a metal chain smashed into his mouth, breaking his teeth. His mouth filled with blood. Time stood still. The pain was filling his head. He looked up and was mercilessly punched hard in the throat. His breath left his body. Samson gasped for air. What had happened? He should have won this easily. No one ever beat him. The guy was hanging from a fucking post two seconds ago!

He raised his face. He had never been on the receiving end before so was surprised to see a flash of a flat hand in front of him. That was the last thing he saw or felt. The blow was so hard, fast, and accurate it smashed the bones in his nose. The impact forced those bones through the lower cranium and up into his brain causing massive brain damage. His head was pushed back so forcibly it snapped the brainstem. Samson was dead before he knew it.

Brody spun as footsteps approached from behind. He lashed out with the chain, hitting Kairu who was staggering towards him. At the last second, he realized it was his friend and pulled back on the chains, but they still caught Kairu a glancing blow to the side of the head. He staggered and fell. It was only as he crumpled to the floor Brody saw the two arrows sticking out of his shoulder and one more from his leg. Naydia came rushing up. "My god Brody, you made it. I was so sure you were dead."

Brody snarled, "You made this happen. Just stay away and do what you are fucking told next time. Actually, there won't be a next time. Now let's sort Kairu. He's hurt."

Kairu was coming to. Brody knelt beside him. "Sorry, friend, you surprised me."

"It's OK, I ran after the poachers and killed them, avenging my fellow troopers. Then the arrows came, just in the wrong place at the wrong time."

"Don't worry. These are not so bad. We'll get you back to the boat and sorted out. Naydia, help Kairu to the boat and don't fuck it up."

Naydia was about to say something, but she had just seen this man ruthlessly kill someone after being tied to a post and beaten, so she thought better of it and helped Kairu to his feet.

Gumbao came out of the jungle. Quai was standing beside him with the barrel of the Ithaca forced into his neck. "So, Boss, what do we do with this piece of shit?"

"That's the easy part. We ship him back to Nairobi with Naydia, kill two birds with one stone. Get rid of them both."

"Sawa, Boss, I'll load him on the boat."

The camp around him was on fire. The Pokomo had decided to burn it to the ground the same way their villages had been, an eye for an eye. After freeing their enslaved friends, the tribesmen went on a rampage, destroying everything. The poachers had run for their lives along the path towards the open plains. The narrow clearing between the bush had been ideal for the Pokomo who lived and hunted in the forest. The small straight track had turned into a killing field as the poachers had run for freedom. Their bodies lay all the way along the beaten path, now stained red. Some had over twenty arrows embedded in their bodies, others had crushed skulls.

Hassan gently pulled *Aminika* away from the bank. She was severely overloaded. Some twenty tribesmen would have to start walking. But he had promised to return for them. Kairu was laid up on the stern seat. Covered in bandages. He had a smile on his face the codeine was obviously working.

Brody looked back at the camp. The flames were still licking the dark night sky. There were pops and bangs as the inferno found the rounds left by the poachers. Then a huge explosion lit the night sky. The mess tent had finally gone up in smoke. In a few weeks, the jungle would start creeping back, the local animals would feast for the next couple of weeks, and all would disappear. There would be no trace left of a camp, just some old broken bones lying in the dirt.

Brody turned to Naydia. "Well, that's it. You can take that Chinese scum bag back to Nairobi and see if you can get him in trouble."

Naydia looked depressed. "Truth is he probably won't even see a prison cell."

"That's true enough. With the amount of money these guys must have spent, they will be protected. He will be in Hong Kong before the week is out I'm sure."

Naydia looked thoughtful. "We'll see. You never know, justice might just be served."

Brody snorted and went back to Kairu. He still felt a bit guilty for hitting him with the chain.

They got back to the Pokomo village just before dawn. The tribesmen full of stories of bravery and fighting, they quickly ran off to find their wives. There would be some babies made today. The two boys Gumbao had found in the village had been waiting all night for *Aminika* on the long muddy beach, hoping to see their father. As the boat rounded the bend just before the village, they started shouting and yelling their father's name. The man ran to the prow of the boat, waving and cheering as he saw his two sons. Brody stood at the back of the boat and wiped his eye. It had all been worth it.

Aminika hit the beach and within ten minutes had refueled and was heading back for the others. Brody carried Kairu onto the bank and up into the village. When they arrived, he was given a place of honor in the long large rondavel and given fresh fish stew with rice and bananas.

Brody greeted the Kijo, "Salaam Alekum, Mzee."

"Alekum A Salaam, Mr Brody."

"Did you finish? Are my people safe now?"

"Yes, Mzee, the camp is burned, and the poachers are either dead or gone. We have the leader here with us, a Chinese. He's on the beach tied to a tree. One of your men is watching him."

"Good. What will you do with him? He can't stay here. He is not welcome in our place."

"Don't worry, the white girl will take him back to Nairobi for the police." The Kijo sneered at this. He knew as well as anyone that nothing would happen.

Quai was not happy. His plans had gone to shit. This white eye had caused so much trouble. He had a broken nose and a massive headache and knew if he got near Nairobi, then his boss would have him dealt with, which in layman's terms meant dead.

Naydia stalked over to him. "You are such a bastard, you know. Killing those animals is inhuman. I don't know how you live with yourself."

Quai just looked at her. How could he turn this to his advantage? "You know, I'm just a worker. Look, I live in that fucking jungle and sweat. I'm nothing. The big guys are what you are after."

Naydia said, "You can't help. You are just squirming, trying to get some favors. I'll take you straight to the newspapers, then when your face is famous worldwide we'll see how you feel."

Quai was not keen on this at all. He was already dead if he got to Nairobi, but if his face was broadcast too, then his family would also die. "Look, I can help you. Bring your boyfriend out. We can talk. I owe nothing to my employers we can make a deal."

Naydia gave him a dark look. "He's no boyfriend of mine. He won't listen to you."

Quai said, "Look, if you want the big fish, then I will help. Get me out of here. Don't take me to Nairobi and I'll give you names and dates. I know where that last shipment is going, even where it will be picked up offshore. You can really stop this trade, not just lock up some low-level workers like me."

Naydia said, "Just sit here. Any attempt at escape, and these villagers will hunt you down and kill you." With that, she stalked off up and over the bank towards the village.

Brody had set Kairu up as best as he could in the circumstances. The ranger had three arrows sticking out of him and a blue chin where the chain had hit him. But the young ladies of the village had often dealt with arrow wounds. Their stupid husbands were always shooting each other. He was being tended to. A potion of leaves, roots and berries was being boiled over the fire, ready to treat the wound.

Brody asked, "So, Kairu, we'll leave you here now. When you are well, the 'Kijo will take you back to Garsen, then you can find the rangers station over in Voi and make a full report."

Kairu nodded. "I'll be OK in a few days. I'll report this whole incident to my superiors. We'll get something done, don't worry Mr Brody."

Naydia asked, "Listen, I need to talk to you. Quai says he will tell us everything. Maybe we can stop this at source in Hong Kong."

Brody nodded. "I'm listening."

"Quai is shit scared, I can see it in his face. I think if we take him to Nairobi, he won't last long. His bosses are not nice people."

"I could always beat the truth out of him. I would enjoy that. I owe him for that bloody giant who wanted my balls."

"Let's talk to him first. If he does not spill everything, then we can move on to your plan."

"Cool, let's get at it. *Aminika* will be back soon, and I still have a date with Faraj."

Quai looked pale on the beach. He had no cigarettes or whisky.

Brody asked, "So, Quai, Naydia here says you want to make a deal. What kind of deal are you thinking about?"

"Look, Brody, if I go back to Nairobi, I am dead. My bosses are shy of publicity. Even if there is none, the politicians will put their prices up, so I want out!"

"OK, saving your own neck. What do you want?"

"You get the info. I give you names, dates, places, everything I have, then you forget you ever saw me. Drop me off in Lamu, and I'm gone."

"You know I could just beat you half to death, then you would tell me anyway, wouldn't you? This is not much of a deal for us."

"Brody, the information I give you freely is much better than the tortured version. This way I'll give you everything: the whole supply chain from Hong Kong to Nairobi."

"OK, I'm listening."

The next two hours, while Brody was waiting for *Aminika*, Quai laid the whole scheme out to them. It was huge, from high-level politicians in Kenya through to the heads of the triads in Hong Kong. Quite a story, but no backup.

At the end, Brody stood to stretch his legs. "There is one more thing. I want Faraj, and I need to find the boat before it loads and the captain disappears."

"No problem, I can give you the exact location. It's about twenty-five miles offshore, directly east of the mouth of the Tana river."

"No way you get off that easy, Quai you will show me as an act of faith. There is no deal until I see Faraj and the ocean freighter loading those tusks."

Quai was sweating. "That's a tall order. So once I do that you drop me in Lamu, and I'm gone."

Brody answered, "Sounds like a deal."

That evening, *Aminika* set off into the west. The setting sun was dropping onto the river behind them, boiling the water as it slowly dipped behind the trees, gone for another day. Hassan was at the centre console driving. The journey would be quick this time. The water was pushing them back towards the ocean. It was about two hundred miles to the mouth, a fourteen-hour journey. Gumbao was up in the bow, shining the powerful searchlight, watching for sand bars. Quai was tied to the bow post. Naydia sat deep in thought. Brody settled down for some shut-eye. He had not realized how exhausted he was. There was nothing to do now but wait.

Chapter Fourteen

Long before the sun broke its golden crown over the horizon to pour its heat onto the travelers, Brody was awake and planning.

The time before daylight was always his favorite. That moment before the sun starts to rise, not dark, but not light. The air was cool, and faint puffs of wind were blowing along the surface of the now wide-open river. *Aminika* had entered the broad delta about an hour ago. The moon had been bright enough to see the glassy river, making it easy for Hassan and Gumbao to navigate at speed. Fresh ocean air beckoned the crew back home as the morning got underway.

To either side of them were broad expanses of flood plain, covered in long green reeds with bright yellow flowers. Huge lily pads floated idly at the water's edge, away from the now sluggish current. The Tana river was in its final stages, slow and fat, heading for the ocean twenty miles downstream. Great herds of hippos sat on the sandbanks, opening their enormous mouths as the boat raced past, roaring mournfully at this intrusion to their peace. Long-necked herons stalked the water's edge, picking the small fry from the shallows, with pied kingfishers inches above them, using the herons to spot the small fish, then darting in ahead and stealing it from their beaks.

Brody sat with Naydia, sipping hot Arabic coffee Hassan had managed to conjure up out of nowhere as he usually did. Next to them was a large sliced mango, with its bright, juicy cubes of orange fruit popping up from the skin. Brody felt a bit bad about the way he had treated Naydia. She had only been trying to help the Pokomo.

He said, "We have a couple of jobs left to do; we know the captain is a little further along the river. First, we have to find him and grab the boat, then I can call in reinforcements to help."

Naydia slurped her mango, the sweet juice dribbling down her chin. "I hope Quai is telling the truth. If the captain is where he says he is, then at least we have something for your soldier friends."

Brody shouted over the engine noise. "Hassan, pull up. Look for somewhere to moor the boat."

As they pulled into the marshy edge of the river, the sun was just starting to rise above the bush to the east, its boiling globe signaling another day. It was already hot and humid. The bugs were hungry.

According to Quai, Captain Faraj would be moored some three miles further downstream, waiting for a signal from the freighter. Brody and Gumbao locked and loaded their weapons and headed off inland, then east. It was a hard slog through the roots of the mangrove trees growing in the semi saltwater. Deep sticky mud stuck to their feet as they clambered inland towards harder ground and the relative safety of the rough sandy higher beaches. After two hours of walking, Gumbao stopped, holding his hand up. "Boss, I can smell smoke. Look over there about three hundred yards. Can you see it?"

Brody shielded his eyes from the glare of the sun with his hand and stared in the direction Gumbao was pointing. Spiraling up through the trees was a thin wisp of smoke, a small campfire. The location was about right. The fire was on a bend in the river where the mangroves thinned.

Brody said, "OK, let's move in slow and steady. I want this bastard alive, at first."

Gumbao as usual just nodded and smiled, then fell in behind Brody, ready for anything, his huge flat feet making no sound as he walked through the dense bush.

The smoke led them across a small flat sand bar behind the mangroves, then down a muddy twisting path cut by fishermen between the tree roots. After one hundred and fifty yards, it was clear they had found the right campfire. The heat of the sun had done its work on the rotting flesh of the tusks. There was no doubt at all this was the boat.

Brody sent Gumbao east to flank the camp. Brody headed slightly west and south. As he approached, he could see the craft was set downstream and downwind of the camp. Gumbao signaled from the riverbank, with a long low whistle, that no one was on the boat.

Brody crept up to the edge of the small campsite. A man was sleeping on a rough blanket in the centre of the clearing. The fire had almost burnt out. It was of no use now the sun was up. He surveyed the whole area looking for another figure, but it was empty.

Brody slowly crept into the open space, sliding the Glock out of his jeans as he moved. The young poacher was surprised as hell to be woken with a pistol barrel in his eye, but soon regained his wits.

Brody demanded, "Where's the Captain?"

The poacher looked with wide staring eyes. "He was here just now. I swapped guard duty with him." His voice was shaking with nerves.

"Well, it seems he up and left you. Where would he have gone?"

"I don't know. He said we could not leave the tusks. I'ave no idea where the fuck he went."

Captain Faraj felt sick to the stomach as he watched the annoying white man come between him and money again. He had walked back from the beach to get to high ground, an old habit of his when he had to wait for anyone or anything. From the top of the rise, he had watched as the two men came into the camp. One down by his cargo, the other straight. They now had his fool of a helper, but he knew nothing, so it didn't really matter.

Faraj watched as the white man tied up his new captive, then stood in the centre of the camp and fired a shot into the air, and after the count of sixty, another, obviously a signal to someone. Twenty minutes later, there was the familiar noise of two powerful outboard engines. The boat pulled up beside his cargo, then quickly reversed back to the camp.

On the boat was the girl, another Swahili, and the Chinese man Quai, an interesting group. He decided to settle in and wait to see what would happen.

Quai asked, "Did you get the Captain? He has the satellite phone for the signal?"

"No sign of him, but he would not leave these tusks, not again."

Brody wandered over to the edge of the clearing, then was gone in an instant. The others did not notice for well over five minutes. By then he was moving stealthily through the thick tangled mangrove roots one hundred yards upstream. The bluff above the boat had caught his eye. There had been a slight movement and maybe a glint off some glass. He cautiously appeared from the thick mangroves, then moved swiftly across the open space between the trees and the small incline, scrambling on his hands and knees. Once he was secure under the edge of the bluff, it was easy to start the long climb to the vantage point above. The Captain would be slightly east and north of him, the best place to get a full view of the surrounding area.

Faraj was tense. The Muzungu must be sitting in the corner out of sight, maybe waiting for something or drinking coffee, but he could not be sure. He drew the Glock from his belt and laid the eighteen-inch knife beside him, just in case. He then sat up, sure he had heard a noise to the west, but it was silent now.

Brody cursed to himself as his foot slipped on a loose rock and sent it tumbling down the incline. There was no way of knowing if the captain was here. He was playing a hunch.

Suddenly, a bullet ricocheted off a rock to his left, throwing splinters up into his face. Brody staggered back, getting his bearings as another bullet came out of nowhere, slicing past his arm just above the elbow, leaving a crease of blood. He instinctively ducked and rolled to the side, falling into a dip in the ground. Another bullet went over his head so close he could feel the heat of the air as it passed. Then the Captain was standing over him, a gun in one hand and the knife in the other. "Finally, my friend, we meet again. You don't know how many times I've dreamt of this moment."

Brody blinked the dust and grit from his eye, then wiped his elbow. The blood was flowing freely into the dust. "OK, Captain. Look, we have you again. My boys will be up here in a second. Just surrender it will be better for you."

The Captain laughed. "And give up my chance to get even with you? Remember you sunk my boat."

The Captain turned slightly to keep an eye on the camp. Brody took his chance and lashed out with his left foot, hitting the captain just below his right knee. It was a solid blow, sending Faraj staggering backwards. Brody was on his feet. His arm was throbbing, and his sight was only just coming back. He blindly lunged at the Captain. They rolled down the bluff, hitting the sand at the bottom with a thump. The gun went skittering off into the dust. Captain Faraj was on top and started raining blows on his opponent's head and face. Several landed hard. Blood started pouring out of Brody's nose. The Captain dived off Brody, rolling across the ground towards the knife. In Brody's stunned and partially blind state, this was dangerous. He dodged the blade as the Captain slashed in a wide arc, then rolled out of the way as it came down to stab him in the ribs. The second roll brought Brody up against a tree root. There was nowhere to go. The Captain kicked Brody hard in the ribs. He buckled and tried to roll out away from the root. Then the Captain came in, trying to stomp on his head. Brody grabbed the foot before it made contact, twisted it, and pushed back with all his strength. The Captain was sent staggering backwards to regain his balance. Brody was on his feet. His head was throbbing, the blood was pouring, and his vision was only just coming back.

The Captain, knowing his opponent was hurt and partially blind, came forward with a scything swing of the knife blade. By instinct and from hours of training in the dark, Brody caught the wrist as it flashed in front of him, taking the appendage, then twisting it a full ninety degrees up. He looked the Captain in the eye as he pushed the last few degrees, feeling the bones of the wrist snap and dislocate. Faraj screamed in pain, then spun around, leaving Brody only holding a jacket. A second later, a bullet ripped past his head. The Captain had found the Glock and was firing with his left hand as he retreated. All the bullets went wide, but Brody still ducked into the mangroves for cover. By the time he raised his head, the Captain was lost in the trees.

Naydia and Gumbao appeared beside him, panting. "What happened? We heard gunshots?"

"The Captain. He ran off that way."

Brody jumped to his feet, but immediately stumbled. His eyes were still full of grit, and his arm was bleeding heavily.

Gumbao said, "Boss, there is nowhere for him to go. Leave it. We need to sort out your arm."

Brody picked up the jacket and went through the pockets. He started smiling. "At least we have the phone now."

Chapter Fifteen

Faraj plunged through the mangrove bushes along the edge of the narrow beach, constantly looking back over his shoulder. So far there was no one in pursuit.

He was reminded of the snapped wrist every time he took a step. A shooting pain fired like a bullet through his body all the way to his brain. The white man had done it again, when he was on the verge of success.

The Captain knew his only chance now was Lamu. If he could find a way back, then his friends there would take care of him. But it was a long trek through the bush, probably sixty miles in total through unforgiving landscape that was only populated by wild animals and the few Pokomo villages. Once anyone left the edge of the life-giving Tana river, the area turned to arid bush with occasional watering holes.

He stumbled on for well over an hour, covered in sweat from the heat and his aching arm. The insects were having a wonderful time on his neck and face, which was soon covered in huge welts from the sand fly bites. Up ahead, a small cave appeared in the limestone wall, an ideal place to lie low and collect his thoughts.

The cave was dry and empty, a perfect place to rest up for a couple of hours. The Captain laid down on the dry, dusty floor cradling his broken wrist as best as possible, trying to support it. Every time he moved, the pain was enough to bring tears to his eyes. The fingers would not move, it just hung on the end of his arm as if it did not really belong to him anymore.

The sun started to leave them for the day. He nodded off into a less than fitful sleep. It felt like every few minutes an intruder was entering the cave. The dreams kept haunting him. A huge smiling face of a white man pushing itself into all of them. Whenever anything started to go well, the face would appear and ruin everything.

He awoke to a start, with a sweat-covered body. A fever was starting to grow as his wrist festered in the heat. Something had brought him back from his restless sleep. There it was again. A pebble hit the wall of the cave twenty feet in front of him. Another cracked his ankle, causing even more pain. Outside the cave, the moon was bright in the sky, illuminating the trees on the edge of the mangrove swamp. The Captain thought he saw a movement, reached for the Glock, and pulled the trigger. But nothing happened. He slid the magazine out to find he had fired all the rounds at that William Brody. He was defenceless. The small stones started bouncing off the walls, some hitting him, others ricocheting off the back wall, making him duck out of the way. It was relentless. He had to do something. The only option he could think of in his delirious state was a mad dash to try to find better cover.

The Pokomo had been out hunting in the early evening, a small group of three middle-aged men looking for some meat to supplement their daily fish diet. Sometimes, if you were quiet and sneaked along the edge of the mangroves, it was possible to surprise a small bushbuck or dik-dik. Menza, the self-proclaimed leader of the group for the evening, had been ahead scouting silently, looking at the ground for any sign of a hooved animal. At nearing fifty seasons, he was an accomplished hunter. Over the last few years, his daily fare of mpunzi, rice and matoke had become boring. His wife Habwoya had not been much use, saying, "Husband, this is what we eat. The river provides for us."

But Menza was fed up. He wanted to taste the tender sweet meat of the dik-dik, then suck the marrow from the bones while the grease dripped from his chin. There was nothing like the smell of a roasting leg on a campfire. His gang had taken to heading out in the early evening to find their favorite snack. If the men were lucky, then a fire would be lit, the animal expertly skinned and butchered, then cooked right there and then. Habwoya could eat her fish. This was men's work, so he reaped the spoils.

Menza was from Kibusu village and was part of the Dzunza clan, a large group of Pokomo living in the final stages of the Tana delta. His family were prosperous with a large rondavel, three kids, and two wives. He lived a happy life, and if tonight he managed to grab a dik-dik, he would go home and make a third child.

The footprints came out of the mangroves. They were deep, as if the person was running hard. Whoever it was had a problem with his upper body. The steps were not even. He or she kept turning around too, looking over their shoulder. The heavy imprints in the soft soil continued into the darkness ahead. There was a smell in the air left by the runner. He was not from around here. The sweat was different. It smelled of rotting flesh, like the person was a butcher.

The others caught up. Oddo, Menza's best friend and neighbor said, "What's this? Who has been walking our trail?"

Menza looked at him. "I don't know. We have never seen tracks here before. There are no villages around except Kibusu. Anyway, this person has shoes."

Oddo looked more closely at the tracks. "You're right. He's injured too. Something wrong with his right arm."

Maro, who had joined them for the first time tonight, came out of the darkness. He was the youngest of the group, a chatty, young lad. He was not very good with the slingshot or the bow, but good company. The elders liked to have a runner along. If they were lucky in their quest, he would make the fire and butcher the animal while they sat smoking.

Maro was also the guy who knew stuff. Any gossip and he was there, right or wrong. The youngster spent his days at the river listening to the women as they chatted or pounded rice into powder.

Maro stepped forward. "Menza, these must be the 'Muzungus' on the river at the moment. I heard they're stealing the elephant's tusks and taking them out into the ocean."

Menza looked at Maro. "Why would they do that?"

Maro looked at him in surprise. "These 'Muzungus' steal them for rings and bracelets."

Oddo chipped in, "I heard there was a big gang upriver. Yuda was having trouble with them. The news was one of the small villages was burned by a gang of poachers."

Menza said, "These must be them. I smelled rotting flesh this morning from the river. I thought it was some animal that had fallen in, but it must have been them passing by."

Oddo said, "The poachers have been killing our women upriver, then taking the men and boys to work for them in the bush. None ever come back."

Menza looked at the tracks ahead. "Well, this one won't do any more harm. We'll stop him and get rid of him."

The group continued in the darkness, the sweet taste of meat forgotten for a while as the hunt for something more important was on.

Deep imprinted tracks led up to a small cave. Menza sneaked inside and saw the man sleeping on the floor. The dirty, forlorn creature's wrist was broken and his clothes were torn. He backed out to report back and make a plan.

Pokomo were not aggressive fighters like the Kikuyus or Massai. It was not their way. Usually, if any dispute erupted in the village, the Kijo would come down with a gourd of mnazi, fermented baby coconut juice. Everyone involved would sit in a circle, legs outstretched feet pointing to the sky and touching. Then a long discussion would ensue. The group would chat one at a time until they had said everything about the problem. At this point, the gourd or gourds were all empty. The Kijo would stand up, if he could, and pass judgement on whatever the problem had been. Everyone would then shake hands and wander off back to their rondavels, happy they had been listened to.

This was different. He was a Muzungu and dangerous. Letting him escape was out of the question, but a full-frontal attack was not possible either. The decision was made to start shooting him with the stones from the slingshots. When he got tired and hurt, the men would tie him up then drag him back to the Kijo for advice.

Captain Faraj burst from the cave in a run, heading inland down a small tributary next to the cave. As he stumbled and ran, the area got wet and boggy. The sides were steep there was no way he could climb with only one hand.

The Pokomo, led by Menza the bravest, kept following him just out of sight, firing the small round river pebbles from their slingshots whenever he slowed down. A rock skimmed passed the Captain's ear, and another cracked against his elbow, causing more pain to his already wracked body.

Oddo was good with the slingshot, in fact in his opinion, the best shot in the group. As children, they would run around the forest next to the village. He could knock a bird out of a tree at sixty feet by the time he was thirteen. But now it was night, and the target would not sit still for a second, just stumbling through the bush dodging left and right as his friends fired their lucky shots.

The Captain was exhausted. His hand had gone gray, the wrist throbbed above the break, and the skin had gone an awful purple and black. The bones could be seen pushing from the inside. And there was a dark line just below the surface forming between his wrist and elbow. It looked like blood poisoning. His head was throbbing. With leaden legs, he stumbled along the path, not knowing where he was going. But every time he slowed, the stones would come and hit him.

The Pokomo tribe hunted this way. It was natural for them to inflict some pain on an animal, then keep pushing it along until it basically ran out of energy. As humans, they could sweat to release the heat from their bodies. An antelope covered in fur could not do this as easily, so soon tired, allowing the tribesmen to catch up and go for the kill. This was the exact tactic Menza had employed on the poacher: get him real tired, when he could not fight anymore, they would drag him back to the village and dump him on the Kijo to sort out.

The waxing gibbous moon came out from behind a large cloud, illuminating the whole area. The Captain could be clearly seen stumbling along the edge of the path thirty feet in front, the hunters following just within range of the slingshots. Oddo took his chance. It was a clear shot. The moonlight was making the poachers white hat glow in the darkness. He swung the thin leather thong around his bent elbow with just the flick of his wrist, making the leather cup hum in the night air. With the precision and timing of a surgeon, he let the three-inch round pebble fly. In less than a second, it struck the Captain on the back of his head. The blow was like a baseball bat coming out of the darkness. Faraj stumbled on the path almost knocked unconscious and fell down the ravine to his right into the mangrove trees below.

He tumbled uncontrollably down the steep sandy bank, rolling head over feet, landing in a heap amongst the mangroves. As the roll ended, his right foot was in front trying to slow the speed of descent. It pushed down into the thick, turgid soup surrounding the twisted gnarled roots. His foot, slick with gloop, slipped between two roots under the surface, they separated to accept the slimy appendage, then slammed shut like a bear trap. The Captain cried out in pain, then cursed as his ankle was seized by the tree. The white grubby Kanzu became stained as he churned up the thick, viscous slop, trying to break free. The white-embroidered coiffure was still sitting on his head, covered in sweat and dirt from the fall. The Captain cried out again, "Don't let me die here, please. I have money. You can save me. I'll pay."

Menza, Oddo, and Maro squatted at the top of the slope some forty feet above the captain. Menza said, "Oddo, why did you hit him so hard?"

Oddo giggled. "Ah, I can't help it. I'm just the best shot."

"Well, you will have to go get him. I'm not going down there; the man is big. How will we drag him up to the path?"

Mora chipped in, "We could just leave him and forget all about it. He's a poacher after all."

Menza nodded in agreement. "That's not a bad idea. It's still early. Maybe a dik-dik will be out and we can grab him. I'm starving after running for so long."

Oddo said, "Hang on, there's something in the trees above the Arab. Look, in the green leaves there above him."

All three sat transfixed. The animal slid along the length of the thick branch some ten feet above its latest meal. The snake's scales shone in the moonlight, its black and brown skin rippling as the python pushed its twenty-two-foot length into the right position to drop onto the unsuspecting man. Finally, the snake was ready. Its tongue flicked tasting the night air, looking for other predators in the area. It was high up in the food chain, but when it started eating, the snake became vulnerable to attack and needed a peaceful place to absorb such a meal.

The Pokomo watched silently from above. Maro was about to shout out, but thought better of it. Menza and Oddo just watched. Living in the bush meant a harsh life and death every day, and this man had caused harm to their tribe upriver. If this was his end, then so be it. Why should they intervene? the snake looked hungry anyway. This was probably a message from the gods to help the snake, then it would stay away from their village.

The Captain was lying still in the mud. He figured if he laid quietly, the Pokomo would probably get fed up and wander off. They were not a violent tribe, more like children really. After a while, they would leave. He could free his foot and find his way out of here. The stones had stopped when he fell down the slope. Another ten minutes and the coast would be clear. Then all he had to do was unclench his ankle, climb up the slope, and find a way out of this place.

Just as he was letting out a sigh of relief, thinking of chancing a look up the slope to see if the men had wandered off, a pale green blur flew out of the tree above, landing on his chest. Within seconds, the huge snake had twisted and wrapped itself around the man's warm body. The constrictor knew its prey was stuck somehow in the mud, as it did not move much. Just a loud scream which startled it, but no matter. This meal was worth the fight.

The python settled into its work. First, it wound itself around the torso of the wiggling, screaming animal, then it started flexing its muscles, slowly pulling them together.

The Captain screamed for help as he felt his body being enveloped by the python. He had never seen one before. The animal was huge: at least twenty feet long with a girth that was as thick as his thigh. The creature was all over him, head to foot, but there was no biting. The snake laid on his frame, sliding itself around him until he was held in a tight embrace.

Then the pain came. His legs first as they were pulled together, he felt them slowly crushed as the animal started tightening its muscles. His chest was next, becoming tight, then ribs were forced closer and closer. When the muscles between the bones were paper-thin, ribs started sliding over one another, becoming a tangled mess. The snake's head was just in front of his own. Its eyes seemed to look into his, watching its prey as it writhed in agony. The snake's tongue flicked out, tasting its latest meal. It wiggled on top of his body, getting more comfortable, slowly pulling its muscles together.

The Captain tried to scream, but the air was pushed out as his stomach was squashed. His lungs came next as the thin ribs collapsed, crushing his heart.

The python settled onto the Captain's chest as it pulled, constricting its body, trying to squash its prey in such a tight embrace that all the bones would be broken. Then swallowing would be easy.

The last thing the captain felt was a thick band of muscle around his neck, slowly squashing his windpipe and voice box, then he went limp as the life was literally crushed out of him.

Menza sat above, watching, looking down at the flat, dead eyes of the poacher. "Well, at least we don't have to take him back to the village now. 'Maseha' always has her way. He tried to hurt the Pokomo. She watches for the evil ones and takes them at night.

The others nodded in agreement. They would never dare interfere in the work of the gods. It was still early enough to get a dik-dik. The Pokomo wandered off in search of their dinner.

Chapter Sixteen

Brody sat in *Aminika*, waiting for his sight to return. The small fragments of limestone from the ricochet had left him in pain and his vision was still blurred. Naydia had immediately taken over flushing his eyes with a saline solution from the first aid kit, then cleaning and wrapping the wound on his arm.

He was angry for letting the Captain getaway. Another failure. Faraj was like a cat with nine lives. Brody swore to himself that if they ever crossed paths again, the man would die.

Two hours later, there was still no call, but on the stroke of mid-day, the phone bleeped twice, and a small envelope appeared on the screen. This was the message they had been waiting for. The rendezvous would be in twelve hours. The coordinates were in the text message. Everything was falling into place. Thirty minutes later, the whoop, whoop of a low-flying chopper could be heard in the distance, coming in fast and low from the west across the long hot savannah.

Lieutenant Colonel Briggs jumped down from the chopper. "Major, you have caused some concern. There is gossip in Nairobi about the ivory trade. What have you been up to?"

"If this works, we will be able to sort out a lot more than some corrupt politicians."

Briggs handed him the small rectangular plastic box. "Here is what you wanted. They're live. We can track them anywhere in the world."

"Thanks. I will let you know how it all goes. You owe me a beer for this."

Briggs smiled. "No problem. Just make sure you come back."

As darkness fell, the long fiberglass boat full of tusks edged out of its hiding place into the river. The current dragged the long low boat along the final stages of the slow-moving watercourse. *Aminika* followed with Naydia and Quai Chan Wai tied to the bow rail. Their first stop was Ziwayu to tie off the speed boat. Quai would be left under the watchful eyes of Naydia and Hassan's uncle.

She approached Brody, who was brooding over the plan, sitting on the rear seats of *Aminika*. "How do you do it, Brody?"

He looked up, "What do you mean?"

"How do you deal with all the lives you have taken? I'm not sure I could live with myself. All those people."

"Once I was a soldier. Then, I did it for Queen and Country. The army sent me all over the world. We went to so many places, not knowing where we were most of the time. The admirals would send us in from a destroyer far out at sea. My team would go into a river or delta just like this. Our orders were always the same: either take the person out or capture and return to the boat. It was simple."

"Why did you leave?"

"It got complicated. I must have been on over a hundred missions, never thinking, just doing. That's what my sergeant major used to say, *'Brody, never think. We do that for you. Just do. Never ask questions. Just do'*. By the time I had finished training, it was like a mantra."

"It sounds like you enjoyed the life. Different places, tons of excitement. What happened?"

"My ideals. After eight years, the world had started to change for me. Some of the missions we were sent on felt wrong. I was not sure how much good was being done or how much money was being made. Iraq was a turning point. We never knew why we were there. After the war, things only seemed to get worse. I started to question my real purpose. When the war ended, terrorism really got going. We were sent into remote villages in Afghanistan to take clerics who did not seem to be doing much. The final straw came on an extraction from Somalia, not far from here, a place called Kismayo. Back then it was a small, dusty, shantytown. The militia were strong but were mostly snot-nosed kids with AK's, not really dangerous, more noise than anything. The clerics were trying to impose Sharia Law into the place to take over. I realize now it is not that easy to rule people, especially Somalis, The culture, the language, and just really the place. Westerners don't think like Somalis. Trying to rectify situations with western beliefs is pointless. I live here now with Hassan and Gumbao. We are totally different in every way. They think I'm mad and I think the same about them. But we get on and find common ground. Violence or just grabbing people off the streets makes us as bad as terrorists."

Brody was silent for a moment, looking at the ocean waves passing *Aminika*'s hull.

Naydia asked, "Was it Somalia that made you change?"

"Not really Somalia. My mind was already moving away from the regimented life where everything was either right or wrong. We were sent into a small village to grab a Muslim cleric who was talking too much. We were told he was dangerous, rabble-rousing the local militia. After two days of watching the dry dusty village, it was time to go in. An extraction is always done as close to 03:00 as possible, because circadian rhythms are at their lowest. The best time for surprise. The village had some visitors, a group of militia, young lads no older than twelve or thirteen. We had come across these child soldiers before. If you shot over their heads, they usually ran for cover. This time was different. We had the cleric and were heading for a vehicle to get back to our rendezvous point. Then it all went to hell. The kids had seen us and started shooting. We tried to scare them off by firing over their heads. But they were different, hardened, not like kids. But they looked like they should be kicking a ball around a field, not carrying an AK. One of my operators was hit and killed. I ended up faced with four of these children. It was either me and my team or them. The hours of training took over. It took less than seven seconds to leave a pile of corpses on the floor. That was it for me. I still have nightmares about it today. The forces just didn't seem the same after that. I lasted about a year, then came here."

Naydia looked at this man. His life had been so different from hers. How could someone deal with killing kids? "It was not your fault. Those children had been taken and brainwashed by someone else. You had no hand in that. Your team could have all died. A Hobson's choice always leaves victims."

There was a long silence, then Naydia reached out and took Brody's hand. "I can never understand how you feel. All I know is you saved us back there countless times. Your acts of selflessness are the only reason we're here. I know it must weigh heavily on your conscience, but just know you are a good man. Without people like you, this world would be a worse place."

They sat in silence, watching the water pass along the hull. *Shukran* was a couple of miles off their port bow, her cabin light glowing like a golden beacon taking them home.

Gumbao and Hassan were subdued. There was a lot at stake. At midnight, the craft had arrived at the agreed coordinates. Hassan was at the wheel. Gumbao was stationed forward as lookout. Brody had the Ithaca out of sight, hidden in the stern.

The dirty craft sat wallowing in the slight swell at the agreed location for well over an hour before the darkened freighter appeared, looming out of the night. All the lights were off. The captain of the freighter hailed them. "Hello, Captain Faraj."

Brody knew this was the tough bit and sat in the darkness with his finger on the trigger, ready to blow the bridge of the freighter to pieces.

Hassan answered. "This is Hassan. The captain is ill in Lamu with a dose of malaria. He sent us with the phone." He waved the flimsy telephone in the air as if it would prove something to the captain of the freighter.

Suddenly they were engulfed in a bright white light, the captain shouted. "Show yourselves, or we'll sink you now."

Hassan and Gumbao walked out onto the deck, two poor Africans just trying to earn a buck. "Faraj said you would pay us one hundred dollars each if we came here with all this stuff. Do you want it?"

The captain's greed took over, he could see half a million dollars of ivory waiting for him. "You standstill. My men are coming aboard."

Brody tied a length of rope to the stern cleat and slid into the dark water, still holding the shotgun. If anything went wrong, he could help his friends.

The men swarmed aboard the small boat. Hassan and Gumbao stood still, hands in the air. In a few minutes, a derrick swung out from the freighter over the fiberglass craft. Nimble hands tied the loads securely before they were hefted to the deck of the larger ship, then straight below. The whole operation took less than thirty minutes. Then one of the crew passed Gumbao some notes. The captain shouted, "Tell Faraj he better come next time, or we'll sink the boat." With that, he slammed the door to the bridge, and the freighter slunk off into the night.

Brody climbed back on deck. He grabbed the whisky bottle from the wheelhouse and took a long slug trying to get his circulation back.

Chapter Seventeen

Satan sat back on his high bar stool in Petleys and took a long drag on the hand-rolled cigarette, letting the blue smoke drift slowly out of his mouth and flared nostrils. "Man, that's some story. You'ave been in the wars. I think you deserve another cold one. How is the blond?"

Brody had been sitting at the bar pretty much non-stop for almost two weeks. After returning from the Tana river, the crew had unanimously decided some R and R was in order. Gumbao immediately disappeared into the back streets, looking for Fatma and the checker's boards. Hassan was staying with his uncle, working on the boats during the day when there were no chores on *Shukran*. They had dropped off the awful little Chinese guy at the airport. Brody had parted with a warning. "Remember, I see you again, and that's it. All agreements are null and void."

Quai had smiled. "Don't worry, Brody, you'll never set eyes on me again. I'm gone from Africa. No more ivory business for me. I'm going back to Hong Kong to work for my brother."

With that, he was gone, wandering up to the small airport looking for a flight out.

William Brody had settled back into the Lamu State House and was enjoying the rich life of his adopted town. He'd get up and run five miles, then eat a huge breakfast and sit in Petleys until midnight most days, resting and drinking the day away.

Naydia had put Kairu on a plane to Nairobi, at her own cost. He called every day and was recovering well. She had decided a holiday was in order and spent most of the day on the long, pure white, sandy beaches of Shella, the easternmost tip of Lamu. In the evenings when the sun had set, she would lazily wander back through the narrow back streets, stopping in the bazaar for a samosa or fresh juice before meeting up with Brody for dinner.

Life was good. They were all getting back to normal. Naydia had decided to head off in a couple of days back to the Ranger Station in Tsavo to carry on with her work. Nothing had appeared on the television or radio about the smugglers, even though Kairu had made an official report backed up by Naydia. The businessmen and politicians had paid to silence everything as usual.

Brody took a long swig from his half-empty bottle of Tusker. "You know Naydia. She lives on the beach, not interested until the sun goes down."

Satan laughed. "We've been keeping a lookout for Captain Faraj, but no one has seen or heard of him. You know that time in the back street here when I saved your ass, that was him."

Brody frowned. "Well, I can tell you, if he crosses my path again he won't walk away. But let's hope a croc ate him on the Tana river." Brody did not believe this for a minute and hoped he would get a chance to meet the old captain quietly in a dark alley. In fact, that was probably why he was so reluctant to leave Lamu.

It was long after lunch. The bright afternoon sun was burning the cobbles of the harbor just outside the bar. Heat radiated in waves from the stones. Although it was hot, the promenade was always busy with donkeys, goats, and tradesmen plying everything from the latest in flashing gadgets to huge fake diving knives that were more like swords. As usual, Brody waited in the bar until the sun started to ease itself into the west. Only then did he move to one of the outside tables to enjoy the noises of the street. As the light was leaving, he could see the blond, sun-bleached hair making its way through the crowds, heading for his table.

"Naydia, you look like you had a good day."

She stood next to the table with a bright white smile. As the town was Muslim, her firm body was covered from head to toe. Brody could see her strong legs and flat belly through the thin cloth. Since arriving in Lamu, they had become firm, if unusual, friends. Each evening would start out well with a few drinks and lively banter. It was as if they really wanted to get on. But inevitably after about an hour, one or the other would make a remark. The next minute there would be a full-on argument. Usually, Naydia stormed off to her room, leaving Brody to continue his hobby of drinking beer.

Tonight, Brody was trying really hard. They sat and ate some lovely mangrove red snapper in coconut sauce with ugali and a spicy salad. The conversation was good. Brody steered clear of what Satan called danger zones.

Earlier in the day, he had spoken to Brody like an older brother trying to get something across to a slightly less than clever sibling. "Look, man, you can't just keep talking to her like that. You'll get nowhere."

Brody looked hurt. "What do you mean? She says stupid stuff and I answer."

"No, man, you got to understand she's a woman. They need to be talked to differently."

"What do you mean? She has two arms, two legs. We are the same."

"Ah, man, you are so stupid. A woman needs you to listen, or learn to pretend to listen. You got to look into her eyes and look like you are hanging on every word she says."

Minor was listening from the kitchen. "Yeah, William, it's all in the way you look. Us Rastas have it made. We know how to give them the look, like we are there, you know."

Brody laughed. "You guys don't know where you are, ever. You smoke so much I doubt if you know what day it is."

Satan said, "That's it though, we don't. But we are right there with them girls, listening all night if necessary. Right up to the bedroom."

Minor high fived Satan. "You are da master, man!"

Satan went on, "A barman never tells, but I can say I have had many adventures just from sitting here and pretending to listen for a couple of days." He winked conspiratorially at Brody, "You mark my words."

So, tonight Brody was determined to pretend to listen, which was already pretty boring, but he was holding in there, and the evening was going well. It had been over two hours. Dinner was finished. He knew a hell of a lot about how an elephant's teeth rotted, but they were still together, no one had stormed off. Satan was watching them, plying Brody with Tusker to keep him calm. He was living the dream. What could go wrong?

He was so engrossed in pretending to listen, the bag ringing next to him went unnoticed. Naydia was the first to say, "Brody, your bag. The phone is ringing." She was instantly on her guard. She knew the only person who could make contact via that telephone was John Briggs.

He rummaged around inside, coming up with the buzzing device. "Hold that thought, I'll be back in a second."

As he stepped outside into the cool moonlit night, he pressed the answer button. "Hello, John, how are you?"

Lt. Col. John Briggs answered, "Brody, how is Lamu? Enjoying the sun sea and sand?"

"It's great, can't get enough of it."

"I hope Satan is treating you well."

"John, is there anything you don't know?"

"Brody, your plan worked. The shipment arrived in Hong Kong a couple of days ago. My guys have been watching the go-down where the ivory is being stored. We have been in touch with the Chinese, they are keen to help us, as Hong Kong still has strong links to the UK. We intend to go and have a chat with the people in a day or so. You made this happen. It could be the biggest ivory bust in the last decade. Do you want to see it through to the end? You could only be an observer, not like the old days' of guns blazing and all that. Just be in on the end."

"Where do I find you, John? I want this over with. Those criminals deserve to spend a long time in jail."

"Don't worry, I have you covered. Be at Lamu airport in two hours. A chopper will pick you and drop you in Mombasa. A plane will be waiting on the runway. See you in Kowloon!"

Brody hung up. Back to the old days. But not quite. He had made a difference. If they could put these guys away, something would have changed. Not for political or monetary gain, but for the betterment of the planet. So, no, not like the old days. He was playing his own tune.

He walked back in the bar, smiling. "You will never guess. The bugs in the tusks worked. Briggs has them in Hong Kong in a warehouse."

Naydia was delighted. "That's awesome news. One for the elephants."

Brody continued, "They want me to go as an observer to identify the tusks when the bugs are removed."

Naydia looked at him. "Is there any danger? You have done more than your fair share."

"No, I'm just an observer. When it's all over, I can gloat over a job well done."

She looked at him with tears in her eyes. "When do you leave?"

"Right now. Got to go to the airport right away."

"Well rush back. And stay in touch."

Naydia grabbed him by the neck, pulling him in close, "Come back, I'll be waiting."

She kissed him long and hard on the lips. When they parted Brody was breathless.

Satan smiled like a grandfather. "You see, just listen, man."

Brody left the bar, hopped on a boat, and headed for the airport about two miles away on the mainland.

Chapter Eighteen

The journey had been long and tiring. At Moi International Airport in Mombasa, the chopper had barely touched down. A smart guy in a white shirt and blue pants directed Brody to a Learjet 60. Two senior looking men were waiting on the plane. They gave a curt nod as he entered. It looked like their journey had been hijacked. The Pratt and Whitney engines threw the small plane along the runway and into the air. It immediately banked to the east, then climbed rapidly to its cruising altitude of 41,000 ft. and settled in at Mach 0.74. Brody wandered over to the bar and mixed himself a stiff scotch on the rocks before settling in for the long journey. His two fellow travelers didn't seem like the chatty type. Five hours later the plane started to descend, heading for a tiny island on the horizon. The jet lightly touched down on Male in the Maldives for fuel and was back in the air again in what felt like a few minutes. The Learjet was soon at its cruising altitude, landing in Singapore four and half hours later. Brody was fast asleep stretched out in the luxury leather seats when the Captain gently shook him. "Sir, it's time to wake up. We're in Singapore International. You leave us here."

Brody staggered off the plane only to be met by a young girl with high heels and very long legs. She greeted him, insisting on taking his army bag, then marched him over to the Singaporean Airlines plane that sat humming on the runway. The hostess smiled. "Enjoy your journey, Major Brody." And was gone.

The Airbus A380 was on its maiden flight. A proud attendant guided him to the upper deck business class, explaining with obvious delight that the seats were fully reclining. Within minutes, he had a scotch in his hand and the Airbus was trundling along the runway. Three hours and fifty-five minutes later, he was in a car speeding through the busy streets of Hong Kong.

The Chinese Military SUV headed to the northwest corner of the Island, an area known as Sai Wan. Brody was dropped off on a busy junction along Connaught Road West. He stood on the edge of the traffic as the dark SUV pulled away and was gone. John Briggs walked up to him and shook his hand. "Major, great to see you. Come in and meet the team."

The comms base had been set up in the corner of a large unused warehouse. Two obvious teams were in the room, sitting a little way off from the techs working the coms for the operation. It was easy to spot the Brits, sat joking with each other, playing cards on a table strewn with ashtrays and empty plastic cups. The other group were all Chinese, sitting quietly, drinking tea and cleaning their weapons.

Lt. Col. Briggs took Brody over to the Chinese. On the way, he whispered, "Be careful with these guys. They are a bit up their own backsides. Take it all too seriously, if you know what I mean."

The Chinese team stood as they approached. Briggs said, "I would like you to meet Major William Brody of the Special Boat Service. We have seconded him, as he has special knowledge of this operation."

The first guy, obviously the team leader, came forward. "I'm Wang Lee, Middle Field Officer and head of the team. Which means I outrank you currently in a joint operation."

Brody nodded. "Sounds great to me. I'm just here to enjoy the sites."

The second guy shook Brody's hand and said with a smile, "I'm Junior Subaltern Ping Foo. It's an honor to meet you, sir. We are grateful to be working with such prestigious British units."

Wang Lei gave him a stern look as if to say he talked too much.

The next guy was a huge man for a Chinese. He stood almost six feet tall and was built like a brick wall, with three teeth missing and a look in his eye, like he just loved to fight. "I'm Nuan Qi, Junior Subaltern." He sat immediately.

The last was a tall slim girl. She looked tough in her black combat gear, but feminine, with a broad smile and a firm handshake. "We welcome you. I am Zhang Xiu Ying, Subaltern. I hope there will be something for you to do after coming all of this way."

Brody smiled. "I'm sure I'll find something."

The Brits were a different bunch: typical special forces, no ranks, no surnames, no respect unless you earned it. Alex was the leader, a battle-hardened veteran who should have gotten out of the game years ago. His second, a youngster full of enthusiasm called Frank, was quieter and more thoughtful, probably a brake for Alex. The other two nodded at Brody, not really wanting to give much up. Briggs said, "These two guys have been in the regiment for more than ten years and have seen most things, a bit like you really, Major. The tall one is Graham and his mate is Andy. They work as a team. But hopefully, we won't be doing much more than arresting and passing over to the authorities."

In the corner of the warehouse, the tech teams were working on the listening posts. They had set up several watch stations around the freighter moored some three hundred yards from their current position. The small harbor had a direct open line to Connaught Road West, then the rest of Hong Kong or Mainland China. Surveillance had shown the captain making several trips to a large multi-storied building on the other side of the quay. The ground floor was an open warehouse, then above were fifteen floors of humanity, mostly tiny, one-bedroom, city apartments. Floors seven and eight were in the process of being renovated into large open-plan offices. The Captain of the freighter had been regularly entering the warehouse, and a signal was being received from the G.P.S. senders with an altitude of 120 feet, putting it on the eighth floor.

Wang called them together just after dark. "We'll kit up now. In one hour, my team will leave and approach from the west. Lt. Col. Briggs you'll wait for my signal, then as agreed you will come and hold position opposite the boat undercover. Only act on my strict orders. Remember you are back-up if we need to retreat."

The short meeting broke up as everyone went to their stations in silence. It did not matter what the mission was, there was always an undercurrent of nervous anticipation. Anything could go wrong. This might be their last night on earth.

Briggs walked Brody over to the weapons table. "Here, take this G36c and a SIG. I'm sure you know more about them than I do."

He picked up the ultra-modern weapon. "These will do, but why am I carrying? I thought I was just an observer?"

"You never know. We have very little intel on how many hostiles are likely to be on the boat. You're more than competent to handle these weapons, and I'll feel much better having an extra set of armed eyes watching my back."

The G36c sat looking at him, slick and black, a lethal tool of death. This fully automatic weapon had been the S.B.S. weapon of choice. He had carried it into battle more times than he could remember. The SIG 9mm pistol was like an old friend, a highly-crafted weapon, the Glock's rich cousin, with an aluminum base and stainless-steel slider. It could take a beating and keep on firing. The trick was to either get the first shot over and done with, as it had a long pull to cock the weapon, or carry it cocked. The SBS's preferred way was cocked, then he could draw and fire accurately in less than two seconds.

The night was warm but overcast, the moon just showing on occasion, spreading a soft glimmer of silver, casting shadows across the wharf. Oily, dark water lapped against the side of the freighter, gently nudging it against its fenders.

Lt. Col. Briggs muttered to himself. "We have been here for nearly ten minutes. What's holding the other team up?" Brody tapped him on the shoulder and nodded towards the western end of the quay. Four dark figures could just be seen flitting from cover to cover.

Wang had insisted on controlling the operation. John pointed out it was their territory, so they had jurisdiction over the British squad. Wang decided his team would take point, approaching from the west, which was most exposed, then splitting up near the ship. Ping Foo and Zhang were tasked with climbing the forward mooring rope, gaining access through the bow. Wang and Nuan would take the twenty-five-foot exposed gangway to the deck.

Briggs' team were spread out evenly on the wharf, hidden around the packing cases. The Brits had been instructed to hold their positions, giving covering fire if needed. It was basically a Chinese operation. Wang Lei wanted the glory.

The tech teams had been watching the freighter since she arrived five days ago. Their current estimate was that there could be up to twenty smugglers on board, plus the boss and the buyer. No one was sure of the firepower, as the boat had not been searched.

Both teams moved expertly through the packing cases at the wharf's edge. Team two peeled off and started climbing the thick mooring rope to the bow. Wang moved like a ghost along the wharf until he was ten feet from the long steep gangway stairs. A lone guard paced back and forth, making sure the meeting was not interrupted. He had a Motorola radio in his pocket to report back to the bridge. Briggs watched through his night-vision goggles as

Wang moved closer to the guard. If anything went wrong now, the whole thing would be a disaster. Wang was an expert in his trade. The guard didn't even know what had happened. A matte black stiletto blade appeared out of the darkness and sunk into his neck without a sound. He fell backwards into Wang, who carefully lowered him to the ground. Nuan efficiently appeared, carrying the guard and hiding him behind the cases.

The first threat was cleared. The two Chinese Special Forces Operators nimbly ran up the stairs and disappeared into the ship.

Brody watched as the forward team climbed the four-inch-thick headline hawser hand over hand, entering the bow of the ship through the cat hole, then merging with the shadows. Now all they could do was wait.

As soon as both teams had vanished, the throat mikes came online. Wang was the first to speak. "Team two, are you aboard? Over."

Zhang replied, "We are on board, moving forward, approaching the main bulkhead below the bridge, over."

Wang continued, "Move as planned to the port side. Cover all exits. Ping and I will enter, thirty seconds to stations, over."

The mikes went dead. Brody looked at John. "Do you think it's wise keeping us this far back? Our teams could have covered the exits, allowing them to have backup inside."

John replied, "We have no jurisdiction. I mentioned that at our initial briefing, but was overruled. Wang is a great officer, but in these situations, the government want to make it look like we are superfluous. good P.R.!"

"Can we move forward? Maybe send one guy to the deck?"

"No, any alterations to the plan have to be agreed with Wang. He's in charge."

Brody went quiet. This did not feel right. He was uneasy. The British team were evenly stationed, but would be able to do little if the Chinese got in trouble.

His mic crackled into life. "Team two, this is team one. We are moving into the hold of the boat hold position." Then static.

"Team two, move forward from your position. We have more hostiles than anticipated."

Briggs broke into the conversation. "Team one, this is back up, teams three and four on the wharf. We can close on position and replace team two for covering fire, over."

Wang replied, "This is team one. Hold position as agreed, over."

Zhang came on. "Team two, we are proceeding towards ship's hold from port, over"

Wang suddenly came online. "We have been spotted. Team two approach with caution, many hostiles armed with automatic weapons."

Zhang replied, "We are now engaged, on final stairs to hold."

On the wharf, there were only slight popping noises coming from the ship, but Briggs looked concerned. "Fuck it, we move in closer to give support." He waved at the British team three. Two men broke off from the shadows and ran to the gangway leading up to the ship. Alex had his Heckler and Koch G36c held at half-cock, these weapons were ideal for this type of wet work, with an optical sight plus red dot, magazines holding 30 NATO .556 rounds, which could be spat out at a rate of 300 per minute. With single and semi-auto, the G36 was a deadly weapon. It could be used in close with the folded stock or at ranges of up to 400 yards with reasonable accuracy. Alex, with Frank just behind him, spent less than a second assessing the stairs for hostiles, then ran full pelt to the deck of the freighter. They knelt at the top, clicked the mics twice then split up, one port and the other starboard.

Briggs clicked his mic. "Team one and two, I have operatives at your back, covering your retreat if needed." But there was silence from the two Chinese teams. Brody clicked in. "Wang, do you read? Over." Silence again. "Zhang, do you copy we need confirmation." Silence.

Brody looked at Briggs. "Maybe the ships hold is too thick and they can't hear us?"

Alex came online. "I have movement coming up the stairs."

Briggs said, "Hold position in cover." Two clicks came back. Whoever was approaching was getting close.

Alex saw the door slam open; the pretty Chinese operative was pushed forward, arms above her head. Next to her stood the huge operative Nuan. He looked pissed and had a black eye and bleeding mouth. It looked as if a rifle butt had hit him hard.

The guy behind him holding a sleek, matte black stubby automatic pistol shouted. "Drop your weapons or these two die as well."

Alex came over the mic. "I have two hostages, one hostile with automatic machine pistol. Can take shot over, but don't know how many more are behind him."

Briggs took over the operation until he could ascertain where Wang was. "Hold fire. Frank, your position?"

"I'm on the port side amidships. I can hear something on the stairs below."

"Hold position. Advise if you see anything."

Two clicks came back immediately.

John looked at Brody. "This has gone to shit already."

Brody cocked his G36c and checked the Sig in his holster, putting a round in the chamber. The gun was very dangerous now. All it took was a half pull on the trigger. But if you were in a tight situation, this was all you needed. He nodded at Briggs, then signaled to Graham to move to the bottom of the gangway and to Andy to stay in the shadows.

Brody raced up the twenty-five feet of gangplank to the deck. He positioned himself slightly further back from the entrance, which would allow the hostiles a clear path to the walkway. Then Andy and he would take them on the gangplank.

The mic came alive. "This is Frank, we have hostiles appearing on deck port side. Should I engage?"

On the starboard side, Alex was facing off the hostiles holding Zhang and Nuan. The situation was tense. Everyone had fingers half pulled, ready for anything. Nuan broke the tension. As the guy behind him switched his weapon momentarily to Zhang, he spun, throwing himself back through the hatch, taking the hostile with him. Zhang took her chance and rolled, expecting fire, landing close to Alex. He grabbed her flak jacket, dragging her into the shadows, then passed her his SIG.

Frank was taken by surprise as four hostiles broke through the door leading to the port deck. He opened fire, taking the first one in the chest and throwing him back onto the second guy. The third was ready and put down a hail of bullets, forcing him to retreat behind a deck ventilation funnel. "Frank port side. I have multiple hostiles on deck. Under fire. Need assistance."

Brody replied, "Am coming from forward. Watch for me."

Frank answered. "Copy, over."

Then the air was filled with the sound of fully automatic gunfire.

Alex and Zhang heard shots from inside the ship. One hostile was bodily thrown through the air, landing on the deck rail, then rolling over. Nuan raced out into the night. A gunman appeared behind him, emptying his magazine into his back. He staggered forward as blood flowed out of his mouth, looked at Zhang, smiled, then fell on his knees. The next shot took the top of his head off.

Zhang lurched forward, but Alex grabbed her, pulling her back as more rounds ricocheted off the bulkhead around them. Alex fired a withering onslaught of rounds, pushing the hostiles back through the hatch.

Frank was pinned down on the port side as Brody dodged from shadow to shadow trying to get close. About twenty yards in front, six guys were holding him at bay, while a large fat man and a short skinny one climbed the rail and started descending a wooden ladder to the water. Brody needed to help Frank first, so let them go.

"Frank, I'm on your 12 'O'clock."

Brody stepped forward, still in the shadows, his G36c on three-shot mode. There were four guys still firing continuously at Frank. He put the first two down with two three-shot bursts. The fourth spun to take on the threat from behind. Frank knew exactly what Brody had planned and stepped out of the shadows, shooting him in the back.

Frank ran over to Brody. "This has gone to hell in a handbasket. I'll go through the ship and help Alex."

Brody said, "Go." He turned to look over the rail as a shot rang out. Frank just stood there with a lost look on his face. The color drained from him as he raised his hand covered in blood. Brody spun round. One of the Chinese was up on his elbow, he drew the SIG like a wild west gunslinger, putting two quick shots into the Chinese's face. Frank fell to the deck. Brody ran to him. The shot was just below his flak jacket right into his stomach. Frank was dead and knew it. He said, "Mate, I don't know you, but we are all soldiers. Tell my wife I love her. "Blood came out between his clenched teeth as his life left him.

Brody laid him on the deck, clicking his mic. "Frank is down, fatal. Am going after two hostiles in harbor."

Briggs came online. "Stay with main team; repeat, do not leave team." Brody tore the mic off his throat and raced for the rail.

Zhang used the covering fire from Alex to move forward. Andy appeared beside Alex. They exchanged looks. One of their team was gone. This was personal now. He moved on to catch up with Zhang. They approached the hatch with extreme caution, covering each other's every step. The door was flung open, and two guys ran out onto the moonlit deck. Zhang took the first one with a double-tap to the chest and a single to the forehead. The second one rolled out, expecting fire, but Andy was ready, waiting for him to stop, then shooting him in the neck, killing him instantly. The three gathered at the doorway. The interior of the freighter was dark, lit only by the dancing beams of torchlight from the operator's barrel Maglite's. They entered the hatch slowly, wary of potential threats from the shadows. Once all was clear, the team moved swiftly through the empty ship. Alex reached the hold first. It was carnage. There were upwards of twenty dead bodies. The firefight must have been extremely fast and violent. Wang sat in a corner. Most of his face was missing. He had taken multiple rounds to his torso and legs. Ping was about three yards away, still holding his gun in lifeless hands. His body had been almost blown in half by a shotgun round.

Alex clicked. "Team leader, this is Alex. Multiple fatalities in ship hold. Will check and secure the area."

Briggs came online. "Understood, have you seen Major Brody?"

"That's negative. He is not with fatalities so far. We'll report as we search, over."

"Over", Briggs let out a sigh. Where the fuck had he disappeared to?

Chapter Nineteen

Brody could see the small boat almost fifty yards away about to reach the far quay. He vaulted over the rail, falling thirty feet into the harbor. Staying underwater, he pushed off the freighter. Surfacing like an Olympic swimmer just off the blocks, then powering through the water. Four men had met their bosses and were helping them out of the boat. Once they were clear, the group rushed into the warehouse.

Wai shouted, "You two, stop that lunatic before he comes through this door. Ying, follow me. We can still do this. I have tusks in my office upstairs."

Ying was a heavy man. He had been dealing in everything from whores to jelly beans since the Chinese had taken over on the 1st July 1997, a good time for him. Over the years, he had become very fat with a preference for skinny young white girls. He twisted a thick gold ring around his podgy fingers. This had gone far enough. "Wai, I don't need this. Just let me have those girls, the ivory is too hot now."

"Ah, come on, Ying. I'll give you a good deal on the whores. Just look at the stuff I have upstairs in the office. They won't follow us now; my guys will deal with them. We'll be long gone before anyone comes looking."

"I'm too old for this." Wai led him into the warehouse.

Brody climbed the ladder two rungs at a time, reaching the quayside dripping wet, the G36 strapped across his back and the SIG tucked safely in its holster. As his head appeared, a shot rang out, striking the top loop of the metal ladder. He ducked down, coming up a second later and fired off two short bursts towards the warehouse. The figure ducked inside, giving him a moment to roll across the hard-concrete floor to a packing case. He took a second to get his breath, then took a look. A bullet hit the packing case, splintering needles of wood in all directions. He rolled and came up on the other edge of the case, letting off another two three-shot bursts, then dashed closer behind a shipping container, giving him an oblique view of the door. The head popped out for a moment. Brody was ready, but his shot went wide. His breathing had not recovered from the swim. As the thug ducked back in, Brody made another dash forward, getting to within fifteen feet of the entrance. The guy's hand came out with the barrel of the machine pistol. Brody slowed his breath and fired two shots, smashing the gun and the hand to pieces. He lunged through the door, rolling across the polished concrete floor, coming up and taking out the other guard with a short burst to the chest.

The two men from the freighter turned to see the commotion. The smaller one shouted, "You two get him. I want him dead this time!"

Brody recognized the voice. It was that bastard Wai Chan Quai. Bullets sparked off the floor in front of him as he dived for cover, then ran between some wooden boxes. The crates were stacked all around the warehouse. Brody quickly climbed up to the top and moved towards the end of the warehouse. Two guards prowled along the corridor between the cases. Brody waited until they had passed his position, then stood up, taking careful aim, he wanted both of them. The first one took two rounds low on his left shoulder. The fragments must have torn his heart to pieces, as he just crumpled to the floor. The second one spun into Brody's next burst, taking his right arm off at the elbow. The final burst finished him, stitching up across his chest. The G36c clicked empty. There were no more mags. He threw it aside.

Brody rounded the last corner before the lift and was met with a barrage of fire. He rolled across the opening, getting cover on the other side in a doorway. The bullets stopped momentarily as he looked out. The fat man was trying to get into the lift, but Wai would not let him. He shouted, "No, it's too late. You stay here and hold off that mad man."

Ying's shouts were muffled as he tried to barge his way into the lift. "I'll kill you myself. You've ruined everything, and brought the authorities down on us."

Four shots echoed off the walls. Brody glanced as Ying slumped to the floor and the lift doors closed. A red blinking number eight showing Wai's destination.

Ying had a bullet in the middle of his forehead, his glassy eyes staring into space. A large pool of blood was forming on the polished grey concrete floor.

Brody crashed through the fire escape door, taking the steps three at a time.

At the eighth floor, he stopped and took a second to get his breath before peering out into the semi-lit corridor. As he checked up and down the wide corridor, he saw a door slam shut some thirty yards further along.

Brody ran along the corridor, stopping outside the closed office door. He slid the action back on the SIG, making sure the hammer was cocked and a round was in the chamber. All it needed now was 6 pounds of pressure, a short pull to release the round. He knew Wai was on the other side of the door. Kicking it in would be risky, but it was the only option. Standing back, he aimed his foot next to the lock and took a deep breath. There was no going back now. He slammed the door, breaking the lock. It swung back on its hinges, hitting the wall. Brody rolled through the entrance, moving into the room, coming up on one knee ready to fire. Wai was waiting for him, standing behind a long wide polished wooden desk. In the center were three gleaming white, cleaned tusks, ready for sale. In front of him stood two frightened, malnourished teenagers, Wai's Glock forcing the one on the right to wince in pain.

"Mr Brody, what took you so long? I've been waiting here for you." Wai said with a slick smile on his face.

Brody remained in the firing position. This had to be a headshot. "Wai, this is over. There are two teams of special forces on their way here right now. You can't get out of here alive unless you give it up now."

"You must be joking. I saw them go down. It's only you left."

"You're a fool, Wai. A laser dot will find you in a few seconds, then your life'll be over." He glanced nervously at the window, adjusting his position further behind the girls.

The white girls were of European descent may be from Croatia or Bulgaria, they were crying and looked terrified. One had bloodshot eyes and was high on something, acting like a zombie with a dumb-looking smile on her face. The other, dressed in a skimpy silver sequined disco dress, was attached to Wai's gun. But she had something left. In her eyes, a tiny bit of obstinance glinted.

Brody said in as soothing a voice as was possible. "Don't worry, I'll get you out of here. He won't harm you. Just stay calm."

The girl looked at him through tired bloodshot eyes. The sniveling stopped. She almost smiled.

Wai grinned. "You have no hand to play. This is not the jungle, Tarzan. It's my turf now."

As soon as Brody had seen the girls, his control of the situation was over. All he was playing for now was time. Nice and slow. Wai will make a mistake.

"Enough games. Put down the gun or I'll blow this ones' head off."

Brody tossed the SIG down and kicked it to about halfway between him and the desk. Wai felt better now. He roughly pushed the zombie girl across the room. She landed on a sofa. The sniveling disco girl he kept hold of.

"Mr Brody, I'm going to kill you now, then take these tusks and the others in our showroom along with these whores and make a lot of money. By morning, I'll be on the mainland. Long gone."

"You will never make it. The Chinese will be on your tail in minutes. You won't even get out of the building."

Wai smiled. "China is a lot like Africa, my friend. Some grease here and there in the right hands and life can be easy."

"You have gone too far this time, Wai. The Brits won't accept anything less than your head on a stake."

"Ah, Brody, my friends are high up, and they love their ivory. I will sell these girls tonight to a whore house. They'll be working within the hour. And you'll just be another dead body."

Brody knew he had little to go on here. Reaching for the gun would be a death sentence. Charging would be worse. He would have to play for time and try to get an advantage.

The disco girl had her head down the whole time. She had been listening to this awful Chinese man. As far as she could see, her life was over. He had just said that within the hour she would be injected and laid on a bed for the next fat Chinese slob to do what he wanted. That was not living. She would rather just get it over with now. Slowly, as if she was trying to scratch an itch in her shin, her foot slid up higher and higher. The disco girl had to warn this man who had arrived. She looked at him full in the face, smiled like a madwoman, and winked.

Brody caught the look. He knew something strange was going to happen as the girl stared into his face.

Then she slammed her foot down on the top of Wai's, twisting her heel with all her weight, then turned and stuck her finger right into his eye. He screamed, pushing the girl away, aiming the gun at her chest with one hand and holding his eye with the other. Brody took the opportunity and threw an ashtray sitting on the table which hit Wai in the jaw, knocking his aim off. The bullet went into the ceiling.

Brody took less than a second to retrieve the SIG, but it was too late. Wai had disappeared through another doorway. He looked at the girl. "Shit, that was a brave thing to do."

The girl looked at him and started crying, he said, "I'll be back to look after you, don't worry. Sit tight."

Brody rolled through the door out across the open expanse of office floor. The open-plan office was enormous and was almost finished. Dark blue carpet tiles covered the floor, and all the walls painted white, with pillars dotted here and there. The owners were waiting for the final plans before fitting the partitioning. There was a large antique table piled high with polished tusks of all shapes and sizes.

Brody came up hard against one of the concrete pillars, instantly letting off three rounds in the general direction of Wai.

Immediately, plaster was being blasted off the corners of the pillar as rounds landed. Brody tucked up and waited for the onslaught to end. He rolled across the floor, shooting as he went, forcing Wai back through the room. Wai ducked behind a pillar, firing back. Brody and Wai dodged across the room exchanging shots. Wai's gun clicked empty. Brody stood up, blasting his last three rounds directly at Wai. He ducked and rolled at incredible speed across the room towards him.

All three shots missed. Wai came up spinning. A hard-round house kick landed on the side of Brody's head. Then he danced away. Brody caught his breath, ready for the next attack. Wai circled him, dancing on the balls of his feet, looking for an opening. "Hey, White Eye, you're a dead man. I eat soldiers like you for breakfast."

Brody grumbled, "Shut the fuck up and let's get this over with."

Wai came in hard landing a fast punch in the middle of Brody's chest, sending him reeling backwards, a second kick was followed to his kidneys. Brody staggered as Wai came in again throwing a straight punch to his face, Brody dodged, blocking the punch and returning with a low right to Wai's body. He took it with a grunt.

Brody moved faster. He lunged in with a straight right for Wai's throat, but was blocked as he had expected. The left hook smacked into Wai's jaw, sending him back three paces. Brody caught his breath, the body punch had hurt like hell. Wai came back, hopping from foot to foot like a boxer. He was changing his style. He dodged and weaved, ducking then coming up with a left jab that caught Brody in the jaw. He immediately tasted blood in his mouth as Wai danced away.

Brody stood his ground as Wai moved around him, looking for an opening or weakness. Wai flicked a kick, aiming for his groin. Brody rolled out of the way, grabbed the leg before it could return, and twisted the ankle as hard as he could, throwing Wai off balance. Brody followed him down onto the carpet. They rolled across the floor, hitting the trophy tusks and knocking them off the table. Brody got on top, landing three good punches to Wai's face, then caught a solid right to his kidneys, knocking him off Wai onto the floor. Wai jumped, trying to run, but Brody caught his ankle, sending him sprawling into a pile of carpet tiles. Brody dived after him. Wai spun around on the floor, pulling a long strip of plastic with him, wrapping it around Brody's face. Suddenly, all the air was cut. Brody gasped for breath, his lungs exploding as Wai hung on pulling the sheet tighter. Brody twisted, his lungs burning. He spun, grabbing at Wai's shoulders, then threw his head backwards, connecting with Wai's nose. The air rushed in. Brody rolled out of Wai's grip. They stood, facing each other.

Wai grabbed a long polished, white tusk, thrusting it at Brody, its point grazing his side. Wai lunged again, then swung the tusk in an arc hitting Brody in the thigh, making him stagger and lose all the feeling from the waist down. Wai was on him. He thrust the tusk. Brody twisted, but the long pointed ivory stake sunk into his thigh. Blood poured out of the gaping wound.

Wai came in again aiming, a killing blow for his stomach. Brody let the long white spike come for him. At the last second, he twisted. The smooth ivory slid over his torso. Then he slammed Wai in the face with a flat left hand. Breaking his already bloody nose. He then grabbed the shaft of ivory and spun it one hundred and eighty degrees like a knight with a jousting pole. He charged Wai. The thick ivory tusk went into his stomach and out the other side. Brody carried on charging like a bull elephant across the open plain, his hand on the flat end of the tusk and Wai back-peddling in front of him. Brody was in a blind rage. He was going to kill this man now in the worst way possible. He was not thinking any more consumed by pure animal rage.

Lt. Col. Briggs stood on the deck of the freighter when he heard breaking glass from the building on the other side of the wharf. Two men came tumbling through a broken plate glass window. He watched as the figures fell from the eighth floor. One angled his body into a swallow dive, swooping out over the dark water. The other rolled and tumbled uncontrollably. He was carrying what looked like an elephant's tusk.

It took an age from so high. The diver hit the dirty water hard, feet first. The other person landed on top of a pasty brown and red four-wheel drive. The roof caved in as whatever the guy was holding went straight through.

The dark water was silent. John Briggs watched, holding his own breath. A head suddenly broke through the surface, gasping for breath. He shouted, "Quickly, get a damned boat. Get that man out of the water."

The   End

Dear Reader,

I sincerely hope you enjoyed this story as much as I have enjoyed writing it. The East African Coast has been my home since 2002, and I love it as much as Brody does. All the locations are based on actual places, islands, and towns; they can easily be found on Google Earth. The people in the story are fictitious, but they are based on people I know and have met over the years.

If you did enjoy the read, or in fact, if you didn't, I would very much appreciate some feedback on this book's page. Just type in the title on Amazon Kindle and let me know what you think. Good or bad, I am always interested, as the reviews make me a better writer for the future. I would also appreciate it if you could put me on Twitter or any other book sites where you think readers would enjoy this story.

Alternatively, my email is steve@stevebrakerbooks.com I would love to hear from you, and I answer all emails personally.

I am now sat with Brody as he gets ready for his next tropical adventure. I am sure if you enjoyed this book, you would enjoy the next. As I am getting to know Brody as a character and his thought process, the stories become more involved, and I hope more enjoyable for you. This series will go on as long as he has interesting stories to tell.

I consider myself very lucky to have lived in East Africa for so long. I have traveled up and down this coastline fishing, diving, and exploring. Most of the descriptions are based on my actual experiences here. This I think puts me in a unique position to be able to give you the best and most realistic view on life in East Africa.

If you would like to sign up for our newsletter, then please click on this link. It will take you to our sign-up page. We don't send out loads of emails, just important stuff like book launches. We also offer free book releases to selected readers. We keep your address personal to us https://www.stevebrakerbooks.com We also have a website which you can visit if you would like at https://www.stevebrakerbooks.com

Yours,

Steve Braker

Copyright

This is a work of fiction. Names, characters, and incidents are either the products of the author's imagination or are used fictitiously and any resemblance to persons, living or dead, businesses, companies, events, is entirely coincidental.

The locations and distances are real. The Tana river delta is a lovely area of the country full of wildlife. The villages are typical of villages on the East African coast, but are fictitious, made from many visits I have made to many villages.

The Pokomo are a real tribe. The customs and rituals I have outlined are correct at the time of printing. The Pokomo have a claim to the Swahili language, as they were the first tribe to interact with the Arabs and probably the Chinese. The National Anthem of Kenya is based on a Pokomo Lullaby.

Copyright © 2017

All rights reserved

William Brody African Slaver

Printed in Great Britain
by Amazon

43040174R00155